BAD BLOOD: A VAMPR NIGHTMARE

PISCES PARANORMAL PR AGENCY: BOOK 1

BEE MURRAY

NIOBE MARSH

EMERALD FERN PRESS

BEFORE WE BEGIN...

Welcome to the dark, twisty, (kinda sweary) world of our new urban fantasy/paranormal suspense series: Pisces Paranormal PR Agency. Surprised we wrote a suspense series? Join the club. Turns out, when two dark and twisty authors decide to write a rom-com that starts with vampires and mass murder and ends up in chaos you get... this. Sooo... oops?

If dark humor, blood and vampire violence gets you excited... you might need to talk to a professional... but you're also our kind of people.

This story is not a love story, but rather an evolution.

It gets complicated, as all evolutions do.

Broken pieces, unavoidable tragedy, explosive chemistry, scathing snark, and fiery tempers.

Violence. Blood. Death. Destruction. History. It's all part of the gig.

Know this: This evolution is too big to fit in just one book. But... stick with us. Pisces Paranormal PR Agency has a lot to say. This is the story of Tuesday Matson, and Tuesday? Yeah. She's worth the pain. We have to do this right and you're gonna wanna be there. We promise.

Allons-y,
    Bee & Niobe

1

———

VINNIE

Test results could be wrong.

False positives were a thing. I'd heard about it on the news as early as two weeks ago. A politician who almost lost her entire career because of a false positive. She'd end up with a nice lawsuit and a chunk of change... That's what usually happened, anyway. A nice pay off for the *inconvenience.* But only the ones who could afford to sue. The rest?

Well... the rest had to deal with the consequences of being a vampire in a town that wasn't quite ready for that kind of diversity.

I squinted at the paper in my hands, convinced if I stared at it long enough maybe the words would change.

I'd done it a hundred times.

They never changed.

A familiar feeling of desperation coursed through me. The worst part of hating reality is when you know, without any doubt, that the thing you fear is real.

I already knew the truth. I had known it for a long, long time. The results weren't wrong.

And nothing was going to change that fact.

If I looked at the damned letter any longer, I was going to go insane. With a growl, I crumpled up the letter and threw it across the room to join the others in the growing pile next to the door.

Each torn, balled up piece of paper in that pile had come in the same baby blue envelope marked *URGENT*.

They're all from the same place: *The Seattle Infectious Disease Clinic: Vampiric Infections Division, Exposure Outreach.*

I don't need to open the familiar blue envelope and read the letter that came today because it's the same as the letter I received yesterday. The same as the day before, and the day before that.

Sure, I'd read the first one; I just refused to believe that this was actually happening. Things like this don't happen to people like me. It's one benefit of being rich and famous. People believe what you tell them. To the world, I'm an eccentric pop star who lives his best life after sunset. Nothing more. Nothing less. I'm not even an anomaly.

But with the truth? That's where my options were limited, and I felt more than a little trapped. I could call my lawyers and set them on it—it would be easy enough to threaten the medical assholes that had dared to put this in writing.

Maybe they would back off, retract their findings. I could call my manager and pay off the testing staff. If threats didn't work, money usually would. But I couldn't bring myself to hit the speed dial.

Plus, if I did anything like that, they might go public with the results.

That's what all the letters were about. I had to confirm their findings and acknowledge that I understood my responsibilities as an infected party—no fucking way. They'd keep sending letters until someone reported my death or I offered the truth.

In order to make this go away, I would have to address the

problem head on. Historically, not my strong suit. I would have to tell them what the letters said and risk leaking a scandal to the press. In order to do that, I would have to expand my circle of trust to include more of my staff, to tell them the truth. That doesn't work for me. The truth doesn't set me free—it crushes my career and might even put my life in danger.

I dropped my phone onto the cushion beside me, ran my hands through my hair, and sank deeper into the leather sofa. A small sliver of sunlight peeked out from behind the cloud and shone merrily onto my house and into my covered porch. It was just a small sliver of sunlight determined to brighten up an otherwise dreary Seattle day when it landed on my leg. I stared at it and willed myself to enjoy the small gift of warmth, but the smoke had already started. Little whiffs rose from my $900 jeans as the heat of that small sliver of sunlight baked through the denim and roasted my skin.

I watched it a little longer, morbidly curious if what I thought would happen would actually happen.

A small lick of reddish-orange flame showed up just a moment later. My leg was on fire. I watched as the small orange flare became a flame that shot across my thigh, destroying my jeans entirely before it clicked in my brain... *My fucking leg is on fire.*

With a roar, I reached for the pitcher of tequila sunrise drink mix next to me and dumped it on my leg, extinguishing the experiment with tequila and lime. *The only sunrise that won't kill me.*

Considering how I got into this situation in the first place, if I'd been in a better mood, I would have appreciated the irony of it all. I dropped the pitcher onto the floor and sighed again as I pressed the button on the remote that closed the blackout drapes.

Not only did I have a burned hole in my jeans and an angry

red welt on my leg, but now everything was sticky, and reeked of tequila. *Great. Just... great.*

Twin flames of rage and intense hunger rose in my core. The emotions were confusing, and I usually ignored them. Deep emotions weren't my strong suit. Not anymore. Not after that night.

Back then, I'd known with every fiber of my being that I wasn't supposed to be there. My buddies and I were supposed to play the set and go home.

That had been the agreement. But when the most beautiful woman I'd ever seen appeared by my side at the bar and offered me a drink, I figured it wouldn't hurt.

Before I knew it, I was drunk. Suddenly, nothing else had mattered. Not even the woman waiting at home, or my buddies in the band.

That night, I was consumed with feelings that wrecked me and lust that blinded me.

A vision in crimson. She had made me crave her with an intensity I had never felt before, and I had been weak. I didn't tell her to stop. Not when I saw her fangs, not when she caressed my neck with such exquisite sweetness, not even when she bit me and drank deeply of the blood that pounded through my veins.

No.

I came alive for her, caught in a web of pretty promises and adrenaline.

Hindsight is a bitch.

How was I supposed to know that one moment would throw my entire life as I knew it away?

When she offered me her own wrist, the deep ruby droplets of her blood glistening against her skin, I didn't even fucking *hesitate.* I drank, knowing it would change everything. I was a selfish prick who wanted to be king of the world.

They say, be careful what you wish for.

I fed from her and relished the taste of the infection electrifying my skin.

She held my head to her wrist and crooned such sweet promises in my ear.

It would be us against the world, she promised. Everything would be ok.

Except that it wasn't. The minute I had drunk my fill, I passed out.

It was the feel of early morning sunshine burning my cheek that woke me up the next morning. She'd taken me to a hotel room, complete with blackout curtains, and abandoned me there.

I waited for her.

But she never returned. Maybe that was her plan. Unleash a monster without a care in the world and then leave me to my own devices.

Either way, it didn't matter. I didn't die. I survived. I built a fucking empire. The selfish prick won and maybe it's time to pay the proverbial piper.

After all, I'd wanted this, right? It was my own damn fault. I *became a* monster.

I have the immortality she promised; but at what cost?

My head snapped toward the locked door as I heard quick footsteps on the highly polished hardwood floor in the corridor.

Bad timing.

A small fist hammered on the thick wooden door.

"Mr. Quake, are you in there?"

Georgia. She knew damn well I was in there. I'd been in this room for the last two weeks. She and Patricia made sure that my fridge was stocked with blood bags and that my laundry was done. I needed little else.

High maintenance popstar, low maintenance vampire.

Get you a guy who can do both.

I looked down at my tequila-stained jeans and swallowed a growl of frustration. My closest staff, the ones in my circle of trust, were there because they only interrupted whatever the hell I was doing on the absolute *rarest* of occasions. They had keys to every room. I didn't even know why Georgia was knocking. *This better be good.*

I stalked to the door and leaned against it. "It's not a good time," I said loudly enough for her to hear.

"I have some mail for you," Georgia said.

"Fan mail? Leave it in my studio."

Ugh. Fan mail. How many pairs of lacy underwear would there be in this shipment...

"It's not fan mail."

"Then what?"

"Mr. Quake, may I come in? I need to speak to you."

I rubbed a hand over my face in frustration and unlocked the deadbolts and walked away from the door. Once my closest staff had learned about my... condition, I took precautions. It was in part because I didn't want to make them nervous. A vampire looming over them in a darkened doorway was enough to make anyone nervous, and rightly so. The monster I could have been loomed just behind the facade of who I used to be. Just under the surface. It was hard to keep him caged, and the more time went by, the harder it was.... I needed the locks for my comfort.

Georgia walked through the door with her familiar, no-nonsense gait. Her uniform was crisp and starched, just like always. I took comfort in the predictable nature of Georgia.

"What is it?"

But she didn't need to answer. I'd already seen the stack of baby blue envelopes in her hand.

"You need to address this." Her voice was measured and

steady, as though she'd been practicing. Probably with Patricia. They were the only ones on my staff who knew my secret.

"Address what?" I replied flatly.

She looked down at the envelopes in her hand and sighed heavily. "You can't just... ignore them."

"Why not?" I pointed to the pile of crumpled and torn paper near the door. "They're not hurting anyone."

"Mr. Quake... You're going to have to—"

"Have to what? Admit that I'm infected? Go down to the clinic and put myself on the registry? Is that what I should do?"

Georgia's calm expression faltered just a little. She was nervous. Maybe even scared.

Good. She should be.

I might've been a tame vampire, but there was still a monster hiding in the shadows.

"Maybe it will be different. It's been a few years and people are more accepting of your—"

"Of my kind?" I hissed.

Georgia swallowed thickly and I could see the vein in her throat throb as her heart rate sped up. She knew she'd made a mistake now.

I let her flounder in the silence for a moment as I walked around her in a circle. "I heard you and Patricia talking yesterday," I said.

"We talk all the time," she said. "She's ordered a new shipment of blood for you. A different abattoir that doesn't ask as many questions."

"You and Patricia always take such good care of me," I said.

Georgia's hands clenched into fists before she forced herself to relax and smile. "We do our best. You're definitely a challenge."

I tapped my finger against my temple as though I was trying to remember something important. "What was it you were talking about," I said. "It wasn't blood. I'd remember that. It's… it's all I think about, after all."

I was toying with her. I didn't need to. But anger welled up inside me and I couldn't escape its clutches.

"I don't know what you're talking about," she stammered. "Like I said—"

I snapped my fingers, and she jumped. "Now I remember," I said brightly. "You were talking about the fang haters… Patricia knows some, doesn't she? She sounded pretty torn up about it. Like she couldn't talk about her life with them. Is this hard for you, Georgia? Working for me?"

"I—"

"You wouldn't sell me out to the hunters, would you?"

My words were soft and dangerous, and I knew Georgia was afraid. I could smell it.

"Never," she blurted out. "Patricia was just — She's worried about you, too."

"So, you both want me to sign on to the vamp registry. Out myself to the world… And for what? So you don't have to sneak around and pretend you're still working for an exciting eccentric pop star instead of a fanghead who can't come to terms with his own reality?"

"Mr. Quake — I said nothing of the —"

"You don't have to say anything," I murmured. "I'm disappointed in you, Georgia. You've been invaluable…"

Her job had been to clean up my messes. There was no way she could have known what state of mind I was in. There was no way she would know what I'd do to protect myself.

That's what I was doing. I was protecting myself. Or, rather, my monster was protecting me.

He reared up and took hold of me as I wrapped my arms around Georgia and held her tight against my chest so that I could bury my fangs into that delicious, pulsing vein in the side of her neck. Her thin scream of fear and pain fell on deaf ears. All I could hear was the rushing of her blood and the pounding pace of her heart as her blood flowed over my tongue.

Giving in to my monster gave me peace.

It felt.... *right.*

Her blood was sweet and light and *perfect.* The more I drank, the happier I felt.

When I felt her life-force leave her as she slumped in my arms? My only regret was that my moment of happiness and this quintessentially primal experience was over.

My monster was insatiable. Once loose, he's hard to corral back into control. The all-consuming hunger burrowed deep into my psyche, blocking out all the work I had done for years to keep it at bay.

Georgia was delicious.

But she wasn't enough.

It's like, if we instructed a human to live on only oatmeal and multivitamins. You get your nutrients and you satiate your body, but it doesn't quell your hunger. Then, one day, you give that person a cake. A delicious, glorious chocolate cake. You tell them they can have one bite and then they have to go back to oatmeal.

Georgia was my cake. And I wasn't ready to stop with just one bite.

The monster was loose again.

All the intense work I had done over the last five years to keep him at bay — gone in a literal heartbeat. That progress vanished the instant her blood touched my tongue. My human brain left me and the primal, monstrous part of me picked up the slack.

My sensitive ears picked up the pounding of the heartbeats in the house, and they called to me with a seductive tempo that would take a man of great self-control to refuse.

I had never been a man of great self-control, and my monster had no time for remorse. I've denied his existence for too long.

All day long, I prowled through the estate. My unsuspecting staff never stood a chance.

Not really.

I hunted them for sport. My thirst drove me into a fever, but the thrill of the capture and hunt drove me into a delirious state.

They never knew the danger they were in. Only Georgia and Patricia knew what I really was. Each victim tasted better than the last.

Their blood sang to me and, one after the other, I tracked them through the house by their heartbeats and pounced.

When I drained them of their life-force, I dragged them to my private quarters and lined them up like cords of firewood. My housekeeper Liliana lay next to Georgia. Those two had always gotten on well. My personal chef, Alejandro, with his food-stained apron was on the other side of my personal trainer, Dan.

Eight staff members lived and worked at my estate, and I killed them all.

The bloodlust faded by the time I got to my executive assistant, Patricia. Efficient, devoted Patricia. She didn't beg like the others. She was resigned to her fate. Maybe her lack of fight was why I got sloppy towards the end. I didn't double-check to make sure she was completely gone when I put her in with the others.

The ding of the text alert tipped me off, but it was too late.

She used her dying moments to send a text to my label, *Cainin Records*. Not her family, or her friends, or her cat sitter— my label.

"Vinnie is a vampire. Household staff dead. Call in the entire team. Get Pisces for PR before it's too late."

She died surrounded by the bodies of her colleagues with her phone in her hand. A small smile on her face.

That's what finally got through to me.

Someone far more deserving of life than I used their dying moments to help me, a monster. There's nothing about me that should inspire this kind of loyalty.

The least I could do, the absolute very least, was get my monster under control. For Patricia. And Georgia. Liliana, Dan, Alejandro, Sue, Ella, and Harris. They didn't need to die.

I sighed heavily as the sounds of vehicles coming up the drive alerted me to my visitors. Judging from the noise, there were at least three trucks. My people were the best money could buy and I was a cash-cow for my label.

Little things like cleaning up a massacre of an entire household-worth of staff wasn't outside their job duties. They might fear me, but they would fix this with the utmost discretion.

The darkness swirled inside me, unhappy to be locked away with my monster once again.

I don't want to be a monster.

If I could, I would take it all back in a heartbeat. I would redo the last five years or, at the very least, just die in that hotel room. But there was no more normal for me, not anymore. If the people who claim to adore me really knew the truth, they would abandon me. That's what people do to vampires. They fear you, abandon you, and treat you like the monster you are.

Vinnie Quake, international popstar, billionaire, global chart-topping narcissistic asshole, is a vampire... And soon enough the entire world would know. Things would never be normal again.

2

———

TUESDAY

In this world, there are a few things that I've learned I can count on. One, making friends with a bartender equals better drinks. Two, if left to my own devices, I will 1000% choose the absolute worst man in the room. Three, they never use a current photo on the apps.

As if to prove my point, I glanced furtively at my date while I sipped some more of my mediocre Chardonnay.

Zach Edmunds.

38.

Divorced. No kids. One dog.

Real Estate owned: one condo.

Job: Wealth Manager.

Credit score: fair/medium.

When we matched on the app, he told me he worked in finance and was very active, loved to paddle board and spent a lot of time pursuing personal wellness. I discreetly pulled his photo up on my phone and glanced at it under the bar.

Technically, the photo was of him. Just a version of him from about ten years ago. The ruddy, windswept cheeks, sculpted biceps and thick brown hair from his picture showed someone with a zest for life. It's why I agreed to meet. But the reality was... disheartening, even by the app standards. He had a receding hairline, an overly inflated sense of self, and the flushed red complexion of someone who spends more time in bars than outside. This man may work in finance, but... he was no outdoor wellness warrior. He's soft, pale and brash; a keyboard warrior.

His expensive accessories impressed but the scuffed, worn down shoes showed he probably lived outside his means. Like every other man I've been out with in my precious little free time these days, he's an utter disappointment. In some ways, the knowledge is comforting. I set the bar low and the men I've found have never, ever exceeded it. Not anymore. Not since... him.

I banished the thoughts of my ex from my mind and refocused on the task at hand. Zach didn't require my participation in this conversation to have a good time. That much was obvious. He, like the ones before him, mainly saw me as a prop for an ego or a notch on his bedpost. In a different life, that would outrage me, but tonight it suited me just fine. I settled deeper into my stool and tried to see if I could tolerate him long enough to get what I needed. If men were this callous about sex, why shouldn't I be?

While he blathered on about something relating to Seattle's wild real estate market and peppered in disparaging comments about the houseless population and liberal snowflakes the bartender set a glass of whiskey in front of me and winked. I nodded at him gratefully. I had scanned him up and down when I first got here. He reminded me of a young Orlando Bloom, and I appreciated the hell out of that look. Unfortunately for me, that golden wedding ring he wore gleamed like a freakin' beacon in the low light of the bar. *Taken.* I took a sip of my whiskey and raised my glass to him slightly and he nodded his head. *Whoever snagged that one is a lucky beeyotch. They really do take all the good ones.*

The addition of whiskey made Zach only slightly more tolerable to my overall mood, but the conversation was growing tiresome and increasingly problematic.

When my best friend, Adrienne, told me to get back out there, I doubted this was what she had in mind.

My whiskey glass was almost empty, and he still hadn't bothered to ask me a single question about myself. *Truly insufferable.* Happy Hour was almost over and the noise of the bar was picking up. The rest of the after-work crowd would be here soon and I seriously considered cutting my losses and finding some nice hipster dude to hook up with instead. I was so frustrated I could scream.

I didn't want forever with anyone.

Hell, I didn't even want the entire night.

I would take one blissful half an hour if that was available. Just... something, anything, to get me out of this impossible dry spell I'd found myself in.

Going home alone, again, was not an option.

I glanced around the bar again, hoping to spot an acceptable alternative to my current date but no one stood out. Maybe it's the bar. It's way more pretentious than my usual stomping grounds. Everyone in here wanted to see and be seen. I didn't. I'm a behind the scenes kinda gal. Fame didn't interest me. Solving problems did.

Zach could solve my problem.

If I could get him to stop talking, he could serve as a means to an end.

Decision made, I drained the rest of my whiskey glass and placed my hand on his knee, a movement which so thoroughly interrupted his current rant that I struggled not to laugh. *God, men are so easy.*

"Zach—can I be honest with you?"

I leaned forward a little more, allowing my hand to slip on the stool and giving him an eyeful of my cleavage as I lowered my voice to a sexier, huskier tone.

His hand covered mine and he zeroed in on my cleavage. *Hook... Line....*

"Of course, babe," he murmured as he licked his lips.

Ew. Babe? Gross.

"I don't give a flying fuck in space about the real estate market. I don't care about your opinion on *literally* anything. I don't. Your thoughts, opinions and mediocre knowledge base is irrelevant to me and some of your views are, frankly, offensive. I would honestly like you better if I never spoke to you again."

He sputtered his outrage but I kept going, and arched my back so that he regained focus on my tits. *Good boy.*

"But here's the thing, Zach... I've been in a sexual dry spell for a while and I have some needs that I'm almost 60% sure you can take care of. I'm going to get up from this stool and I'm going to walk out that door. If you're interested in *exploring* my needs for one night, and let me stress this, *one* night only, you can follow me. Otherwise... enjoy your evening."

I straightened up and stifled another laugh at his dumbfounded expression... and the visible arousal in his pants. I threw a $50 bill on the bar, waved to the bartender, and waltzed out the door, my hips swaying side to side as I went.

I counted softly under my breath as I stood at the taxi stand, and was unsurprised when it only took until the count of four for the breathy, excited broker to appear at my side. *Snicker.*

So predictable. Some men like to posture that they're the Ultimate Alpha, but whenever I let my dominant side out, they come crawling. Turnabout is fair play. If men can talk to women this way, I might as well return the favor.

I tucked my hand into the crook of his elbow, and waved

down a cab. My intention was to take Zach home to break my
dry spell in the most unimpressive way possible. The key was to
set my expectations low enough—that way I wouldn't be disappointed. I had learned that the hard way and I'd never forget it.

***

Unfortunately, I was overzealous in my estimation of how
low I have set the bar. I didn't actually believe that such a
thing was possible, but good old Zachary was much worse than I
had originally thought.

Not only was he unable and *unwilling* to accept direction, he
insisted on giving me a running commentary on the situation,
drank half a bottle of the whiskey I'd been saving for my birthday, and then attempted to mansplain women's pleasure to me.
Complete with a rant about the 'myth' of the multiple orgasm.

I didn't even get my stockings off before I explained, as nicely
as I could, that we—regrettably—*weren't* compatible and then I
threw him out of my condo on his ass.

At the rate I was going, I'd be better off dating myself. Men in
this city were severely overrated if Zach represented the cream
of the crop.

Ugh.

I laid in bed, stared at the ceiling, and watched the oscil-
lating ceiling fan go round and round.

I'd spent the better part of the last five years grieving my last
relationship. Five years of feeling the betrayal daily. Five years of
being afraid to let myself be vulnerable, and I still couldn't break
my celibacy streak no matter who, or what, I tried.

A small jolt of pain twanged in my heart when I allowed
myself to think of *him*.

We all have one.

That one ex you spend an eternity trying - and *failing* - to get over.

It was hard to be happy with 'Mr. Safe & Boring' when your heart craved the explosive passion you used to have. Adrienne likes to tell me I'll find someone better. But she's an eternal optimist, and I just can't bring myself to that level of... cheer.

But I wouldn't find anyone better.

Not really.

And if I was being *truly* honest? I wasn't sure I *wanted* to find something better.

The only downside was that rage had replaced passion in my heart. Pain and hurt lived where love used to. I'd closed myself off and turned that heartache into jet fuel. Really, getting over my ex would mean I would have to deal with that shitstorm once and for all. And I just was not ready.

Fuck.

The memories crowded my mind and I dragged my hand through my hair in frustration. I desperately wished that I could zap his presence from my brain. Temporary amnesia would be a blessing. I could live with rage, but the memories of his sweetness, the way he used to hold me—those were the ones I had to watch out for.

With a groan, I dragged myself off the mattress and pulled a robe over my shoulders. I stretched, cracked my back, and threw my hair into a messy bun. Once again, sleep would be in short supply tonight.

I sat down at my desk and turned on my laptop. The best way to distract myself out of a problematic vault of memories was always the same. Take a deep dive into someone else's problems. That's what I do best. I can fix almost anything... except myself.

An email marked **URGENT & CONFIDENTIAL** flashed on

the screen as my laptop loaded and I frowned at it. Getting a work notice around midnight was certainly not unheard of, but something truly urgent would normally have been preceded by a phone call.

I scanned the email and my eyebrows raised through to my hairline and a tingle went through my body. Someone fucked up really terrible.

The idea of digging into whatever horrific mess one of our clients created excited me twice as much as anything Zach could have come up with. I saw two other names next to mine in the email header and realized that Carlyn, my boss, had sent it out to the three most senior Client Relationship Managers. A fierce sense of competitiveness and possessiveness flooded me and I reached for my phone and punched the speed dial for my boss.

My colleagues Frankie and Daiya were good at keeping clients happy and spinning stories. We actually got along great. But this kind of mess wasn't their cup of tea. They didn't have the hunger for it or the... flexible ethics... required to deal with the darker, messier side of it.

I did.

This case had my name written all over it from the very first word.

Carlyn answered on the first ring and jumped into the logistics without so much as a greeting. She's efficient like that. It's why we get along so well.

"Tuesday. You called first, the case is yours."

I pumped my fist in the air with victory.

"Be advised: the situation is time-sensitive, involves rumored criminal activity, and will require a... creative approach. You'll need to debrief the client team within the hour. This is a Level 10 situation. Rules of engagement will be forwarded to you."

I shivered in excitement. Too often, we got called in to massage public opinion about a politician's mistress or help spin rehab stories for the rich and famous. This one was different. I could feel it.

I moved around my room with practiced efficiency, throwing changes of clothing, notebooks, and my spare battery packs into my tote bag.

By the time I hung up with Carlyn, I was dressed and moving out the door.

The cool night air and gentle breeze brushed against my skin. It was a full moon and I bounced from one foot to the other as I waited for the Lyft. My excitement for this assignment grew with each moment.

Some people had an innate desire to help people. Those people made wonderful teachers, social workers, doctors, and parents.

I had a desire to win, no matter the stakes.

Each case I took was a game with high stakes for my client and for our agency. My adversaries were whatever problem these rich assholes got themselves into. I didn't need to agree with their choices or even like them, but by God, I would win for them.

When I had landed at Pisces PR Agency a few years ago, I had thought I would just be spinning political bullshit for a few years to gain experience.

But Carlyn took a chance on me and showed me a whole new world was out there. One filled with things outside my wildest dreams and problems no one else would touch.

After six months, I was a regular on the emergency fixer team. By a year, I was leading my own. And now? Now I was the one they called in when it's bad enough to cause an international incident.

This job was the dream I never knew I had, and I was damn good at it.

. . .

***

What was it about people who did bad things and abandoned office buildings on the outskirts of town? They couldn't be more cliched if they tried.

When the Lyft dropped me off at 11:48 p.m., I smiled to myself. *Show time.*

A man in a well-tailored suit waited for me just inside the door. He was barrel-chested and built like a Mack truck, dwarfing the ficus plant he stood next to. There was an aura about him that screamed "do not fuck with me" and I immediately liked him and nicknamed him Truck.

"Name?"

I smiled at him and pulled out my card. "Tuesday Matson, Client Relationship Manager for Pisces PR Agency."

He grunted and pulled out his phone to take a picture of my card.

"Follow me, Ms. Matson. The client is waiting for you. When we get inside, I have to search you."

I nodded quickly and followed him through the double doors. Another man in a suit, somehow bigger and burlier than Truck, waited beyond. In my mind, he immediately became Tank. *Tank and Truck. Perfect.*

Tank and Truck searched me quickly and efficiently. These were not rent-a-cops with a careless attitude and a badge from eBay, they were professionals with a lifetime of experience working in security and protection.

"She's clear." Tank called out and Truck nodded and dug a small badge and lanyard out of one of his cargo pockets.

"Ms. Matson, you must wear this at all times while moving about the building."

I examined the badge as they escorted me into an elevator, hoping it would give me a clue who the client was, but there was nothing written on either side. Just a QR code and some numbers.

Carlyn hadn't been overly verbose in our conversation earlier. She insisted I would get all relevant information from the client. The situation was, in her words, *evolving.* The only thing she told me was that the client needed help to stay out of jail and manage their public image. It wasn't outside my scope of practice to assist with discreet cleanup missions. Given the security they employed, the client was probably a highly-ranked politician, a criminal, or an A-list celebrity. If I was lucky, it's all three. *Yeah, yeah, I know I'm weird.*

The elevator lurched to a stop, and the doors slid open to reveal a standard office building floor with a big reception desk and a lobby waiting area. A harried-looking man in a floral button-down shirt and skinny jeans paced the carpet beside the desk. The poor man looked as though he was one step away from literally wringing his hands.

"You the PR guru?" he asked, his voice high and anxious.

I smiled at him, trying to put him at ease. The high-strung ones always responded best to displays of confidence. "You bet. My name is Tuesday and I'm here to help solve your problem."

His smile looked forced as he grabbed my arm and led me into a small office area just behind the lobby.

"You must sign an NDA before we go any further." He dropped a thick folder onto the desk in front of me and held out a pen.

I flipped open the folder and scanned the documents. It was a standard non-disclosure agreement, and I knew, regardless of what it read, I would sign it with no issue. Absolute discretion was the bread and butter of our business. I ignored the pen in his hand and pulled an elegant fountain pen out of my purse to sign the documents before sliding the folder back over the table to him.

His smile was a little more genuine this time.

"Thank you for coming on such short notice, Ms. Matson. Your reputation precedes you, and we're *very* grateful that you would consider our request. My name is Baldwin Kennison, and I am the client-by-proxy. Will you come with me, please? We have a great deal to discuss."

My curiosity piqued, I followed him out of the room. We didn't do client-by-proxy much anymore. *Someone really must have something to hide.*

Perfect.

3

TUESDAY

Another set of doors led to yet another conference room where several other people were already waiting. I sat in the chair my new client indicated and looked around the room expectantly.

"Good morning, everyone. Let's get started, shall we? Who wants to brief me on the situation?" I made eye contact with everyone around the table as I pulled out my iPad and a stylus, prepared to take notes.

A small, mouse-like woman spoke first.

"Thank you for coming so quickly. We're... eager to get on top of this situation. My name is Kelly and I work with the client's management team. Recently, we learned the client has... developed a permanent medical condition that has resulted in a total turnover of his household staff. He is currently refusing entry to anyone from his management to his home with the exception of a discreet clean-up crew. Due to the... number of individuals... involved in the... turnover... we're seeking a PR strategy to help us keep their career intact."

I blinked at the tiny woman in confusion, trying to read

between the lines of what she was actually telling me. *Client did a bad thing and is blaming a medical condition. Interesting. This should be fun.*

I tapped my stylus on the table briefly and tried to think of the best way to ask the questions I needed to ask.

"What was the exact number of staff members involved in this... incident?"

Pisces PR had handled many situations over the years, some for the good guys and some for the bad. Depending on the body count, covering up murder comes with a significant surcharge.

The silence in the room was so heavy that I got a terrible feeling about this.

"Eight," someone at the table said in a choked voice. Two more people sniffled and a wash of icy dread swept over me.

One or two was easy enough to explain. It sounded callous, but people died every day. I could usually fix three with a tragic accident, but *eight*? Eight was a massacre, and massacres rarely just went away.

"And the client is public-facing? We have a brand image to worry about?" I couldn't stop the cringe as my brain worked frantically to think of how I could spin this. *Maybe a gas leak? An accidental explosion? Food poisoning? God, what about the families... this was going to be complicated.*

Kelly looked up at me with unshed tears in her eyes and confirmed my assumption.

"Very. Our client is a household name and has contractual obligations that greatly interest my employer. We would like this... medical condition.... addressed in a way that allows them to complete the terms of their contract." *Typical corporate interests. Their client kills a fuckton of people and they are worried about their image and money.*

"How long has it been? Where are the bodies?" I'm done

being polite. If I had to spin the deaths of eight innocent people, it's time to get really blunt. I stared at the members of the client's team, crossed my fingers under the table and hoped for a break.

"Best guess is eight to ten hours. The staff involved were all live-in, and none had dependents we were aware of. The client makes that a requirement of employment."

Ok. We can revisit the legality of the dependent thing later. It's been less than a day. Ok. We can work with this.

Confident that we at least had a starting place, I sat up straighter and exhaled slowly. Under a day, live-in staff, no dependents. Unless whatever happened attracted a lot of outside attention, chances were we could intervene before law enforcement. Maybe.

"Are you prepared to disclose the medical condition the client has that... impacted this situation?" I asked, glancing over at Baldwin. *Please, not a serial killer. Please, not a serial killer.*

Unsurprisingly, Baldwin's cheeks paled, and he cleared his throat awkwardly. Grabbing the NDA I signed earlier, he held it up in the air and made eye contact with me.

"You understand the terms of this NDA will destroy you if you so much as *whisper* the idea of anything we tell you in this meeting to anyone outside these walls, correct?"

Oh, clients. They never get it.

With great personal strength, I resisted rolling my eyes. Barely. I got this question a lot, especially from our more... unsavory... clients. But they had nothing to worry about. I was a vault. I'd served as the secret keeper for so many people in the greater Pacific Northwest that few things shocked me anymore. However, only half my job was wrangling images. The other half was talking worried handlers off the edge. To appease the man across the table, I nodded my head vigorously in acceptance.

"Of course."

Kelly shared a long look with Baldwin before she leaned toward me, "He has…"

A large bang and loud voices shouting from the hallway outside the door interrupted us.

Before we could react, the conference room door slammed open and a tall figure wearing sunglasses and a hoodie barged in, flanked by Truck and Tank.

I blinked as a sense of déjà vu rose in me. *What's happening?* I stared at the newcomer curiously.

"I think I should be a part of this conversation, don't you, Baldwin? Since it's my fucking mess you're cleaning up."

The stranger's voice made me freeze in shock. *Oh. Oh no.* I couldn't stop the audible gasp that escaped me.

The stranger turned his head toward me slowly. With one fluid movement, he pushed his hood back and took off his sunglasses. His full face was on display for me.

Nope. Uh huh. No. Not a chance.

I blinked again hard and something deep and powerful, an emotion almost like fury boiled in my stomach. The one man on this god-forsaken planet who could make me go from calm, cool professional to raging banshee in 3.4 seconds flat stared back at me.

Vinnie-The-MotherLoving-Asshole-Quake. International Pop Star. Seattle's Bachelor of the Year three-years running. General Dick-face. Ex-Fiance.

My body reacted on instinct.

I would swear in court, I didn't even feel myself rise out of my chair and move towards him until we were standing nose to nose. My hands shook. That familiar face that I loved, cried over and hated with every fiber of my being for the last five years. Here. *Here.*

He smirked down at me and the fury erupted.

The slap rang throughout the room when I cracked him

across that stupid, perfect face. The noise snapped me out of my trance, as did the unusually cold temperature of his skin and the pain in my hand as I took another step back.

"I probably deserved that," he whispered, his red eyes flashing at me as he gestured to Tank and Truck who hovered next to me, guns out, to sit down.

"You deserve that and so much more, *Vincent.* You look like *shit*, by the way. A killer now? Really? Thought you were too much of a coward for something like that." The rage powered through me, further fueled by his complete lack of reaction to my presence in the room. And my greeting.

Tank and Truck appeared at my side again and they looked upset. In unison, their big beefy hands dropped onto my shoulders and pushed me back into my chair. I couldn't tell if this was to protect their client or to prevent me from storming out of the room. Probably both.

"Tell your goons to unhand me, *Vincent*, before I make sure your problems get MUCH more complicated."

Vinnie smiled and waved his hands at Tank and Truck and they stepped away from me.

"Now, will you hear me out, Tater-Tot?"

Tater-tot? How dare he? Self-preservation intervened before I could do something more drastic than baring my teeth at him for his casual use of my old nickname.

Arms crossed in front of me, I gave him the frostiest glare I could manage. He looked almost exactly the same as the day he left me. His face still resembled a classical sculpture, with chiseled cheekbones, broad shoulders, and powerful hands. I hated how attracted I still was to him.

"My "medical condition" is complicated. We could spend a long time discussing it but I know you like the details. Here they are. I'm a vampire. I turned five years ago."

His soft voice pierced through my rage as the implications sank in. *Vampire. Turned. Five years. The same year we broke up.*

I shook my head and focused my attention. *Red eyes. Pale complexion. Holy... vampire?* Whoa.

"My team ordered a physical for my world tour. I'm not exactly... out... to everyone. There was a mixup at the clinic and they ended up doing a full workup, including blood work. Long story short, I tested positive for the Vampiric Infectious Disease. There are regulations in place to prevent the doctors who discovered it from going public... but I don't expect any of this to remain a secret for very long." Vinnie sighed heavily.

"Patricia was my lifeline. She and Georgia helped me more than I deserved. Patty found blood sources for me to feed on and always checked in on me." His next pause was longer and felt heavier. "It wasn't the perfect system, but we had a balance. It worked. Until it didn't. Earlier today, I experienced a severe lapse in control and... my household staff died because of it."

His tone was completely blank as he gestured to the people sitting around the room. No one moved, it was almost as though the act of explaining what had happened— that my ex-fiancé, the biggest pop star in the world, was a secret vampire who had eaten his household staff as a pre-dinner snack was perfectly normal. It blew my mind. Eight people died and we categorized it as a 'loss of control'.

Which, as a vampire, it could very well be. *Dodged a bullet there, Tuesday. Criminey.*

A headache burned behind my eyes as I tried to make sense of the entire situation. I pressed my palms against my face and took a few deep breaths. That was supposed to be calming, right?

1. If what they said was true, they contracted me to spin a mass murder into something... less murdery. Check.

2. The murderer was a vampire and living a double life as possibly the most well-known music star in the world. Whatever I spin had to stand the test of many, many press outlets.

3. Said vampire was also the ex who ruined my life five years ago and just admitted to eating his assistant and his household staff without a bit of remorse.

I'd done 'Mess Clean Up' before. That's what we called it when one of our clients did something illegal and we're called in to make it go away. Mess Clean Up covered up a multitude of sins. There were always boundaries and rules for what we would clean up: No kids. No rape. No animal abuse. But murder? Sure, we'd made that go away. It horrified a small part of me that this was my life now. I made a living by categorizing how terrible something was and put a price tag on it before I decided whether I would make it go away, legal or not.

But a different, more sinister part of me, the part I didn't admit to in public, was happy that I'm so good at what I do. There's a peacefulness that comes from being called to a situation and being allowed to drop the ethical lens and just solve the problem at hand. It's like a giant jigsaw puzzle with real-life consequences. *Does that make me a sociopath? Maybe.*

The tension in the room was overwhelming. I could feel the stares of every single person at the table burning into me. They were waiting for me to say something.

I could walk. Carlyn would understand.

Probably.

But if there was anything I hated more than Vinnie, it was the idea of giving up. To give up would be to let him win.

He was never, ever, allowed to win. Winning was my thing.

Without me, they were... in the crassest of terms: royally fucked. I knew it and they knew it. Without me, every single person in this room would go to jail.

I was a professional, and this was not my first uncomfortable case, it definitely wouldn't be my last. It was more than clear that the time to turn my emotions off and focus on the issue at hand was well overdue.

"According to Pisces PR contracts, concealing felonies comes with a surcharge. Given the number of people that Mr. Quake has... eaten and killed in cold blood this evening, that surcharge will be substantial, as will the extra fees for me having to deal with his pathetic ass. Consultant rules."

Vinnie smirked at me and everything in me wished I had a spray bottle of Holy Water to spritz on him like a misbehaving demonic cat.

With vampiric infections on the rise, local drug stores sold really cute pressurized Holy Water canisters—Vampire mace— but I had never seen the need to carry one. I would change that as soon as humanly possible. I was pretty sure that a boutique near my apartment sold a range with Swarovski crystal embell- ishments...

Vinnie's manager smiled in a way that felt far too familiar for the situation. "We both know Mr. Quake's profile is high enough that money is no object. Thank you for agreeing to help. We anxiously await your plan."

I bristled at Baldwin's simpering tone as he pushed a blank check across the conference table toward me. They'd already made it out to Pisces PR. I was nothing more than a service provider to these people—a way to solve a problem that their crazy client had created.

At least they had the sense of self-preservation to come to us. No other agency would touch this mess. We're the only firm in town, hell, in this section of the world that even had the capa- bility and stomach to deal with this.

But that didn't mean they got off easy.

Oh. No.

Not by a long shot.

They were going to pay. *Vinnie* was going to pay. Big time.

Against my better judgment, I pulled out my folder and tucked the check inside.

It was time to get to work.

4
____

VINNIE

I watched Tuesday take a deep breath and knew we'd hooked her. She prided herself on being a steel trap that never showed emotion, but I knew what buttons to push to break through that facade.

It's hard to hide from someone you once knew better than yourself.

Hearing her voice again was surreal. She steadfastly refused to make eye contact with me and the brush off, while warranted, stung a bit. Watching her work was a special pleasure. Her professional mask and the cool, confident, competent problem solver was in complete control and she was managing my team like an expert. You would never guess that she had lost control only a few minutes before.

"Are you planning to go public with his diagnosis at some point? Am I preparing to have him do a public 'coming out' moment, or are we just managing him and this incident to achieve contract compliance and keep him out of jail? What is being done for the victims and any family they might have? Even if they were loners, someone will eventually come looking for compensation if it's being offered."

I slipped my sunglasses back on while she went through her checklists and contingency plans. Her movements were professional, but I knew that under her cool exterior she was seething like a volcano about to erupt.

Her long brown hair was piled into a bun on top of her head, and everything in me ached to pull out whatever pins were holding it in place and run my hands through those mahogany waves.

I sniffed the air and the familiar scent of ginger and jasmine wafted towards me and my cock twitched. It didn't matter to my cock that I was a monster and deserved to be put down like a rabid animal. The sight of my ex-fiancee stirred my desires and caused me to react on a primal level. Baldwin never should have called her. She was temptation personified, and my control was hanging on by a thread.

The moment I realized she was in the room with me, I tuned my senses into the steady thrum of her pulse in her neck. My fangs longed to plunge deep into her veins.

My monster wanted her.

I wanted her.

I didn't care *how* I had her, as long as I did. If I could taste her again, plunge my fangs (or my cock) into her until she cried out in ecstasy? Then I could die a satisfied man.

They say every superhero has a weakness. But I'm no superhero. I'm the villain and villains have marks.

Employing Tuesday to solve this problem was a mistake, and this whole thing was probably going down in flames, but I couldn't bear the thought of not having her here.

I'm a selfish, murdering prick. I don't deserve her or anyone else.

We used to talk about the future we would have during the day and lose ourselves in each other when the sun went down. I'd fucked that all up.

"Earth to Vinnie. I need your input, oh supreme jackass."

Tuesday frowned at me with a familiar look of exasperation on her face. Apparently, she had asked me something. I doubt it was to go into the broom closet and fuck. More's the pity.

"Yes?"

I forced myself to pay attention to the situation at hand.

"I said, do you have any enemies who would attack you or have reason to harm you?"

Baldwin and I laughed at the same time.

I was no saint.

People who would want to attack me? A dime a dozen. Such is the life of an international star. But the more I thought of it, the only person with any *compelling* reason to harm me was sitting right in front of me.

"Have you said anything particularly offensive to anyone of late? Had any threats? Do you have *anything even remotely helpful* we can use?"

I pondered for a full minute, trying to think back on my previous interviews. Finally, I shrugged and shook my head. My public persona was carefully designed so that I always appeared aloof and mysterious. I rarely gave interviews, especially not in person, and was never seen around town without a scheduled event to attend.

Tuesday's lips pressed into a thin line and her narrow gaze had me wondering if she was plotting my death. *Good luck, cupcake. It might do the world a favor.*

"Baldwin," she finally spoke, "What was the reasoning behind keeping Vinnie's *condition* a secret?"

My manager glanced at me and then back to Tuesday.

"We did some polling—test marketing, focus groups, that sort of thing. There is a lot of anti-vampire sentiment out there. We believed at the time that alerting the public to his status would be detrimental to his career."

And the label's bottom line.

I knew all of this, but it still rubbed me the wrong way.

Tuesday nodded thoughtfully. "Yes, but surely that sentiment has died down a bit? We're hearing of more and more vampires in high-visibility positions. People in the public eye. Politicians. Industry players. Was there any other reason that factored into spinning him as a reclusive eccentric, rather than a jackass who happened to be a blood-sucking vampire? Sales of vampire fiction and cult TV shows featuring sexy vampire love interests are at an all-time high."

I looked at Baldwin in surprise. I had never considered that I could go public and be well-received, but my manager just pursed his lips and shook his head.

"Do you know how many hate-groups that target vampires are active in the Seattle area? Twelve. They boast substantial membership, their social media followings are skyrocketing, and they're actively recruiting. Two of them, *Outlaw Vampire Alliance* and the *Vanquish Vampire Vigilantes* have had highly publicized incidents where they attempted to stake ordinary vampires going about their business. Assassination attempts. Kidnappings. And that's just in the Puget Sound. Cainin Records and I agreed we would not court any... *controversy* unless it was absolutely necessary. His status as a vampire is on a strictly need-to-know basis."

Tuesday nodded and pursed her lips as she tapped away at her iPad to make more notes. I used to love watching her when she would get like this. Tuesday had always had a brilliant mind. She saw the world like a giant puzzle, and I knew she was enjoying putting together these pieces.

The pulse point on her neck drew my attention again. The sound of the steady beat of her heart and the rush of blood in her veins was like listening to the sweetest melody. It called to me and I knew there would never be any lyrics I could write that would do that beauty justice. My monster perked up, suddenly interested in exploring the object of my intensity and I gritted my teeth to keep him at bay.

"I've got it!" She sat up straight and tapped her stylus against the iPad triumphantly. A pile of loose papers covered in her handwriting spread out in front of her and I blinked in confusion. "Here's what we're going to do!" She looked over at me, not bothering to hide the scorn on her face as she gestured towards her pile of papers. "Pay attention, dickface. I'm only going to explain this once."

She turned her attention to the pale man in the expensive, but still somehow ill-fitting, floral shirt. "Baldwin. The bodies of his... victims... they're still in the house, correct?"

My manager nodded; his expression grim.

"Good. Your clean-up crew is going to put them all back in their beds," she said firmly.

Her face was devoid of all expression. Detached. It was like she was talking about taking out the laundry, not... bodies. *Impressive.*

"Make it look natural... as much as possible anyway. Any vampire paraphernalia must be removed from the house. No blood bags or issues of *Vampire Monthly* or anything else. Find out if anyone on staff had strong vampire political feelings or opinions—either way. Once they set the stage, no one goes in without checking with me first. This may take a day or two to pull off and those bodies are going to get rank."

Baldwin got out his phone and started barking orders into it.

"Tank and Truck..." She pointed at my bodyguards and then grimaced. "Sorry, I don't know your actual names, but you two look like resourceful men of action. Do you think you could find some explosives on short notice?"

The bodyguards froze the minute she addressed them. A small, grim smile flashed across Tank's face and he turned to talk to Truck. They had a brief, whispered argument with vigorous hand gestures. But in the end, an agreement was reached. Truck turned to her and gave her a thumbs up while Tank pulled out his phone and started texting furiously.

"I'm Sergio, and that's Cole. We can get explosives. Do you know what kind you need and how many?" Truck, otherwise known as Sergio, looked at her expectantly.

She smiled and made eye contact with me. My fangs descended without warning, and I struggled to stay seated.

"Enough to level the entire house."

Sergio grunted his assent and turned back to Cole. The conversation between the two of them was too faint for me to follow. Tuesday's little announcement stunned me to my core. I couldn't begin to care much about their logistics discussion while I was still processing *that. Blow up my house?! That's preposterous! It's a custom-built, multi-million dollar property with private waterfront access. My first purchase as a megawatt star. Who blows something like that up?!*

But she wasn't done.

"Kelly, get your content and social media teams ready. Wake up whoever you need to. We're going to get ahead of this and start some rumors. Coordinate with my office so we can leak an article, maybe a blog post, and attribute it to Vinnie. Post-date it so that it can be pulled up and they can talk about his pro-vamp views surfacing. Make it appeal to the common good. Something... innocuous that expresses sympathy for the vampire-infected population. If you can, Photoshop him in front of one of the vamp clubs downtown. Get that trending on Twitter and the morning rags ASAP. I want it to hit the wire immediately." The woman with pink hair nodded and started making calls.

"Sergio and Cole, as soon as the explosives are ready and the clean up crew has left, you'll go in and put them into position. You need to set them so it looks like an amateur got really, *really* lucky." The two men exchanged meaningful looks. "If it were me, I would attach them to the gas line and maybe let the gas leak into the house first, but you're professionals. Just remember, we want a *big* fireball and *no* survivors. Set it for a timer and remote detonate. Use a burner phone, but, and I cannot stress this enough, you *have* to make it look like amateur hour. I want that in the papers when the Fire Marshal's office releases their findings. Be mindful of security cameras and don't waste any time. I need them ready to go at a moment's notice. We're going to pick a fight."

Tuesday was beautiful any time of day but when she was giving orders? Casually ordering the destruction of a murder scene to save my sorry ass? She was resplendent. The only thing better was when she got mad. I slid my sunglasses off my face and made eye contact with her.

"That's your grand plan, Tuesday? You're going to blow up my house? Somehow, I expected something a little... cleaner? Where am I supposed to live during all this?"

She whirled on me and the white-hot anger written all over her face made me take a step back.

Be careful what you wish for, man.

"Oh, I'm *so* sorry, *Vin-Vin,* here I am trying my damnedest to clean up a *mass murder site* for my *ex-fiancé* who is now a *vampire.* It's the middle of the night. If you don't like this plan, fine. It's the only one I have. Just say the word and I'll go. Good luck out there. Someone just might stake you on sight if they learn the truth, you walking blood-borne pathogen."

"You're right," she continued in a voice that dripped with disdain, "you are *clearly* the one being inconvenienced here. I should have given more thought to the creature comforts of the murdering, lying, cheating, smug bastard billionaire who had no choice but to hire me because he couldn't control himself for one unsupervised second."

The entire room fell silent, and I knew they were all waiting to see if I lost control again. No one had ever spoken to me that way. No one except Tuesday.

"Your goal is to have a reason for someone to hurt you. We are giving you an alibi tonight, an opportunity to make a public statement with accessories and schmooze with your fans while the rest of us build the case and provoke a substantial reaction. Can you control yourself long enough to get this done? Do you have someone you can spend the night with?"

She looked at me so sternly that I hoped to the Gods above that I could do this, if only to please her for just a small second. Two of the women working the phones threw thumbs up as they continued with their frantic conversations.

"Good. They'll take care of your social calendar tonight," she pointed at the assistants who were chattering amongst themselves.

"You need to be seen out and about. Get your ass into some clubwear and get downtown. Mermaidia has last call at 2:00 a.m. and that's in 1 hour and 27 minutes. You won't have time for a stylist so you're on your own. Make it provocative, Vinnie. That shouldn't be too hard, should it?" She scowled at me and turned to one of my assistants.

"You. Find him some accessories that show his newfound vamp sympathizer status. Bracelet? Necklace? Giant glowing fang-studded crown? I don't care. Just get it. He needs to make a statement. The blogs and paps need to get many, many, photographs of this. Go. Now."

I watched in amusement as my terrified intern nodded and scurried out of the room, her phone already glued to her ear.

Another assistant started writing on the white board, making a list of confirmed paparazzi and media contacts. *Tuesday knows how to inspire action, that's for damn sure.*

"Ok. Let's recap. Vinnie is unavoidably high-profile, and tonight he is going to poke the bear. This, along with our ability to spin public opinion, will give us the fuel we need for our firestorm. That gives us a motive, people. The key to this is to not do it ourselves. We need there to be proof, beyond reasonable doubt, that someone wants him dead. Preferably a lot of some-ones. Only then can we blow the house and take care of the rest of this situation."

Baldwin looked paler than normal and a few of the assis-tants gulped. It struck me that Tuesday (and, by extension, *me*) was asking my staff to do something truly terrible. If I were a good person, I would acknowledge that or do something for them. But the words stuck in my throat.

"That means trading on the increasingly prevalent anti-vamp bullshit and purposefully antagonizing some violent and unstable people so they can take the fall for this. Does anyone have a problem with that?" Tuesday's voice rang out clearly and the room quieted as my team looked at each other nervously.

"Um, what does that mean?" Kelly asked timidly.

Tuesday looked down at the table for a long moment before meeting everyone's eyes as she spoke.

"It means that we are going to wage virtual warfare. There are groups here in the Puget Sound that actively foster discrimi-natory behavior. Their numbers are small, despite their disorga-nization, the fervor of their anti-vamp sentiment is loud. If they knew what Vinnie is, they wouldn't hesitate to wish death, destruction, or a quick stake to the heart upon him. Or all of the above."

She paused for a moment, but no one moved or said anything. It felt as though the whole room was holding its breath.

"As it is, he has never taken a public stand for, or against, vampires," she continued. "I checked. If he takes a stand that is pro-vamp, they are literally going to shout for his blood. He will be the highest profile individual to publicly support the vampire community. They'll view him as a traitor. This will allow us to explain why Vinnie is missing public appearances later and explain why his *multi-million dollar waterfront property* is targeted in a domestic terrorist attack. Vinnie will, of course, survive but his staff were all viciously murdered. Unfortunate casualties of anti-vampire sentiment. This puts us in complete control of the narrative."

I smiled at her and clapped slowly. Tuesday Matson had always known *exactly* how to take things to the next level. I stood up but didn't bother to hide my fangs, or my boner, this time. I couldn't tell her how I really felt so I did the next best thing: I made her mad.

"Tuesday. That is. I have no words. You're the best. I bow to you. You're simply *the best*. Your plan is solid. I accept it. Baldwin, Sergio, Cole, and I will leave for my penthouse in the city, I'll get ready for Mermaidia there. You are, of course, welcome to accompany us to *supervise*. Just like old times."

She glanced down at my crotch and then met my gaze with a raised eyebrow and a smirk on her face. "You can fuck right off with that. I never make the same mistake twice, and you, Vincent, are a mistake. Why are you even here? You have an hour and 22 minutes to pull off being photographed in public. Go." She dismissed me and turned to the rest of my staff.

"It's time to get to work, people. Come over in groups for your assignments."

The entire room erupted into activity, eager to obey the flurry of orders Tuesday was dishing out.

My bodyguards nodded at me and stood to escort me to the door. They appeared completely unbothered by the request to level a building and hide evidence of murder. I should have leaned on them more. Maybe if I'd been more honest with them, they could have prevented my monster from getting loose.

Hindsight, it is a bitch.

Tuesday sat back as the room exploded into action again. I could hear her pulse racing. She was excited to see it all come together. Of course, she was. This plan was either the most brilliant thing she had ever come up with or it was all going to blow up in our faces... literally.

"I think that's everything to start," she said. "This will be our command post and we'll monitor the situation from here. I want status reports on the hour. Everyone needs to be using burner phones as soon as possible and someone needs to bring me the biggest coffee they can find. Go!"

I shook my head and followed Sergio and Cole out to the waiting SUV.

On the bright side, if this actually worked? It would give me a way to support the vampire community without formally coming out.

Only time would tell.

5

VINNIE

Baldwin arrived at the penthouse after us, and I could only guess that he'd stayed behind to speak to Tuesday in private. He was uncharacteristically quiet as he helped me choose my clubwear and only spoke to me to go over key points of the plan.

I was only half-listening to his droning. Tuesday had told me to be provocative and I was in the mood to be as literal as possible.

A neon mesh shirt combined with tight leather pants would be a statement that was sure to provoke some conversation. A black leather pageboy cap sailed across the room and clipped me on the shoulder. I flashed my fangs at Baldwin in annoyance but put it on. The cap combined with the mesh and the leather pants gave me a very... bondage club vibe.

"Here, you need to drink this." Baldwin interrupted my trip down memory lane and shoved a to-go cup in my face. "The last thing we need is another *incident.*"

Baldwin looked tired and he refused to make eye contact with me. A small part of me wondered if I had finally pushed my long-suffering manager too far.

Frowning, I examined the straw that protruded from the cup, but the familiarly coppery smell inspired a happy growl that startled Baldwin as I took a long sip.

"Must you?"

I smiled at him, my teeth stained red from my pre-game snack. "This was your idea," I said with a shrug.

Baldwin shook his head and stomped away from me. There *were* benefits to my lifestyle, and having a team of people dedicated to making sure I didn't screw up my life too badly was definitely at the top of the perk list.

Where had they been on the night I'd been turned...

I couldn't help but wonder what Tuesday would think if she saw me now. My fangs extended at the thought of her.

Tuesday. Seeing her again was like a stake through the heart. The burn of a shaft of sunlight on my skin.

She'll always be the epitome of the 'one who got away.' And there was definitely nothing I'd be able to do to fix that now. Especially in a neon mesh shirt.

If I could trust the notifications on my phone, my social media team had already accomplished a lot more than I'd expected.

#VinnieQuakeVampLover and #VinnieVamper were already trending on four platforms. The plan to leak pictures of me dressed like this would definitely accelerate the situation. The idea made me cringe in distaste.

The idea of going out like this, of tempting fate, actually horrified me. It had been extremely difficult hiding my identity as a vampire for five long years. Flaunting it went against every part of my being. But the luxury of having that choice disappeared when I lost control. *That can never happen again.*

Baldwin returned and handed me a leather bracelet that read: *Vamp Community Justice.* The steel clasp felt cold against my already icy skin and I rubbed at it as I thought about the fallout coming my way.

Ready or not, I was overdue to face the masses.

Operation 'Distract and Dominate' was officially underway.

Another assistant with a clipboard and a Tuesday approved can-do attitude appeared in my doorway.

"Mr. Quake, I'm glad to see that you're ready." She checked her watch and frowned slightly. *Tick-tock.* "Ms. Matson has arranged for you to meet up with Sandrina this evening. I've arranged for photographers to catch you taking Sandrina home to your penthouse apartment. You'll meet her in the VIP section of Mermaidia." She kept her eyes on her clipboard and didn't look up at me. *Fair enough.*

"This should keep you in the news and amplify the pro-vampire messaging. We received some intel from her team that Sandrina is working through a break-up and has an interest in making her recent ex jealous. They were very excited to work with us. Sandrina has no official stance on vampires, but she frequently advocates for peace and love. Her people want a love connection. Negotiations are between you and Sandrina on how that plays out, but her team ideally wants photos of you two kissing and dancing closely. They are not opposed to her staying the night and being photographed leaving your penthouse around midday tomorrow." The assistant finally looked up and met my eyes, but her expression was steely and emotionless.

I sighed and nodded. Sandrina was lovely but she was just so... young. Barely 21, she was the current darling of the up-and-coming glitterati—the hungriest of the sharks—and the amount of drama she could fit into one interaction was truly stunning.

I supposed beggars couldn't be choosers, and I was grudgingly thankful that she was willing to help. Obviously, she was getting something she wanted, but that was beside the point.

Her message delivered, the assistant disappeared. They

never bothered to wait for me to actually verbally agree to anything. It was part of being *managed.* Baldwin and Co. made sure each assistant was trained to simply announce information to me and then move on before I could complain or ask questions they couldn't answer. It used to piss me off, but I'd figured out that it's the best way to get anything done.

Baldwin joined me in the elevator and clapped his hand against my shoulder encouragingly when I stepped out into the parking garage. My shiny red restored Corvette was idling at the curb, and I couldn't help but smile to see it there. I loved cars. Anytime I had an excuse, I brought out this baby instead of riding around in the standard issue limousine or SUV.

I slid behind the wheel and Baldwin closed the driver's side door firmly.

"Tuesday said to tell you not to fuck this up," Baldwin said with a smirk.

I pressed my foot on the gas quickly and the engine roared gently.

"Of course, she does," I said. "Stop touching my car."

Baldwin pulled his hand away from the door as though it was red hot. I shifted the car into drive and pulled away from the curb, headed toward downtown.

Tuesday said...

Tuesday used to be mine, and I'd thrown it all away.

I thought I had come to terms with the fact that losing her was my fault. There'd been no other alternative... But that reason was feeling more and more hollow every day. It didn't help that I still hadn't figured out how to let her go.

Something that felt like loss gnawed at my guts and I sucked on the straw of the to-go cup Baldwin had given me and tried to forget as the highway stretched out in front of me and my foot pressed down on the gas.

· · ·

***

The crowd outside Mermaidia was larger than I'd expected. Judging from the amount of press hanging around the door, Tuesday, Kelly and their merry crew of social media minions had done their job of dropping hints as to my whereabouts.

I hate this.

I slipped my sunglasses on and stepped out of the Corvette. A practiced smile slid across my face as the flash of cameras and camera phones burst in my face. As I eased through the crowd, I was careful to flash my bracelet when taking selfies with fans and gave the paparazzi lots of angles to photograph it and my cheeky peace signs.

When I finally made it into the club, I scanned my surroundings, immediately thankful for Baldwin's foresight in giving me a blood bag before I left the house. The entire club was a writhing, gyrating feast.

An intoxicating buffet.

The blood of each person who moved in that club had its own special aroma. Some were spicy, others were gentler, sweeter, with almost floral tones.

I hastened to the VIP area, anxious to escape the general club population and took refuge in the more exclusive and less populated luxury tables. Sandrina was holding court in the center of the VIP balcony, and she blew me a flirty kiss as I caught her eye. I wiggled my fingers at her and struck a pose that made her giggle and wave me up.

I heard the whispers around me as I made my way toward her. The glow of cell phone screens and flashes told me that Tuesday's plan was working as fingers tapped on screens. They spread the word that Vinnie Quake was out on the town...

wearing mesh and leather, but most importantly, supporting vampires.

As much as I fully understood the reasoning behind this plan, something about the fact that the universe knew what I was wearing anytime I went out in public freaked me out.

From germs to gossip, people couldn't resist spreading shit around. They just couldn't resist. Little did they know, I was a carrier for both a germ, and the prime subject of the gossip. *Overachiever.*

I stepped across the velvet rope separating the VIP area from the general club goers, and Sandrina launched herself out of the booth to give me a big hug. She held me slightly longer than absolutely necessary and tilted her face up to press a kiss on my cheek. I could feel, rather than see, the camera phones being tilted our way and the buzz of the club as the news spread. *Show time.*

Sandrina was a pro at playing these games. She made it seem so easy. For a woman in this business, it was probably more than a game -- it was a survival tactic.

I winked at her suggestively. "Wanna give these assholes a show?"

She grinned up at me and then turned slightly to move us into the light so that it hit us perfectly before she tapped a finger against my jaw.

"Dance with me," she said in a business-like tone. "You can grab my left breast—but not my right one. I like neck kisses, hair pulls, and if you're feeling really bold, you can take a tequila shot off my body later. We'll have one full make-out session in front of the cameras in approximately a half an hour. You'll drive me back to your place in that sweet little Corvette and then we'll go upstairs. When you walk me into your building, your hand can be on my ass, but you are not to touch anything else below my waist. We want to make it believable, but not so much so that

Bruno has a conniption fit and breaks down your door at 5 a.m. Does that work for you?"

I blinked at her as I processed everything she had said. This petite dynamo had already beautifully choreographed our evening to best take advantage of the press, and her ex. She truly had this down to an art form and I looked at her with renewed respect. I leaned down and pressed a kiss to her cheek.

"Game on," I whispered into her ear, before I dropped another kiss tantalizingly close to the pulse point on her throat.

She returned my smile and ran a bold hand down my chest as she pushed me onto the couch. As soon as my thighs hit the cushions, she straddled me in a quick motion and pressed her face close to my ear as she swayed her hips gently in time to the music.

"So, are we trying to distract the press from an ex or from those vampire lover rumors I've been hearing? Which is it?"

I grunted, unable to concentrate on both her subtle lap dance and the frank business conversation she wanted to engage in.

"All the above?" I managed.

She nodded sympathetically and her gaze landed on the vampire rights bracelet around my wrist, but she said nothing. The song changed, and she flipped around just as quickly as she had straddled me, content to use me as a chair as she reached for her champagne and then leaned back against my chest.

"For the record? I think it's brave. That you're willing to go public with the vampire rights views. It's a risky move, but a bold one." She drained her champagne glass and glanced at her phone.

"Oh! The first photos of us have hit Twitter!" She squealed and all of her friends crowded around to see the latest buzz.

I took the moment to check my phone.

Tuesday had texted just two words: *Go Time.*

I glanced down and saw Peter Dawson, renowned purveyor of the daily gossip rag "The Dawson Dirt" hovering just outside the velvet rope of the VIP area and an idea to expedite the situation came to mind.

I pulled Sandrina close and embraced her as I leaned down to whisper my plan in her ear. Her sweet giggle was all I needed to get started. With a quick text to the DJ, I grabbed her hand, and pulled her off the couch to get started on the escalation of our distraction campaign.

Hand in hand, we let ourselves out of the VIP area and walked down the steps. We sashayed through the crush of people until we reached the dance floor. With a wave of my hand, someone trained the spotlight on us and the DJ played one of Sandrina's more sensual hits.

The crowd moved away from us and formed a circle as we danced around each other—the beat pulsed through us as we moved our bodies together. The sexual energy of the room made me sweat as I tried to keep hold of my monster. I could feel my fangs already trying to descend as the smell of Sandrina's arousal filled my nostrils every time she brushed up against me.

The beat became stronger, and our movements more fluid. We danced, bumped, and ground on each other—both of us breathing hard as we lost ourselves to the music for a moment. As the last beats of the song played, I pulled Sandrina close. I dipped her back before I slammed my lips down on hers, my hands curved protectively around her body as I groped her left breast, as requested, not her right.

The crowd around us burst into applause as we came up for air, looking, for all intents and purposes, like a couple that had been caught in a private moment. Sandrina was even blushing as she smiled at the people around us.

"Wanna get out of here, baby? My penthouse has an incredible view," I stage-whispered to her, loud enough that Peter Dawson could hear me.

"I need you to take me home," she whispered back before she launched herself into my arms and wrapped her legs around my waist.

I held her there, her body pressed flush against mine as we moved through the club. She was close enough to feel my arousal, and I tried to shift so it didn't stab her. *Common courtesy, really.* But she just giggled and stopped me as she ground against me enticingly and threw her head back as if in ecstasy. Little black spots appeared in my vision while I struggled with the temptation of her creamy neck exposed so close to me.

"Oh, Vinnie! You're so naughty!" she called out and giggled as some of her fans screamed provocatively when we passed by. She blew kisses to them over my shoulder. I growled and slapped her ass playfully, relishing the screech of surprise she let out.

"Would you have me any other way, babe?" I said through gritted teeth, thankful to the Gods that we were almost to the car.

The facade weighed on me, and the terror of slipping up plagued my mind.

I knew from experience the gossip rags were already debating our couple nickname. I fully expected to see something nauseating like 'Vandrina' or 'Sinnie' trending at any moment.

But that was infinitely better than the alternative.

We had accomplished what we'd set out to do. Yet a part of me wondered what Tuesday would think when she saw the photos. *She hates you, dude. Stop thinking she's going to get jealous. That ship has sailed, caught fire, and sunk in the harbor. Seriously.*

Safely in the car and briefly blinded by the barrage of

camera flashes, I checked my phone, but there were no more messages from my new PR manager.

I pressed my foot down on the gas and grinned as Sandrina squealed with excitement as the engine roared. Music pulsed through the Corvette's updated sound system and we headed back towards my luxury penthouse uptown.

Phase one, complete.

6

———

TUESDAY

It wasn't until I heard the roar of that Corvette as it pulled away from the curb rip through the air that I felt free to let my breath out fully and sit down to assess the clusterfuck of a situation that I got myself into. This plan wasn't my best. It wasn't even a solid second-place effort. This plan was bottom-of-the-barrel-crisis-response thinking. But, even if it wasn't as glamorous as my plans usually were, I felt confident that it would work. *Probably.*

Antagonizing the hate-groups was a risk. If that went wrong, a lot of innocent vampires and others would be caught in the cross-fire. My sense of ethical responsibility warred with my desire to win at all costs.

I already broke one rule when I failed to disclose to Carlyn that the client was the previous love of my life. I could still call her. There was still time. Mistakes were going to be made during this case, and I would be lucky if they didn't cost me my job or possibly my life. *What's that saying? In for a penny, in for a pound. Fuck.*

I didn't have to stay.

Vinnie was already out and about dancing with some tart at a club.

No one would blame me. Not really. Not when the truth came out.

The man killed and *ate* his household staff.

I could end this in a myriad of ways. I could call my boss, the police, the feds, hell. I could call the press. Yet, my hand never reached for my phone.

Vinnie. A *vampire. Whoever runs this sorry universe sure has a sense of humor.*

To think, all those nights when I prayed to any and every deity to curse his sorry ass. All those days when I cried over his photos in the magazines and indulged in toxic 'what if' spirals. The man was singing his heart-out to thousands of screaming fans at nighttime concerts and living a double-life as a fucking bloodsucker.

Strangely, I wasn't afraid of vampires. Not really. Even when he admitted to me in a room full of people that he 'lost control' and turned into a literal monster who murdered and consumed *eight people* in the last 24 hours. I should be afraid. I should walk or better yet, run away.

But I didn't.

I stayed.

Hell, I'd even signed on to help the psycho bastard.

Maybe, when all this is over, I would take Carlyn up on that offer of a vacation. Go somewhere extra sunny where there are no vampires and get my head on straight.

Because with Vinnie, I can't make rational decisions.

He fucked me up big-time... possibly forever.

All the rage and the hurt and the sheer pain that I'd spent five years pouring into hours upon hours of hot yoga and tear-filled therapy came roaring back the second I saw him. It was still so *fresh* that it felt like I might burst into flames at any moment.

I sipped my coffee and frowned at the shaking hand that held my oversized cup.

There was a moment right before everything went sideways five years ago when I believed everything was literally *perfect*. Like it couldn't get any better, even if I'd wished for a thousand years.

Life was much simpler back then. We weren't rich. I had just finished grad school and spent all my time hunting for jobs and going to Vinnie's gigs.

Back then, he was just another kid in the Seattle music scene trying to make it, singing in cover bands and contests. It was us against the world and we were *happy*. Or at least, I was. Until he walked out of my life without a look backward.

The alert on my phone rang and snapped me out of my reverie. *Right. Work.*

The little notification popped up and I clicked it mindlessly. A photo loaded and I stared at it, breathing shallowly.

It was Vinnie holding Sandrina up against him and walking through the club. Her tight dress was riding up enough to show off a very toned ass and the hint of a thong. The visible tent in his pants had sent the gossip rags running with frenzied speculation about his cock. Vinnie had his hand on Sandrina's ass and they were smoldering at each other.

My breath caught in my throat and I wheezed, my emotions taking over.

I tossed my phone across the table and exhaled heavily.

I literally choreographed this and then leaked it.

I orchestrated this entire scene. These photos were absolutely, unequivocally my idea. I glanced down and saw a gallery that was trending on Twitter and fiery rage filled me. *Tuesday, pull yourself together.*

Yesterday, if you'd asked me if I was jealous of my ex's groupies, I would have told you to fuck right off with that noise.

But today?

Not today, Satan.

Today, I felt the glacial pulse of jealousy run through me each time I saw a fresh shot of Vinnie and the saucy singer who climbed him like a tree in the middle of a crowded club. *I can't do this.*

I slammed my phone down, put my head in my hands, and tried to breathe.

Vinnie left you. He left you and became a literal monster. He has killed people. Killed them, drank their blood, and then asked you to hide it and clean it up. He cheated on you instead of supporting you during a terrible time in your life.

You. Deserve. Better.

My stupid, traitorous heart wouldn't listen to reason. It never did. But the problem was, I couldn't dwell on the night we lost each other without thinking of the hundreds of nights where we found ourselves in each other. The good times we had, the raw animal chemistry, the promises we'd made—they all came flooding back to me one after another.

"Ugh!"

A notification dinged on my phone and I glared down at the screen as an update from *The Dawson Dirt* popped into view. An exclusive, shocking new video was available featuring Seattle's own Vinnie Quake and singer/actress/philanthropist Sandrina.

I hated myself for clicking on it, but I needed to see my plans at work.

The recording wasn't high quality, and the lighting was dim until a spotlight clicked on and I saw him.

He was standing in the middle of the dancefloor, tufts of his chocolate-brown hair sticking out from underneath a black leather pageboy hat. His shirt was 100% mesh, and he's wearing tight leather pants that cup his ass like a lover's caress. His sculpted cheekbones and muscled arms made him look like some sort of bondage-wet dream. When he moved, he glided effortlessly, his body gyrating with the beat of the music.

He stalked her around the dance floor. His predatory nature would be obvious to anyone who knew what he was.

Everyone else in the club probably thought he was just putting on the same act he pulled on stage. He pulled the petite beauty into his arms and leaned forward to inhale her scent at the base of her neck. His bracelet flashed in the light before they whirled away from each other, each dancing, gyrating, pulsating with the music like magnets separated before crashing back into each other.

The video ended when he dipped her into an embrace, his hands covering her body and his lips on hers, and I sat down and bit my lip so hard it bled.

My mind screamed at me; *The asshole isn't worth it! Go back to hating him!* But my heart, my dumbass heart shouted back: *He is mine to hate, mine to love. Mine. Mine. Mine.*

I may not be the best person in the world, but I always, always do whatever it takes to protect what's mine. *Back to work.*

History or not, I needed to see this through. I moved through the hallways of the deserted building like a ghost, making my way to the conference room we had set up as a command post. Someone went and retrieved cots and pushed desks together in the main cubical area and staffers were sleeping in spurts.

Each of the team leaders gave me status updates, filling me in thoroughly on what they had accomplished. They surprised me with the thoroughness of their work. As unimpressed as I usually was with corporate minions, Vinnie had the cream of the crop working for him.

Kelly was the most impressive. In less than five hours, she made Vinnie the top trending topic in five countries. Using primarily hashtags and several pre-programmed bots that our IT department deployed, she incited a small group of vampire-haters into a frenzy while simultaneously dropping vampire rights topics into the news cycle at all levels. Her assistants had been diligent in the leaking of multiple photos of Vinnie and Sandrina's night out.

Local news stations were already talking about the subtle-but-not-subtle-at-all symbol that Vinnie flashed about Vampire Rights. The talking heads on the network news are bringing in experts that are for, against, or generally apathetic about the idea of recognizing this growing community.

Overnight, Seattle was bitten by vampire fever. All was going beautifully according to plan. I should have been impressed. Yet, I couldn't shake the feeling of unease and dread that permeated every interaction.

This ride was just getting started, and I knew from experience it would not be smooth sailing. If the anger from the anti-vamp crowd was half as intense in real-life as it was behind the safety of a computer screen, we would be lucky to get out of this with no one else getting hurt.

I took another long sip of coffee and picked up my clipboard. The conversation had begun, it was time to set the stage for the next action.

Sergio and Cole answered on the first ring and gave me a status update.

The bodies were in place. Check.

Vampire related paraphernalia removed. Check.

The house primed and ready. Check.

All that was lacking was a group of assholes to pick a fight with.

This was the part I had been dreading. Picking a fight on the internet was easy enough, but this wasn't just an argument. This was something bigger that had long-ranging implications for an entire group of people.

As much as I wanted to win, I knew I had to approach this with razor-sharp precision. The three laptops in front of me were already loaded with software designed to post comments to dozens of news stories at a time, all under unique usernames.

I started small.

When you are trying to deflect attention onto another group, create a viable source of something to blame. For the anti-vampers, everyone knows who they blame. I commented on several news articles, blaming the vampire community for taking funding from the human community. I highlighted the emergence of new private clinics catering specifically to vamps and suggested they took up space previously designated for immediate *human* community needs.

But the Seattle community hit back at me, countering my argument with science-based links and data proving my theory wrong. I smiled to myself. Some days, I loved my city.

If deflecting with blanket statements doesn't work, I remembered that personal anecdotes often left a lasting impact. Historically, people loved to quote things they hear that fit their personal narrative. I posted a story about a sick relative that didn't get the care they needed because caring for a vampire took most of the blood supply that day.

People started upvoting my story and the outrage was picking up. While a few people argued that my story wasn't relevant—several others picked up the slack and started sharing commentary about how their sick relatives didn't get the care they should have gotten because a vamp took their space. It probably had nothing to do with vampires in the first place, but that didn't matter — I started the conversation. The sense of unease that dogged me all night came back with a vengeance.

I've done a lot for my clients, but this felt wrong.

By 7 a.m., the outrage picked up.

Humans are so predictable. And utterly disappointing.

I quickly added text to a few photos of Vinnie and his bracelet and shared them on Twitter and Facebook, knowing that they were just the kind of images to go viral.

The comments quickly rolled in, each more explosive than the last. My guilt weighed on me. I've had nothing against the vampire community as a whole, and I knew our actions were going to make their afterlife harder.

I logged into the dredges of social-like-media and started dropping comments about Vinnie Quake and his vampire bracelet. I trolled him mercilessly on Twitter, Instagram, and Reddit. I even dropped some comments on LinkedIn. Soon, #VinnieTheVampLover and #TraitorVinnie started trending. With one strategic email to my hacker friend, Vinnie's personal home address was leaked all across the dark web.

We set the stage. The general public could take it from here. *Gods help us.*

I was grateful to step away from my computer command post and focus on the logistics of blowing up a house full of bodies.

Baldwin provided me with the information on all the staff members who had been in the house on the day of the incident. I steeled myself and looked through the folders, my heart in my throat. I didn't normally get emotional at work, but this case wasn't normal. Eight lives gone. Exsanguinated at the hands of someone they'd trusted and looked after. Their employer. Their friend.

They weren't bad people. They didn't deserve this.

In my line of work, I regularly interacted with people who deserved violence and pain. Cartel leaders. Criminals. Warlords.

Not the housekeepers and chefs and assistants who busted their asses to keep the lives of the rich and privileged worry free.

Nothing would bring them back. If I was successful, that meant justice would never be served in this case. The man who killed them in cold blood would walk free.

The best we would be able to do was something to honor their memory and even that felt cheap and inadequate.

I debated calling Carlyn and asking for help. She'd been around for a long, long time. Surely, she would have advice that would be pertinent to the clusterfuck I found myself in.

I glanced at the TV and did a double-take.

Live camera crews gathered outside Vinnie's building as Sandrina popped out wearing a large hat and the same clothing from the club. Vinnie was obscured in the shadows but Sandrina went up on her tiptoes and pressed a kiss to his lip. His hand drifted towards her ass and gave her a friendly squeeze. Sandrina turned and waved to the paps, blowing kisses and posing for photos in all her morning-after glory. The press ate it up, shouting questions at Vinnie who just waved and disappeared back into the lobby, ever mysterious and eccentric. A little idea percolated in my mind as I watched him avoid the sun as much as possible before he slid behind the wheel of the Corvette.

What if we hid the crime, but not the man?

What if... Vinnie came out as a vampire?

I yawned, turned to my minions and gave them orders to wake me the second anything of note happened. Satisfied they could take the reins; I crawled under one desk and pulled my tote bag to me. I pulled out a travel pillow and a small blanket and promptly fell asleep, secure knowing that the world would probably still be a dumpster fire when I woke up.

***

. . .

I was right.

When I woke up again it was midafternoon and the dumpster fire was still blazing away.

Sometimes it sucks to be right all the time. Someone had ordered a variety of snacks and I gorged myself on Hot Pockets and coffee while each of the team leads gave me an update.

The media was enthralled by Vinnie and reports that he had ties to pro-Vamp groups was dominating the news cycle. His connection with Sandrina was creating a lot of buzz that only increased when the first connection between a public statement advocating for vampires and Vinnie appeared linked to his social media.

The teams debated on whether or not to make a statement. Baldwin was adamantly against it, convinced it would ruin Vinnie's brand. Kelly and the assistant squad advocated that it was a calculated risk that would eventually pay off because Vinnie himself was a vampire. We eventually agreed to like and comment on a single Instagram post from a pro-Vamp organization and see where it went.

Baldwin grudgingly found us an organization he could live with being associated with.

Sanguine Sunsets was a tiny local independent bookstore. They had a popular vampire book club that was held at night so that actual vampires could attend. At Baldwin's direction, Vinnie liked their post advertising the vampire book club and commented on it with: "This looks awesome! Would love to check it out sometime!"

That was all it took.

The bookstore was overwhelmed with attention and after two hours, we had secured a spot for Vinnie at the club meeting tonight. A book club meeting that would be heavily photographed? That had all the makings of the perfect alibi and I sent a text to Sergio and Cole to stand by.

Vinnie's house plans were spread out on the table in front of me. According to the blueprints, all the staff rooms were in the same wing which made this plan even easier than I'd hoped. I circled the gas line that was closest to them and sent a reminder text to Sergio and Cole to turn it on.

Georgia had a room with a wide window—perfect for a Molotov Cocktail to make it through and ignite the place. They would cut the power and security system approximately 15 minutes before the house blew. That's how long it would take for a luxury customer to get a tech on the road to make any repairs.

I wracked my brain, trying to think of what else the little pissants in the anti-vamp groups would have a wet dream about if they could pull it off. Those little dicks loved drama... and what's more dramatic to a vampire than a stake? Or... blood?

I sent a quick text to Sergio and asked him to pick up a sizable amount of pigs' blood and some garden stakes. Humans took things at face value. Realistically, it would be weeks before they untangled the mess enough to realize that pigs' blood had been mixed in. CSI in a city plagued with Vampiric Infections was hard enough, and I was about to make it a lot harder.

If there's anything I've learned, it's making the scene as believable as possible. Our city's finest won't try too hard to see something else. Especially if it takes the heat off them and focuses it elsewhere.

That settled, I checked back in on my burgeoning little riot and felt a strange, perverse sense of pride at how quickly it had escalated.

According to the internet, both Seattle and Vinnie Quake were going to burn tonight. It felt surreal that I was in control of it all.

I closed my laptop with a flourish and replaced it in my ever-present bag. If the city burned tonight, then there was no reason to deny myself any longer. There was one more fire I needed to put out, once and for all. If nothing else, I needed closure.

My phone buzzed in my hand the same way it has been for the last 24 hours. Notification after notification—but this wasn't something I'd been expecting. My caller-ID read "Mansplainer Zach" and I stared at it in confusion.

"Zach? Who the hell was Zach? Oh—" I muttered out loud before realization dawned on me. *Oh.That Zach.*

We didn't exactly leave things open-ended, so I couldn't for the life of me figure out what he wanted. He couldn't possibly believe we were ever going to be a thing after that "date."

I hit *Ignore* and focused on the task at hand. Closure. Or something like it.

VINNIE

Over the rush of water that poured over my head and pounded into my back, an insistent knock on the door of my penthouse suite thundered behind an already powerful headache. I slapped the shower control off and stood there, a hand braced against the cold tile as water dripped off my body and pooled on the floor. I was tired and cranky.

The irritating knocking continued unabated, and I gritted my teeth. If whoever was outside wanted to talk to me so badly, they were going to regret it.

I stepped out of the shower and strode across the apartment. I didn't bother with a towel. Instead, I ripped the door open with a furious scowl, bare-ass naked.

This could very well go down as the biggest night of my life and I was not pleased to have my private time interrupted. Whoever dared to break into my inner sanctum could deal with my nudity or get the fuck out. Except, when I opened the door, it wasn't one of my legion of assistants or even Baldwin. It was the one person with the power to strike me speechless.

Tuesday.

She looked me up and down with a tiny smirk on her face.

"Does your medical condition include sensitive skin? Have to air dry now?"

I missed her humor in my life. Always laced with a certain edge that I couldn't quite pinpoint. I stood there, stunned, as she stepped around me and into the hotel suite I kept as a permanent apartment.

"Love what you've done with the place. Very minimalistic. Have a nice time with your little friend last night?"

She dropped her enormous bag on a tacky silver couch and walked over to the window to peer down at the view below. I let the door slam with a loud *bang,* but she didn't even flinch, much less turn around.

A possessive, primal feeling pooled in my gut that defied my self-control and caused my fangs to descend against my will.

Tuesday doesn't owe me a goddamn thing.

I'd left her.

I'd hurt her.

I had also created this giant mess and then begged her to clean it up.

I owed her a life debt.

She deserved a gentleman, not a monster.

But I couldn't let her go. Not yet.

She came here willingly, knowing full-well the nightmare that I'd become. I might as well play this one out and see what happens. I growled and stalked toward her, but paused long enough to grab a throw blanket off the couch to wrap around my waist like a towel.

"If you are trying to intimidate me or seduce me with your vampirey pheromones or whatever they call them—it won't work."

Tuesday pivoted, and her breasts brushed up against my bare chest, further awakening my monster. I should have warned her she was playing with fire, but Tuesday's never been one to back down from a fight. Her nipples were hard and she leaned into me slightly. *Game. On.*

"No? Your nipples seem to think otherwise. Maybe you should let them know."

I stepped closer to her and pushed her back up against the window, fully invading her personal space.

She didn't say a word, but then again; she didn't have to.

"I can smell your arousal, Tues. I may piss you off, but I'm also turning you on. Or do you want to lie and deny it?"

I watched gleefully as she struggled to control her facial expression, but little bits of rage escaped through her neutral mask.

"Move."

Her voice was cold and authoritative, and she followed it up with a heavy push against my chest. When I didn't comply, she raked her fingernails down my bare skin and left long, red scratches.

My self-control was already teetering on a wire, and I had to back up to avoid losing it on her. The pain she caused made my blood sing.

Tuesday moved around me with quick steps, grabbed her bag from the couch and then sat in the lone armchair to face me. She guarded her expression and fumbled with an envelope that she pulled from the depths of her massive purse.

"I wrote you a letter, Vincent," she said shortly. "You don't have to read it. But I needed to write it. It's how I get closure. Because how we ended? The way you left me? That messed me up for a long time. You made it so I couldn't trust anyone for years. Hell, I didn't even let myself be *touched* again by another person until literally hours before I got the call to come rescue your sorry ass. I can't talk through this with you. Not right now. Not when we have so much in the air, but... I wrote it down, and now you have to take it. I don't care if you read it, but you have to take it out of my hand... like right now."

The monster in me went into hiding at the thought of emotional healing and wellness, and whatever part of me that's still human looked at her warily, and reached out to take the letter that she offered.

"I need to forgive you, Vinnie," she continued. "If... if we survive this. I want to do that. I don't know if we'll ever be friends, but I have to move on. The last five years—"

She blurted out the words and her face turned a delightful shade of pink as she looked down at the floor and over at the wall, anywhere but at me.

I ambled towards her as though I was in a trance, I stood before her, my hands outstretched to her in invitation. She placed her palms on mine cautiously and I hauled her to her feet so she stood flush against my body. Her breath was uneven and I smelled fear intermixed with her arousal.

She *was* afraid. Afraid, turned on, and exhausted.

I moved slowly and wrapped her into a hug. The top of her head nestled under my chin, and my hand came up to rest against her glorious dark brown hair.

"I just want you in my life, Tuesday," I whispered as I dropped a featherlight kiss onto her head. "It doesn't matter if you take another five years, or fifty, to forgive me. I'll take it."

She relaxed against me just a little as her arms wrapped around my bare torso. The warmth of her skin was a dramatic contrast to my coldness. The longer I held her, the more my fangs ached to drop and my cock twitched; but this moment was hers. I would rather die again than lose control and prove her trust in me was misplaced.

I lost track of time as we stood there, two exes locked in a nameless embrace, holding onto each other as though we were lost at sea.

She moved first, and my stomach tightened as her head shifted slightly. I loosened my arms to let her have more freedom to move. I didn't know what I was expecting—a kiss? I wouldn't dare—

But I definitely wasn't expecting a sharp stab of red-hot pain when she grabbed my nipple in her teeth and bit down.

My fangs descended, and I growled as I pushed her away and held her at arm's length. It took immense effort to refrain from retaliating in kind or throwing her to the ground to have my way with her.

She laughed, slapped my hand away, and stepped closer to me. When she reached out slowly to touch my cheeks and trailed one finger ever so slowly toward my mouth, I gulped. Slowly, she leaned forward and rubbed her thumb over the edge of my fang.

"My, my, my..." she whispered. "What big teeth you have!"

Without warning, she pressed her lips to mine in a searing kiss that had the monster in my head roaring and demanding freedom to play, too.

Her hands roamed all over my body. She violently ripped the blanket away from my hips and grabbed me by the balls. Her grip was firm. Unexpected. Borderline painful. My eyes rolled into the back of my head and I groaned in pleasure. She pulled her mouth away from mine and looked at me. There was a fierce glow in her eyes that stoked the flame in my guts that still burned for her. *Is this really happening?*

"You know what we never did, Vincent?" she purred. "We never had the hate-fuck. Let's remedy that, shall we? After all, you're supposed to die tonight. *Again.* Ground rules: Rule #1: No biting. Rule #2: No blood. Other than that? It's fair game, fangface."

I growled, picked her up, and strode towards the bedroom. I kicked open the door and launched her onto the bed. She bounced on the wide mattress and struggled to gain her balance.

With a graceful leap, I pounced on her and held her still with my body as she squirmed beneath me. My hands roamed her body, ripping her clothes off viciously.

My monster had agreed to her terms, albeit reluctantly, and we were both ready to play. From the looks of her? Her monster was more than willing to jump in the fray and battle it out as well. Neither one of us wanted to be gentle with the other, not really.

I leaned down, smelling the unique bouquet of her blood as it pumped through her veins. She bit down on my ear and I roared in pain and dropped my hand to her throat.

"Oh, is that how it's going to be, tater-tot? Be careful how rough you get with a vampire," I said through gritted teeth.

Tuesday smiled sweetly as her knee connected squarely with my junk. Not just a glancing blow, either. A full-throttle, no holds barred, knee to the cock.

Time froze for a split second.

I suppose, in hindsight, I should have expected that she wouldn't fight fair, but in my defense, no one anticipates getting kneed in the balls during consensual hate-sex.

Well, at least *I* hadn't gotten that memo.

Cursing her, I curled into myself as my vision blurred and black spots danced in front of my eyes. I tried to breathe through the pain, but I sounded more like a wounded animal and it wasn't helping in the slightest.

Tuesday wasted no time. As soon as I was vulnerable, she jumped on my back like a wildcat. Her arm encircled my throat, and I choked out a strangled laugh and pulled her over my shoulder in a smooth motion. Flipped back onto the mattress, she glared at me with murderous rage in her eyes.

"Vampires don't need to breathe, babycakes, we're dead. But nice try. Really, valiant effort."

The knee had hurt, though.

I brought my palm down on her ass with a resounding smack. She squirmed out of the way; her muffled curses shouted into the bedcover.

I grinned when I saw her one hand wriggle out from where it was trapped beneath her to flip me the bird.

That's my girl. That's my Tuesday.

I spanked her again as she wriggled farther away from me. She launched herself toward the headboard and then flipped around in some sort of yoga-gymnast bullshit move.

"Getting over you took a lot of yoga, hot stuff," she snarled.

We grappled and clawed at each other, neither one of us particularly concerned with hurting the other, but indulging in the release of five years of hurt.

Five years of betrayal.

I shredded her clothing, ruining it as I ripped it from her body. She used her stockings as a gag when she snuck up behind me. She stuffed them into my mouth and pulled them tight, gagging me until I bit through with my fangs.

We fought.

We yelled.

We called each other every terrible name in the book.

Breathing heavy, we perched on opposite sides of the bed, two predators staring at each other with eyes full of distrust and anger.

And then, something clicked in me and I dropped my head, hoping she'd recognize, and accept, my submission.

"Tuesday, I—I could wrestle and hate-fight with you all day. We could rip each other, and this room, apart, but... that's not what I want. My monster does. He loves playing with you. He gets excited to provoke all that glorious anger and passion you keep bottled up inside. We could destroy each other so easily. It wouldn't even hurt. But I want to be different with you. You deserve more than that." I shook my head and dared to meet Tuesday's glare. She needed more. I took a breath.

"The day I left you. I owe you an explanation. I know I do. I was turned that day. You probably already figured that out. If I could go back and change it, I would. I should never have left the apartment that day. I would have been there for you when you needed me. But I can't change the past. I can only offer my truest, most sincere apology for how it ended between us."

She didn't answer me, she just sat there stunned and I sighed. It was probably for the best.

Leaning over, I pressed the softest kiss to her forehead before I slid off the bed and left her there, sitting cross-legged on the mattress staring at me, the bruises from our catharsis already blooming on her skin.

My phone vibrated and skittered across the table as I entered the living room. Apparently, Tuesday's plan was still in motion —the Seattle Police just offered protection for the Vampire Rights book club I was supposed to be speaking to tonight. They wanted to let me know that there's been an uptick in online hatred for vamps, and I should use caution as a high-value target.

I thanked them but I couldn't help but wonder if we were doing the right thing.

8

———

TUESDAY

I sat on the bed and stared down at the fingermark bruises on my thighs. I hadn't expected the fervor with which I had launched myself at Vinnie. I hadn't expected the anger to come pouring out of me as I pinched, slapped, hit and scratched my way through that encounter. And I *really* hadn't expected him to bow out and leave me panting, bruised, and aching with a need that only he could fill.

Freakin' A. Men are the worst. Even the undead ones leave you wanting.

In the other room, my phone buzzed in my bag as my alarm went off. It was almost go-time, and I was still naked. My joints ached as I pulled myself off the bed and shuffled to the bathroom. There was no way any of Vinnie's clothes would have fit me, so I took one of his black t-shirts and wore it as a dress with one of my old stockings as a belt. It's all the rage in the fashion niche of *walk of shame chic.* Was it even a walk of shame if it was just to the living room?

I made my way out to the living room and found Vinnie sitting on the couch. He was dressed like a fashion icon and sipping something out of a large black goblet. He looked like

Dracula's much hotter, much younger cousin. *Ugh, why is he so pretty?*

It was awkward. The words said and the ones left unsaid ate away at our ability to talk. We acknowledged each other silently, but we didn't engage. Perhaps, even after five years, our pain was too fresh and our wounds too deep. *Maybe we can't come back from this, after all.*

"Why didn't you go public back then? You could have dragged my name through the mud a thousand times with our history. A woman scorned? The tabloids were always on the hunt for stuff to make me look bad. You probably would have made a fortune, Tues." Vinnie came up behind me and smoothed the flyaway hair on top of my head and looked down at me expectantly.

He had a valid point, in his own way.

He'd walked away from me, but I didn't chase him. I still remembered the first magazine cover I saw with him smiling on the glossy cover in the checkout line at the grocery store. It was like an ice pick to the heart.

"I'm just not that kind of person, Vinnie. What would I have gained? Public intrusion into my life? Notoriety as one of the many notches in your bedpost. You were too busy being Vinnie Quake, superstar. It was pretty obvious you weren't the man I fell in love with anymore. Why would I put forth that kind of effort for no reward?" The words tumbled out in a rush, one after the other. When I finished, I drew in a shaky breath and hugged my arms to hide the tremor in my hands.

It wasn't a lie.

Outing Vinnie as a womanizer and unfaithful fiance would have done exactly nothing back then. It likely would have back-fired and made him more popular. *Boys will be boys, after all.*

Uncomfortable with the direction this conversation had taken, I gave him a terse nod. There were phone calls to make and plans to set in motion. Memory lane was a useless exercise.

"Tuesday," he called out softly, "You were never just a notch on my bedpost. You're the one I let get away and regretted every day since."

But right now, none of that mattered. It was time for *business-face*. I pushed back my shoulders and lifted my chin. No time for fluffy bullshit.

I grabbed my bag from where I'd dropped it on the silver couch and pulled out my phone to shut off the alarm and bring up the itinerary for the night's events.

"Let's get to it," I said briskly. "At 7:00 p.m., you'll go to the Book Club and speak about your interest in Vampire Rights. I don't really care what you say, but make them believe it. At 8:00 p.m. you'll leave the bookstore and we'll start the countdown. By midnight, your house will be a smoking pile of rubble and you will be seen dancing the night away with your new girlfriend Sandrina, oblivious to the destruction."

It all sounded so simple. A logistical juggling act all for one purpose: making sure my undead ass of an ex could still have his multi-million dollar empire by the time the sun rose.

"We expect a small-to-medium brawl will block the south-western corner behind the coffee shop where the book club is. Be advised, our intelligence tells us they plan to come armed with stakes, Holy Water, and silver. Many are 'True Believers' and they are expecting a fight. Your address and confirmed attendance at the event were leaked on the appropriate channels and Kelly has three of her little proteges ready to keep poking people to get the results we want. The explosion will be hot enough to burn the remains beyond recognition and then... It's done."

Vinnie nodded, but he wasn't looking at me, I didn't even know if he'd heard anything I'd said. He stared out the window at the sunset. The sky was red. Dark and dangerous. He took another long slurp of his drink.

"It won't be. Done, that is. Blowing up the house was just a step," he said grimly. "I decided to make an announcement in the next month about my status as a vampire. I want to launch a foundation to honor the lives of my staff. If I make life more difficult for the vampires of Seattle because I'm covering my ass, then I need to put myself out there."

His words struck a chord within me. Knowing he was willing to make amends with real action healed a small portion of the hurt that he'd caused so many years ago. *Had being turned actually made Vinnie Quake into a good guy?* I walked toward him, pulled the ornate goblet out of his hand, and looked into his eyes.

"Thank you, Vinnie. Thank you for making it right."

I leaned forward and pressed my lips against his. This moment was just ours. A stolen second in time with no hidden agenda, no anger, no revenge. Just Tuesday and Vinnie, just like old times.

He let me lead and my tongue teased against his lips until he opened his mouth to me as I deepened the kiss.

My tongue touched the sharp points of his fangs and the coppery, metallic taste of the blood on his tongue surprised me. I froze, unsure of what to do but unwilling to stop this moment. *It's only blood.* I teased him again and nipped at his lower lip. He groaned his approval and I felt his body react to mine. He reached up to pull me into his lap and crushed me against his chest as we dueled for dominance and enjoyed each other.

He pulled back first and I reached up to touch his now mussed hair. I liked how he looked disheveled and sex-drunk. His lips were slightly swollen from where I nipped and nibbled and his eyes were red, almost purple. We studied each other, imprinting this moment as a memory, frozen in time.

"Can we be kissing friends?" he finally asked and I burst out laughing.

I pressed another kiss to his nose and pushed myself off his lap, ready to face the rest of this clusterfuck and get it over with.

"Let's go save your fine ass from jail or insta-staking, 'kay?"

He grumbled something I couldn't hear and begrudgingly got to his feet. I reached for my bag and ran into the palatial bathroom. I always had a change of clothes with me. The outfit I wore over here was ruined beyond repair so I stuffed Vinnie's shirt into my bag and pulled on my jeans and t-shirt.

Together, we walked out of the hotel suite and took the elevator down to the main floor. A blacked out SUV waited at the curb.

"Now or never," I muttered as the door opened. Vinnie smiled, flashing his fangs at me as he climbed into the back seat.

This was, hands down, the craziest night of my life.

I needed an enormous coffee. And someone to slap some sense into me. *Just the basics.*

***

Vinnie walked into that bookstore so confidently, it made my throat tighten. He greeted his fans and stopped to take selfies and sign autographs. It was a little surreal that he'd successfully hidden being a vampire from all of his fans for so many years.

He told me his inner circle was extremely small and loyal, with iron-clad NDAs that threatened all kinds of repercussions if they told his secret. His late assistant, Patricia, was his primary procurement specialist, ordering a seemingly limitless supply of pig's blood and other blood mixes to stave off his hunger. Until one day, that hadn't been enough to save her, and she became the meal instead.

That thought was enough to bring me back to focus on the task at hand.

Business face. Get in the game.

The press loved this new side of Vinnie, and a quick check of my phone notifications confirmed that this little book club visit was trending on an international level. Gotta love the human fascination with a celebrity, it works every time.

I was grateful that Carlyn insisted her staff always carry a go-bag with us. My tote bag had quite literally saved my life in the past and I was grateful for the change of clothes. The cozy fleece jacket and jeans were a welcome respite from wearing Vinnie's old shirt.

The Bluetooth headset in my ear beeped, and I answered.

"So, that scuffle you ordered? It's bigger than we expected."

Baldwin sounded nervous, but he'd have to get over that.

That's the other thing you can count on—people are more than willing to be dicks to anything that is remotely different from their shared experience.

"Good. Just keep your distance," I said, and ended the call. I didn't have time to hold Baldwin's hand through this process. There was too much at stake.

Stake. The anti-vampers had probably brought their own.

Great, now I was making vampire puns.

I took out my headset and concentrated on the noises outside the bookstore. Sure enough, there were low rumbles of shouts and marching drums coming up one of the side streets. *Here we go.*

Sergio and Cole reassured me via text that everything was ready and I slowly exhaled.

My phone beeped again and I looked down in surprise. Four

missed texts from "Zach-The-Boring"? *What the hell? I never would have pegged him for a clinger. Ugh.*

I hit ignore. I was not remotely prepared to deal with that. Zach could wait.

My phone alarm sounded and a shiver wracked my body. 7:00 p.m.

Show time.

Vinnie sat in the circle, his legs crossed as he dipped his head in conversation with a tiny elderly woman who wore a giant hat covered in flowers made out of yellowed book pages. He laughed at something she said and his entire face lit up with the superhuman ethereal beauty that was so uniquely *Vinnie.*

The vampiric infection may have supercharged his natural charm and looks, but Vinnie could hold his own. He looked up suddenly, as if he could feel me staring at him, and smiled in my direction. A little wink, subtle and just for me, made me feel stupidly warm and fuzzy inside.

Get a hold of yourself, woman. This is not the time, and definitely not the place. He. Broke. Your. Heart.

My silent scolding was only lukewarm. Vinnie Quake held a piece of my heart for years now, and whatever happened tonight, he'd probably still have it in the end. *Damn him.*

The screaming and yelling from the melee outside dragged me away from mooning over my bloodthirsty ex, and the hair on the back of my neck prickled up.

Showtime.

The first wave of angry residents came into my line of vision, and they were just as virulent and repulsive in person as they were online. They carried a wide variety of homemade signs attached to wooden sticks that were sharpened like stakes at the end.

Not unexpected.

We *had* provoked them into a frenzy. Still, the sight of them in-person sent another shiver down my spine.

Vampire Hysteria had hit Seattle. *I hope we know what we're doing.*

The press wasted no time filming the interlopers, and I knew this incident would drive national conversation for days to come.

A large man with a dirty beard and stained trucker hat stepped to the front of the line. Before anyone could stop him, he reared back and hurled a brick at the front window of the bookstore.

Someone screamed, I ducked, and the plate-glass window shattered into a thousand pieces that rained down over the beautiful book display and skidded over the hardwood floor.

"Hey, Vinnie! Get fucked, you vamp-loving scum!"

A roar of approval rose from the crowd and they surged forward, the mob mentality ignited. The security forces Carlyn hired and the police protection that had been offered closed ranks. They raised their riot shields to provide some protection for the book club members, but they couldn't stop every rock, brick, and bottle hurled at the shop.

I glanced frantically at the crowd of book club members and saw Vinnie crouched over the body of the elderly woman he had been talking to. Her unique hat was on the ground, crushed beyond repair by running feet, and his face was a mask of rage.

Another bottle sailed through the broken window and struck another woman in the face. Blood poured down her face as she fell to her knees.

Oh no.

Vinnie and two others whipped their heads around as soon as they smelled her. Three hungry gazes laser-focused on the ruby red drops that dripped down to the hardwood floor.

Shit. Shit. Shit. Shit. SHIT.

The situation was already volatile but now it was threatening to be outside of our control. I sent a quick text to Baldwin and muscled my way through the press to get to Vinnie. I could see how red his eyes were from across the room. This was *not* good.

His monster was shimmering just beneath the surface. I could tell that it was taking all the self-control he had to rein it in. There were two more people on the floor, their blood pooling beneath them as others struggled to bind their wounds and help them up.

Even a very well-fed, very self-control-oriented vampire would have an issue with this. I lost sight of Vinnie as smoke bombs from the security forces went off to force rioters to back away from the doors.

Rough hands grabbed my ponytail and pulled *hard.* I let out a thin shriek of surprised pain as hands gripped my forearms and forced me toward the melee. The scent of stale cigarette smoke, b.o., and the sour odor of beer vomit invaded my nostrils as they flung me towards the crowd.

"Here's Vinnie's little whore, boys! She's a traitor to her own kind. She's hooking up with a vamp-lover! Maybe we should teach her a lesson!"

I looked up and saw that I was being held between two young men with anti-vamp slogans printed on their shirts. They leered at me and licked their lips suggestively as I struggled.

"Let. Me. GO!" I screamed at them and kicked out at whoever I could reach.

A man with a carefully trimmed beard and a "Vamps Should Stay Dead" shirt twirled a baton with a sharpened end between his hands and glared at me with cold, calculating eyes.

Where were the cops? Where was the extra security? This couldn't be happening.

"I don't think we will," he said with a smirk that I hated instantly. "I think we'll play with you first."

A bitter sense of dread sank into my stomach and I struggled harder against the hands that held me.

"Help! Help me! Someone, please! Help!" I screamed again. I bit down on the hand that tried to muffle my shouts and then a vengeful slap rocked my head back and I tasted blood on my tongue.

No one was listening. No one could hear me over the noise of the riot all around us. Someone grabbed my wrists and upper body, and someone else grabbed my legs and I was carried out, farther into the crowd. Farther away from Vinnie.

I blinked hard to fight against the tears that filled my eyes and as my vision cleared a face appeared above me. Glaring down at me with an expression of undisguised hatred was —

"Zach?"

Confusion flooded through me.

What have we done?

Before I could say anything else, something hard hit me in the face and red spots danced in my vision, obscuring Zach's face for just a moment before darkness swept me away.

The pain in my head threatened to split my skull in two. Everything hurt—including my eyelids as I blinked and tried to focus on my surroundings. Muffled voices and a strange ringing pulsed through my brain. My hands and feet were tied, making it almost impossible to push myself up to a sitting position. I flopped around like a fish, each bump sending a jolt of pain through my whole body. If anything, it just made my headache worse. I groaned and rolled onto my side instead, it would have to do for now. A dark stain on the floor beside me looked suspiciously like blood, and I swallowed thickly. *This is bad. This is really fucking bad.*

"Ah, the vamp-whore is awake."

I winced as I lifted my head to look toward the cruel voice that taunted me.

I don't know what I had expected to see, but it certainly wasn't Zach and Baldwin. They sat on a luxurious leather couch like old friends, a gun and a knife resting causally on the cushions between them. I remembered Zach's angry face, but my heart sank as I stared at Baldwin and his self-satisfied smirk.

"You? Really? Why are you doing this? Where are we? Where's Vinnie?" My voice was hoarse from screaming and my mouth was dry, but I tried my damnedest to inject as much authority as I could into my words, which was hard to do while lying on my side on cold concrete with every muscle screaming in agony.

Zach stared off into space and ignored me while he played with the knife in his hand. Baldwin grabbed the gun from between them and stood, the weapon held loosely at his side.

"Tell me, Ms. PR Guru, did you ever think of the *human cost* when you spun this so-called *accident* into the pro-vampire movement?" Baldwin asked. "Did you even give the tiniest bit of consideration to the people left behind when you took the side of a murderous vampire? Did you think of them as people, terrified in the final moments of their life, or were they just numbers to you? Eight little problems to be solved. Are there no limits to what you do for your clients?" His tone was conversational, but I caught the pain behind his voice. I had never been so confused in my life.

"*You* hired me to do a job. I did it. What do you want me to say?"

Instead of an answer, Baldwin reached down and wrenched me into an upright position. I struggled against his grip and he rewarded my efforts by smashing the butt of the gun against my temple.

My vision flared white, and then blackness slipped over me again.

. . .

***

When I regained consciousness, the room was silent and dark. I was still tied up and lying on the floor. Seattle's skyline was visible from the window, and the coppery tang of blood hung in the air.

I struggled to get myself into a sitting position and my face rolled in something wet and sticky. This smell was overpowering and I gagged before squirming away from it as fast as I could. My body collided with something cold and hard and I screamed when the cold, hard thing groaned weakly.

I was surrounded by blood and I was definitely not alone.

Carefully, I eased myself away from the other person. It took a monumental effort that caused my entire body to scream out in pain, but I shifted myself into a sitting position.

A pool of blood surrounded us on the floor. Tremors rocked my body as I turned my head to look next to me. Staked to the wall was a vampire, mouth open, frozen in mid-roar—two bloody gaps in his otherwise straight teeth were enough for me to know that the mob who took me out for more than just blood, they were taking trophies, too.

Baldwin's betrayal came rushing back into my mind, and suddenly I knew exactly where I was.

This was Vinnie's house.

The house I had prepped to blow up at midnight.

Bastards.

9

VINNIE

When Tuesday explained her plan for the evening to me, it seemed straightforward enough. Do a press appearance at a vampire book club, lend my celebrity to the pro-vampire community cause, take some selfies with the press, and see and be seen with Sandrina on a dance floor.

Easy. *Well. Everything but the Sandrina part. She's more annoying than she looks.*

Sure, there was some high-powered explosive stuff to deal with, but I didn't have to touch it—I just had to act horrified when it all went down. Other than that small detail, it was simple.

But when that first brick smashed the bookstore window and the angry protesters became a larger brawl than anyone had planned, my monster rose to the surface.

The smell of blood had flooded the room as they caught innocent humans in the destruction.

My fangs descended immediately, and it took everything in me not to lap up the beautiful, precious blood that poured out of the victims and stained the floor.

A quick glance was all I needed to know that I was not the only one having issues with the amount of blood being spilled. I lived on pig's blood for five years, but now that I've had a taste of the human vintage...

No. Keep a leash on that monster, Vinnie. You have to.

This was an opportunity to show I was different. To pay penance for my past sins. I refused to lose control again.

I swallowed my own cravings and tried to emulate my new role as model vampire citizen. The other two vampires in the room followed my lead, but I could see they struggled as hard as I did to keep their fangs in check.

It was going as well as could be imagined, until I heard Tuesday scream.

The note of panic in her voice ignited my bloodlust in an instant, and the predator in me snapped to attention. I was no longer in control. The monster craved the hunt, and it was way past time to let the vampire out to play.

I moved to the side of the room with lightning quickness and I scanned the crowd to take an inventory of the situation, not to mention look for any sign of Tuesday.

A group of men carried what looked like a body through the crowd and I felt my senses sharpen as I let go of what little control I had left.

With eyes closed I tried to hone in on the specific scent of Tuesday's blood, but the environment was too chaotic and the smells were too intermixed for me to get a read on it.

A dark blue hooded sweatshirt on the floor next to the fallen coat rack caught my eye. I snatched it up off the floor and pulled it over my head.

I pushed through the protesters and jumped through the broken window just as the cops and security guards began to beat the crowd back. Safely beyond the front line, I pulled up the sweatshirt's hood and followed the direction I thought the men had gone in.

If anything happened to Tuesday, there would be no survivors.

***

When the crowd thinned and my eyes stopped watering from the tear gas bombs, I reoriented on the scent of the men who had taken Tuesday. It was hard to pick them out amid the chaos, and I couldn't smell anything but smoke and pepper spray. My ears rang with angry shouts, terrified screams, and the wail of sirens.

"Where did they go," I muttered.

People ran in the opposite direction while others surged forward with their signs and weapons held high. The ignorant bastards didn't even know what they were fighting against anymore. I was in the crowd, I wasn't in the bookstore anymore.

I felt terrible for the shop owner, I'd have to remember to get Baldwin to reimburse them for the damages and maybe have the social media team promote them for a while. Indie bookshops had enough troubles without adding something like this to it.

Baldwin.

Tuesday had said that he was close by. She'd been talking to him on her Bluetooth headset. Baldwin would know what to do.

It was too late to go back to the bookstore, and the damn thing was likely destroyed by now.

"Fuck."

A hand grabbed my elbow, and I spun around with a snarl.

One of the vamps from the book club meeting stood behind

me. He dropped his hold on my elbow and raised his hands defensively. "Hey, I'm not trying to start anything!"

"You should get the hell out of here," I snapped.

The other vamp shook his head, and I wondered if I'd seen him around town before. Then again, I didn't mix in the vamp circles. Or with anyone, for that matter.

"I —"

He looked panicked, and I didn't have time for a tag along. I had to find Tuesday.

"Look, maybe it's safer if we stick together," he started.

"I doubt it," I said without looking at him.

"Do you? I know you think you're hot shit, Vinnie Quake, but you don't know what it's like out there for vamps."

I met his pale gaze quickly and then looked away in case he noticed my fangs poking out. "Yeah, yeah. Look, I need to find someone—you need to get the hell out of here before something happens."

"Something has already happened," the blonde vamp said desperately. He gestured at the bookstore behind us. "They attacked a *book club*! These people are deranged and they hate us. Do you honestly think they will stop here? *You* did this! We've been meeting here for years without anyone bothering us."

"It's not my fucking fault," I snarled. "I didn't ask for this."

"None of us did," he snapped back. "But this is who we are now, and we have to deal with it. Even someone like you."

I couldn't let that slide. "What's that supposed to mean?"

"You know exactly what I mean."

I had no intention of fighting this guy. I'd never fought another vamp before. While I would admit to a certain *curiosity* about how it would go down but finding Tuesday was more important.

"I'll take a rain check on kicking your ass," I muttered. "Now, get lost."

"Vinnie!"

I spun at the sound of Baldwin's familiar voice.

Thank *fuck.*

Relief flooded through me as my manager pushed through the crowd of people and ran toward us.

"Someone took Tuesday," I shouted at him.

"I know," Baldwin replied. "I heard it on the headset. I couldn't get here fast enough to help." He glanced at the vampire at my side and his eyebrow rose slightly. "Who's your friend."

"No one," I growled.

"You're an asshole," the other vamp snarled.

"Yeah, I know."

I looked back to my manager. His face was pale and I could hear the pounding of his heart against his ribs. He was scared. And rightfully so. An explosion from behind us made me duck, and Baldwin let out a surprised yelp.

"There goes the bookstore," the other vamp said in a tired voice. "Are you happy now, Quake?"

"Shut the fuck up," I snarled. The faintest scent of jasmine tickled my nose and I inhaled deeply. If I didn't know any better, I'd say I smelled Tuesday's blood.

"I know where Tuesday is," Baldwin choked out. He rubbed at his eyes — that goddamned tear gas was everywhere. "But we have to move fast."

"Why are you still talking," I roared. "Take me to her!"

Baldwin's eyes widened slightly, and he glanced at the other vamp quickly before he nodded and ran away through the crowd. I followed him, keeping pace easily. *My manager needed to hit the gym more often.*

The blonde vampire ran at my side.

"What are you doing?" I growled at him.

"I'm going with you," he said firmly. "The fact that you've hidden this for as long as you have man, it seals the deal. Wherever you're going is sure as hell gonna be safer than out here."

"Piss off."

Even though I wanted nothing more than to drive my fists into his face, I didn't have time to argue. Besides, he was right.

Baldwin headed straight for a moving truck parked against the curb. It was painted flat black and badly. It looked like someone hired a couple of kids with spray bombs in a back alley to paint it.

Classy.

"When did you upgrade your wheels?" I asked incredulously.

"Are you going to make jokes or get in?" Baldwin snapped.

Baldwin's reaction took me aback for just a moment. He never raised his voice to me, he never dared. But this wasn't about Baldwin, it was about Tuesday's life, and I'd do anything to save her. Even if it meant traveling in a moving truck that looked like it was about to fall apart on its axles if someone slammed a door too hard.

The cab door opened, and a man I didn't recognize stuck his head out. "Get the fuck in!"

No more arguments. No more stalling.

The other vamp pushed past me and leapt into the truck. I gritted my teeth and glared at Baldwin. "I don't know him. First chance we get, he's out."

Baldwin said nothing and I leapt up into the back of the truck and pulled the grate down.

The truck lurched forward as the engine roared to life and took off from the curb.

The back of the truck was dark and cavernous. The breakneck speed and lack of seatbelts or handholds threw my balance off. When we turned a sharp corner, I stumbled against the other vamp, and he growled in the darkness.

My eyes adjusted quickly, and I pushed away from him. We weren't alone in the back of the truck. I counted three men and one woman braced against the walls of the truck box.

"What the hell," I muttered and tried to find my balance again. The truck swerved again, and the tires squealed against the pavement. "Baldwin, where are we going?"

He didn't answer me, and the truck turned again before it picked up speed. Whoever was driving was pushing the rolling bucket of bolts to its limit.

It would be a miracle if it didn't burst into flames before we got to our destination.

There was a scuffle behind me, and a grunt of surprise. I turned to see what had happened, but before I could react, something solid collided with the back of my head. The force of the blow dropped me to my knees, and I reached up to protect myself. A cloud of cold mist settled over my face and I coughed as it invaded my lungs.

Whatever it was, it burned.

Rage filled my chest, and I tried to draw enough breath to roar, but they had sprayed something in my face that was making my throat close up.

"Stay down you fang-faced bastard," a voice growled.

A boot connected with my back and drove me onto the rough plywood floor of the truck. I tried to roll away, but the pain in my throat and the pain in my head made it impossible. Passing out was not on my list of favorite things, but it didn't seem like I had a choice in the matter.

***

. . .

A strangled scream pierced through the darkness that had enveloped me. It sliced into my skin and jolted me back to consciousness. My head ached, my throat burned, and my stomach rolled. Whatever they had dosed me with was like getting run over by a freight train. *It had to be a drug. What else would lay me out like that? I'd tried almost everything, but whatever that was... I did not want to ride that train again.*

"Get another stake into him!"

Where the hell was I? Everything sounded strange, and there was a metallic ringing in my ears and the taste of blood and something else in my mouth.

I shook my head and tried to force my eyes to focus. "What the f—"

"Hey, Baldwin... looks like your boy's waking up!"

I coughed hard and spat a mouthful of blood onto the concrete floor.

Coarse laughter made my headache pound harder.

"Shut up," Baldwin's familiar voice growled.

"What — Baldwin, what's happening?" I croaked.

"What's happening?" my manager replied smoothly. "I'll tell you what's happening. Your little PR maven's stunt worked. Better than she'd expected, I think."

He chuckled and pressed something hard against my temple. I flinched away and realized that I couldn't move my arms.

"You told me — Where's Tuesday?"

"Don't you worry," Baldwin said soothingly. "She's right where she's supposed to be. In the middle of a mess of her own making. Well, it's your mess, really. Isn't it?"

"What? I don't... I don't understand."

Baldwin shoved against my temple again, and it occurred to me he had always talked about owning a handgun. I'd never seen it, and I'd always doubted that he was telling the truth. But there was something unmistakable about the feel of a muzzle pressed against the side of your head that you just didn't question.

"Don't you?" Baldwin whispered.

"Get him again! There's still space!" The sudden shout rips through the air and I wince at the sound—like a fist slamming into a side of beef.

Another scream tears through the space, and I closed my eyes to try and focus.

Where was I?

It smelled familiar, but I didn't know what to trust anymore.

"Where is Tuesday?" I asked through gritted teeth.

"You really see nothing you don't want to," Baldwin sighed. His hand gripped the top of my head and my eyes flew open as he turned me to the left.

A huddled figure lay sprawled on the floor. All at once, I recognized Tuesday's jaunty ponytail. Her face was pale and marred by a smear of blood from a wound at her hairline.

"You bastard," I snarled. I strained against whatever held my arms to my sides. "What did you do?"

"You brought this on yourself, Quake," another voice growled.

I turned my head to face this new opponent, but as I did, I saw what was making the horrendous noise.

The blond vampire who'd hitched a ride with me to escape the mob at the bookstore was pinned to the wall. Blood soaked his chest and arms, and blood-tears streamed down his face. Long pieces of wood, like lawn darts, pierced his body in more places than I could count. Everywhere but the heart.

Everywhere but where it counted.

Bastards.

His chest heaved and shuddered as the men laughed. These

men weren't the beer-soaked conspiracy-theory believing die-hards. They were clean cut and well dressed; they were the ones who wrote the conspiracy theories and spread rumors that set the internet on fire.

These were the people who hated for the sake of hating. That was what got them off.

"What the fuck are you doing?"

"This is what all fang-heads deserve," one man shouted. His fist slammed into the other vamp's face, and I struggled harder to free my arms.

Where the hell was my super strength?

Why couldn't I get out of this?

"It's the silver," Baldwin said mildly. "I wasn't sure if it would work, but the guy who sold it to me said it would be effective. You inhaled more than was probably healthy, but it's not as though I give a shit."

I coughed again and tasted blood.

Silver.

"You're next, Quake!"

More laughter.

"Baldwin, you can't let them—"

My manager shrugged. "I'm not making the rules here, Vinnie. You brought this on yourself."

10

VINNIE

Desperation clawed at my stomach as another man punched the helpless vamp pinned to the wall.

I was next.

An undead dartboard.

"What the hell are you talking about? I don't understand!"

Baldwin shrugged and stepped aside as another man strode toward me. "Of course, you don't understand, you selfish prick," the man snarled. "All of this is your fault. All of it!"

I mean, he wasn't wrong. I had killed my entire staff—all of them. Without a second thought or moment of remorse... That all came later.

"Do I know you?" Panic wasn't a familiar emotion, and I hated the way it made me feel. The sooner I could get out of this, the better. "Look, whatever you want from me, take it and go. Just let Tuesday out of here."

"The only thing you have that I want, I'm going to take from you before the sun comes up," the man said. His smile was strange and unnerving, and I swallowed hard.

"What is it?" I asked as boldly as I could. "Money? No problem. Baldwin can write you a check."

The man's fist collided with my jaw, and my head rocked back. Someone laughed, and I glared at the man with as much venom as I could muster.

"Ow."

"You keep it up, fang-head," the man snarled. "I'll wipe that look off your face if it's the last thing I do. You didn't care about any of them. They gave *everything* to you."

"What are you *talking* about?" I shouted. Desperation wasn't a good look for me, but I was running out of options. "Who?"

"My sister!" the man yelled. His boot slammed into my stomach and knocked me sideways onto the floor.

"She literally dedicated her entire life to you, and how did you repay her? By draining her blood and leaving her for dead! You vampire bastard!"

More blows rained down on my body and I closed my eyes and took the beating, unable to roll out of the way or protect myself.

All at once, the beating stopped and I dared to open my eyes.

"You know that won't do anything," Baldwin said mildly.

"I know, but it makes me feel better," the man panted.

The only other sound in the room was the strangled breathing of the blond vampire.

The man wiped his hand across his sweating brow and nodded to the other men in the room. "Do it," he commanded.

A scream echoed through the room, cut off by a wet ripping sound that I knew would echo in my dreams for centuries to come... I knew what they'd done. I'd heard whispers about vampire trophy hunters. But I thought they were just that. Whispers.

There was no scream to accompany the acquisition of the second trophy. Just a shuddering moan.

"He's no fun," someone complained.

"Finish him," my attacker said. "We have more work to do."

The man's face loomed over me.

"My sister Patricia. You murdered her in cold blood."

I blinked in confusion. "I — I didn't know she had any family."

"Oh, but it was ok to kill her when you thought she was alone? That's fucked up logic, even for a bloodsucker. You don't give a shit about anyone but yourself."

The man's spittle flecked my cheek, but I didn't turn my head away. I deserved this. He was right. I *hadn't* cared. I hadn't given a single solitary shit about anyone for the last five years.

"Do you have anything to say?" the man demanded.

I shrugged helplessly. "I'm sorry."

Sorry didn't bring Patricia back. Sorry didn't bring any of them back. And it wouldn't save my neck, either. But it was all I had.

"Not good enough," the angry man snapped. "Pick him up!"

The bonds that held me were released and rough hands dragged me up to my knees. I smiled grimly as feeling rushed back into my fingers. He was going to regret this. But they were one step ahead of me. My revenge was halted when something hard slammed into my chest just below my collarbone.

I looked down in surprise. A wooden stake. How original. Nothing like an old faithful to get the job done. But why didn't it —

Pain streaked through my body and my back arched, bending me almost in half as I writhed in the grip of the men that held me upright.

Four more strikes slammed into my torso. I heard rather than felt my bones breaking. Ribs shattering. Organs punctured. But the pain. Oh, holy fuck, the pain.

They dropped me and I writhed on the floor, unable to escape, unable to roll away.

I roared in rage and frustration as the nameless men descended on me.

"Zach!"

All at once, everything stopped.

Through the red and black fog of my pain, I heard Baldwin's voice and the panic in it.

"Zach, we have to go!"

"What? But we're just getting started," someone complained.

"Shut up," Zach commanded. "Why? What's happening? There's no sirens. You took care of the alarm. We're fine. The cops aren't coming."

"It's not the cops," Baldwin hissed. "It's the house... it's rigged—"

"Cameras?" one man asked in a panicked voice.

"Explosives," Baldwin said grimly. "We have to get out of here..."

Zach looked down at me. His expression was unreadable.

"Leave him," Baldwin urged. "The fire will take him, and all the evidence, with it. Please!"

Zach frowned and then shook his head. "Come on. You heard the man."

"But what about the fang-head?" another guy whined.

"Leave him!" Zach barked.

He aimed a vicious kick at my head, but I barely moved when it struck my temple. Every inch of my body burned as though it were already on fire. What was a little kick to all of that?

I'd actually forgotten about the explosion. The carefully planned demolition of my beloved home was scheduled to happen while I was across town being photographed with Sandrina at some dance club while Tuesday monitored everything from the command post.

We were still together, but this was not how the plan was supposed to go down.

Fuck.

I leaned back against the wall and listened to their boots thump down the stairs. The slam of the door confirmed that my attackers had fled my house. There was a sick sort of justice that they left me here, of all places. This was the floor my own victims had laid on just a few days ago.

I was the world's worst vampire.

I must have been to let myself get blindsided by a bunch of humans.

But the minute they took Tuesday, none of that had mattered.

I acted on impulse when I ran after her kidnappers. It was a blind fit of passion. Backfire. *Total fucking backfire.*

Tuesday groaned and my cold, undead heart lurched in my chest. *Tuesday was alive.*

I rolled to my side to face her. She's pushed herself up to a sitting position, but before I could call out to her, she focused on the body of the blonde vampire and let out a scream.

The sharp sound felt like someone was driving stakes into my ears and rendered me unable to speak to let her know I was there.

With careful movements, I crept forward. Silver-tipped stakes, drenched in Holy Water, I could feel every inch of them. Every movement I made was excruciatingly painful.

"Tuesday."

My voice sounded hoarse as I whispered her name, desperate to get her to stop screaming.

"Tuesday, it's me. It's Vinnie."

She turned to me slowly, and I felt a fresh surge of protective anger to see her skin so pale and her face marred by the smear of dried blood from the wound on her forehead. They'd hurt her, and they would have done worse if they'd had time. I didn't doubt that they would have woken her up to make her watch them do to me what they'd done to the poor bastard pinned to the wall behind her.

Rage filled me as I dragged myself toward her with purposeful movements.

She sat there as if frozen to the wall. Shock had rendered my tough warrior princess temporarily unable to move.

I grimaced as I edged my body inch by inch across the floor until I lay close enough to touch her. I was panting with the effort of that movement and the pain had caused blood tears to drip down my cheeks and onto the floor.

Tuesday still said nothing. I wasn't positive she even knew where she was. I worked as quickly as I could to untie her hands. I gently massaged them, hoping to get the feeling back there. She flexed her fingers, one by one and woke up just a little. Her breathing was shallow but her heart was beating strong. She pulled her feet to her chest and untied the cord around her ankles herself. I leaned back on the floor and tried not to focus on the pain that rippled through my body.

I'd died once, but it hadn't felt like this.

"Baldwin. Baldwin betrayed us," she choked out. "And... someone else I know. I don't know why, but this felt personal." Her voice was calm, but there was a tremor underneath her words that I didn't quite recognize.

"You're not going to say anything about the stakes?" I asked.

It was supposed to be a joke, but Tuesday's eyes filled with tears and I instantly regretted my flippant attempt at humor. *Bad timing, pal.*

She turned to me and reached down tentatively to brush the blood tears off my face. My entire body buzzed at her touch and I willed myself to remain still, unwilling to share this moment with the pain of movement.

"Vinnie... I'm so—"

"I need you to pull the stakes out," I whispered.

Her eyes met mine and this time the fear took over her face, but she nodded and her shaking hands moved to the first stake just below my collarbone. I closed my eyes and inhaled deeply to prepare for the rush of pain that I knew would accompany the removal; but nothing happened.

Instead, the most intoxicating smell filled my nostrils. A drop of something hot and forbidden hit my lips and my fangs descended automatically. My tongue darted out to taste it.

Blood.

Slightly citrusy with just a hint of jasmine...

My eyes snapped open and my bloodlust ignited as Tuesday held her bleeding wrist to my lips.

"You drink," she chided, "I'll pull."

Her eyes were bright as she pressed her wound toward my mouth. I hesitated, dragging my eyes away from the pulsing vein beneath the tender skin of her wrist to look into her eyes. They met mine with a clarity I envied, and she smiled briefly before she rolled her eyes and shoved her bleeding wrist against my lips again.

The first taste of her blood exploded on my tongue and I let out a little moan of pleasure. Gently, I pierced her skin with my fangs, careful not to gulp too quickly as her blood rushed into my mouth. Her breath came fast, but she didn't pull away.

She waited a moment before she pulled the first stake out and I was thankful for it. The pain was white-hot and coursed through me like wildfire. The shock of it forced me to bite down —hard.

"OUCH! Vinnie, what the hell?!" She thumped me on the head with the bloody stake she had just pulled from my chest. I released my hold on her wrist and withdrew my fangs carefully.

Her eyes blazed at me with the same rage I knew so well,

before she grudgingly offered me her wrist again and prepared herself to pull the next stake. "Be. More. Careful." she hissed.

We fell into a rhythm. I fed, she pulled. She wiggled the stake a little before she pulled it out, a signal to me to let go of her wrist, and soon we were both panting with the effort and a pile of eight stakes lay on the floor next to us.

Eight.

One for each sin. One for each dead body.

My healing kicked in as soon as the last stake left my body, and my super-charged senses rushed back, powered by the extra boost of her blood in my veins. If I couldn't admit it before, I could now. I'd been dreaming of this moment for five long years.

I rubbed a hand over my face and sat up. Tuesday wobbled a little on her knees, weakened by the loss of blood. I stood up and pulled Tuesday to her feet. She leaned against me and her eyes closed for just a moment. "My turn," my voice was husky as I looked down at her, "Let me heal your head wound at least?"

Her eyes snapped open, and she glared up at me.

"I should have left that last stake in for a little longer," she said. "If you think, for a goddamned second, that I'm going to let you turn me into a vampire, you are *utterly* brain-damaged."

"I would never turn you against your will. I just want to. Well... lick you. My saliva can heal you. That's it. I'm offering nothing but spit... Well... at least until we get out of this."

"I am not having a spit or swallow debate with you right now," she grumbled, but she didn't pull away as I wrapped my arms around her bend drew her close. I cherished the feeling of her warmth against my chest. In all the horror that we'd experienced in the last few hours, this was my sanctuary.

I pressed small kisses to the cuts and bumps on her face and head and smiled to see the wounds close. I couldn't replace the blood she'd lost, but I could make them stop bleeding, and stop hurting. That had to be enough for now.

For the first time since I became a vampire, I was grateful for my extra abilities.

"Can we do anything about — him?"

She was looking at the corpse of the other vampire again. I cradled her face and turned it away from the nightmare pinned to the wall. She was thinking about how it could have been me —I didn't need to ask her to know that much.

"There's nothing we can do. Even if we pull out the stakes, it's been too long. He's lost too much blood and that last stake—"

Tuesday closed her eyes and nodded. I looked back at the unfortunate vamp and said a silent apology to him. He hadn't deserved what they'd done to him. I hated that we couldn't change what had happened. All I could do was vow to see the responsible parties were punished.

Suddenly she gasped and pulled away from me, panic clear in her expression.

"The house, Vinnie—we wired the house to blow. We have to go. We have to go *now*."

We ran through the house together, checking the doors and windows on the main floor, but Sergio and Cole had sealed them shut. The window glass was designed to filter out maximum amounts of sunlight and was too thick to break easily.

Detonation cords and explosive devices were wired together at each potential exit. Sergio and Cole had artistic flair when it came to blowing shit up. But I recognized that someone else had put the last touches on the house. Best guess? Baldwin and his band of merry assholes wanted to cover their tracks before they'd abandoned us to the inferno that was about to engulf my house.

Tuesday turned to me, desperation and fear written all over

her face. I summoned all the strength my vampire abilities could give me. There was another sound approaching. Shouting and screaming from down the road. The mob from the book-store discovered my address on the dark web. They came for me, ready to unwittingly play their part in Tuesday's scheme.

We had to move fast. If the inferno didn't get us, the mob would finish the job.

No pressure, Quake. No pressure at all.

11

———

TUESDAY

I'm known for being the calm one in high-pressure situations. I've assisted countless celebrities, businesspeople, minor members of European royal families, and even a few criminal players with their own unique set of problems. Through all of that I've never lost my cool. Until now.

I was about ten seconds away from losing all semblance of control.

Why? Being locked in a deathtrap of a house with eight dead bodies, my vampire ex, a dead vampire, a pool of blood, and a huge crowd of rioting bigots (that I incited) on their way to burn everything Vinnie had ever touched to the ground was panic-inducing.

I had never felt more empathy for Frankenstein's monster than I did at that moment.

Vinnie muttered to himself as he paced back and forth in front of the wall. He'd said something about making a door, but that just seemed—stupid. It had sounded stupid. And impossible.

I *should* help him strategize. That was the entire reason they hired me for this job. But I couldn't do it. Fear paralyzed me and I just... stood there wringing my hands like some sort of damsel in distress. I spotted my tote bag scattered in the corner and rushed to retrieve it. The dickheads had stolen my iPad and cash but everything else seemed to be fine. I clutched it to my chest as the one piece of comfort in this shittastic situation.

The clock ticked ever closer to our doom, and I couldn't tell if it was the gas leak, the stench from the bodies, the blood loss, the head wound, or even just the stress from the last 48 hours but dizziness struck me at every turn. I just watched on unsteady legs while Vinnie paced.

There was usually a comfort in knowing how a particular scenario would play out. But in this case, all those details were eating away at me.

Vinnie's hand snaked around my waist, and I yelped in surprise. Half-grateful for the distraction from my thoughts, and half-terrified with worry that I missed something crucial that could save us.

He moved so silently; it was like being locked in a room with a panther. A very sexy, very rage-filled panther who was ready to kill for you. *I actually don't hate it.*

"Do you trust me?" he asked. His voice was soft like velvet. When he looked at me like that, I almost forgot the fact that we were about to be incinerated along with all of his expensive possessions.

I nodded. Seeing as our deaths were imminent, trust was slightly irrelevant. But underneath that, I *did* actually trust him. Weird how that worked out.

"Good. I am going to need you to do exactly what I say."

He handed me a small flashlight and led me over to the grand river rock fireplace in the formal dining room. It took up the entire side of the wall and was larger than anything I had ever seen outside a lodge-themed hotel. He carried a length of rope in his hand and my eyebrow rose slightly as I noted the color and texture of it.

"Where... Where did you get shiny purple rope? Who has that on-hand in their house? Is this from a sex dungeon? Is it clean? Oh my God."

He looked down, shrugged, and shoved it into my hands. "I will neither confirm nor deny any of that other than to tell you I can personally verify it's load bearing. Hold this."

With purposeful steps, Vinnie strode to the fireplace and grabbed the decorative poker. With a roar, he reared back and smashed the poker into the glass front of the fireplace. I let out a small scream, more out of surprise than anything, as the glass scattered over the stone floor. Without hesitation, he reached in and ripped out the metal grate. It clattered across the floor as he kicked it away. He turned back to me and grinned.

"It's like Santa! But in reverse!"

I looked at the glass and the fireplace and sputtered. *Surely, he doesn't mean we are exiting the deathtrap by going up a chimney?*

He grabbed the rope out of my hands and knelt before me, measuring the rope around my waist and hips before wrapping me into some sort of harness. His hands moved quickly and I could barely keep up.

Standing quickly, he kissed my forehead gently, swiping his tongue over the cut above my eye and making me squirm. "Stay next to the fireplace," he said.

I moved into position. Where else was I going to go? I'd lost track of time, I didn't know how far away we were from death. I didn't want to die like this. I didn't —

Before I could protest or say anything at all, he looped the remaining rope around him like a professional rock climber and crawled into the fireplace and disappeared from sight.

"Vinnie!"

My voice was barely a squeak, and I giggled wildly as a cartoonish puff of soot fell out behind him. I crouched down to peer up into the chimney, but it was pitch black.

I heard muffled profanity as he climbed up the chimney. That vampire superstrength was something else. A scraping noise sounded from somewhere behind me and I whirled around to see what it might be. *Help? Firefighters? Anyone?*

No. Don't be stupid. No one's coming to help you. It's just the friendly mob outside baying for Vinnie's blood.

Nothing popped out but I couldn't shake the feeling I was being watched. "Hello?" I called out.

No one answered.

A deafening *crash* drowned out my voice as a deformed piece of metal hurtled down the chimney and collided with the stone base of the fireplace. I jumped back, crunching the glass under my shoes.

With shaking hands, I pulled it out of the way just as the purple rope in front of me jumped around.

"Tuesday! They are at the driveway. We gotta go, baby. Come stand in the direct center of the fireplace grate and hold your hand on that knot at the top of rope. When you're ready, pull on the rope twice and I'll pull you up. The harness will hold you. Just sit back into it and try not to move a lot."

His voice echoed down the chimney, and I hurried to comply. I ignored my pathological fear of heights in favor of my survivalist fear of dying.

Armed with a plan, I hoped the rope was sturdy enough to hold. Dying in a raging inferno was one thing, but suffocating to death in a chimney or falling to my death was an entirely different kind of nope.

Standing in the grate, my precious tote bag hanging off my

shoulder, I took a deep breath and tugged on the rope. There was barely time to register what was happening before the rope jerked and lifted me off the ground. My eyes squeezed shut while I eased through the chimney. The rough sides brushed up against my arms, coating me in a thin layer of soot. I ignored it all and held on to the rope as tightly as I could.

I only opened my eyes when Vinnie's hand closed over my arm. His silhouette against the velvet dark sky, wreathed in moonlight, took my breath away. With quick fingers, he untied me and steadied me on the solid metal roof and led me over to lean against the chimney.

Even though it was late summer, there was a chill in the night air. The breeze off the water felt icy cold against my skin and made it difficult to focus. I didn't have my watch but I guessed we only had minutes, if that, before the entire house exploded into a carefully arranged fireball.

People were visible, gathered at the base of the driveway, with more headlights tracking down the private drive. Shouting and cheers were carried by the breeze. The smaller flashes of light bobbed around the fence line. Flashlights. The crowd was trying to breach the gates and make their way toward the house.

I essentially planned this, but it still shocked me how brazen they were. Standing beside me, leaning up against the chimney, Vinnie vibrated with rage as he watched them.

"We have to go," I whispered as panic gripped me again.

Without a word, Vinnie nodded before offering his hand to steady me as we sat down and slid carefully down the angled roof toward the back porch.

Vinnie released my hand and slid effortlessly to the ground. He landed like a cat from the one-story drop, but something in my head screamed that I wouldn't survive the fall. My heart beat wildly in my chest as I fought to slow my descent.

Stop it. Stop it. Broken legs or die in a fireball.

Breaking glass and a roar from the crowd spurs me on and I closed my eyes and launched myself off the roof, praying to whatever deity in the sky that may or may not exist that either Vinnie caught me or I died quickly.

Being caught mid-fall off a roof by a strong, sexy man was romantic only in movies. Real-life was painful and awkward. When Vinnie caught me, I let out a grunt of pain so loud, he crushed me against his chest to muffle the sound. As soon as I could breathe again, he picked me up and held me tight, running across the carefully manicured lawn towards the boathouse.

We reached the small stand of trees just beyond the house when the first explosion ripped through the building and set off the chain reaction I'd arranged so carefully.

Vinnie put on more speed, and I clung to his shoulders as we tried to outrun the fireball that lit up the night sky. The heat from the explosion stung my exposed skin as we raced towards the water.

I panicked when Vinnie bypassed the beautifully crafted dock and walked straight into the water, wading through the icy cold bay until he was waist deep.

"Vinnie!" I hissed, hiking myself up higher on his body, "What are you doing? I can't swim!"

I chanced a brief look behind us and the fire was raging so beautifully that I felt a small surge of pride that my plan actually worked the way I intended it to. Sort of.

Sergio and Cole did outstanding work. I should poach them for the Agency.

"Wait here," Vinnie whispered, carefully setting me on the floating platform. The breeze blew water up on me and I shivered from the cold. Vinnie disappeared under the surface, popping up a few yards away on the other side of a floating buoy.

I looked around nervously, but none of our visitors seemed to have noticed us. Yet.

The fire burning Vinnie's luxury mansion was really kicking up, and I knew we only had minutes before this entire property was swarming with first responders.

The sound of gentle splashes drew my attention away from the fireballs and back towards the place I last saw Vinnie. A dark shape moved through the water towards me and I squinted to make it out.

A boat.

An old, rickety, row boat. *You've got to be kidding me.*

Vinnie popped up out of the water and pulled himself onto the platform next to me, tossing me the line for the rowboat with a satisfied smile on his face.

I looked at him for a long minute before looking back at the boat. It barely looked seaworthy, and it reeked of rotting fish.

"Ok Poseidon, you're richer than God and *this* is your escape boat?" I groused, wrinkling my nose against the smell when the wind shifted.

Vinnie's look of satisfaction shifted, and he looked at his rowboat with slightly less enthusiasm. He reminded me of a kid who just lost his puppy, and I immediately felt like a bitch.

"It's... great. Far quieter than a ski boat!" I half-heartedly proclaimed, nudging the decrepit vessel with my foot. *We survived all of that, and now I'm going to drown in Puget Sound.*

Vinnie brightened and looked over my shoulder at the blaze that lit up the night sky. The amount of destruction we had managed took my breath away.

It had worked.

It had really worked.

Well, the house had exploded, but everything else had gone entirely to shit.

I turned to Vinnie, ready to figure out the next step of our plan, but he wasn't interested in speaking. Heat flashed in his eyes before he pulled me against his chest with a growl.

His mouth crashed down on mine, and my eyes drifted closed. This was the Vinnie I remembered. All power and sensuality. But the sharpness of his fangs brought me back to reality. We had just covered up a mass murder with an explosion that had probably taken a few other lives in the process—sure, they might have been people who would have been more than willing to murder the two of us, but that wasn't the point.

I turned my face away and pushed back against his chest.

"They'll find us," I choked out, my heart hammering in my chest. "We have to go."

Vinnie looked at me like he wanted to argue the point, but the sounds of shouts from the house changed his mind.

Without another word he picked me up and tossed me into the rowboat and then pulled himself in, pushing off with an oar.

"Duck down and hide under the tarp," He whispered, pointing towards a crumpled up blue tarp in the boat's stern.

"Uh, no?" I gagged when the smell from the tarp reached me. "I'm good. I'll just sit right -"

"Get. Down." Vinnie ordered, reaching over to yank me down off the bench seat.

"Old Mr. French fishes most nights out here by himself. If they see you, they are going to want to investigate." He continued, muffling my outrage with his hand.

His logic was sound, although I suddenly had a disturbing thought about how Vinnie had acquired said boat from old Mr. French. Vinnie read the questions in my eyes and glared at me.

"I didn't kill him. I knocked him out and put him under a tree. He's fine."

I glared back and sank my teeth into his fingers, biting down as hard as I could.

"What the fuck?" He let go of me and shook his hand out, nudging me away from him with his foot. "You almost drew blood, Tuesday! Who's the vampire now?"

I didn't dignify that with a response. I curled myself into as small of a ball as I could and huddled next to but not under the offensive tarp, my precious tote bag clutched to my chest.

"Start rowing, asshole," I gritted out, counting to ten in my head to stay calm.

I really, really hate surprises.

Vinnie fumbled around and pulled the oars he had dropped out of the bottom of the boat and inserted them into the oar locks. Before I could say anything, he pulled back, leaning into the stroke with his considerable strength.

The rickety boat moved backwards, and then we listed starboard.

Vinnie looked down at the oars and then back at the water and shrugged.

He pulled back again, and we spun in the water.

"What the...?" He muttered, pulling back harder and harder.

The boat rotated more until we made a full circle.

"Vinnie..." I croaked, the motion and spinning making my stomach lurch.

He kept pulling, his considerable strength rocketing the boat from side to side and around and around.

"Stop!" I scraped my fingernails down the skin of his ankle and sat up slightly. "Your oars," I struggled to get the words out, "Fix your bloody oars so we go straight or I swear to God, I'm going to break that off on your thick head and stake you myself. Do. You. Understand. Me?"

We stared at each other for a moment before he let go of the oars and adjusted the placement. The motion — and the persistent smell of rotting fish from the tarp - proved too much for my fragile stomach. I hung my head over the side and threw up.

A soft hand rubbed my back and tucked my hair behind my ears in an act of sweet comfort.

"Oh Tuesday, what are we going to do?" he whispered as we floated and watched the distant figures gather in front of the inferno we left behind.

"We have to figure something out," I choked out. "We can't just hide —"

Vinnie rubbed a hand over his mouth and looked at me incredulously. "But hiding is easy," he said.

"Not when your manager, the guy who's in charge of your bank accounts and credit cards and everything else, was the one behind a plot to have you killed!"

He grimaced. "Good point."

"Any ideas?"

"Well, we definitely can't let those bastards live. Not after what they pulled."

His face broke into an evil grin, and my heart leapt in my chest. I knew what to do, but I didn't know if I was strong enough to make it work. But there wasn't any time for doubts.

"Get me back to dry land and we will make a plan," I said firmly. "Pisces maintains property all around the region. If I can get a hold of my people, I can get us to a safe house that is off the grid. Everyone involved in that little shit show thinks we're dead, and we might have some time until the fire department releases their report."

"Have I ever mentioned how hot you are when you're all murderous and shit?"

"Save it," I snapped. "We're still neck deep in this mess."

Vinnie grabbed my hand and brought it to his lips, sending a small jolt of fire all the way through me. His touch was comforting, and I needed all the comfort I could get right now.

Together, we rowed across the bay—partners again, for now. But all that could change in a heartbeat.

***

The last remnants of the warm fuzzy feelings I'd had on the beach evaporated by the time we landed on some abandoned dock near a downtown beach, and cold, hard reality had set in. The last eight hours had been.... eventful. We'd caused a riot and demolished a house. Now we were on the run from people who, hopefully, thought we were dead.

Knowing Vinnie was going to come out as a vamp when this was all said and done— No. I couldn't think about that. But if I'd known, shit would have gone down a little differently.

We needed to get out of town. And for that, we needed wheels.

Thankfully, Vinnie had cash in his wallet and he'd snagged a burner phone and a data card from a corner store. But no one was answering the line at Pisces PR. Someone always answered that phone, and when every second mattered, it was incredibly aggravating.

If we couldn't reach Pisces, I wouldn't be able to use one of our safe houses. We would have to go underground without support, and that thought scared the crap out of me.

"Here we are!" Vinnie sang out, oblivious to the world of trouble we were in.

Men.

My feet hurt and every muscle in my body ached. The last place in the world I wanted to be was here, but Fate wasn't really asking me what I wanted these days.

We stood in a dirty alleyway in front of an abandoned warehouse. Not my first choice, but that was my fault for letting Vinnie be in charge of directions.

"Where exactly are we?" I looked up at Vinnie, but he wasn't paying attention to me. He frowned at a hidden keypad and then punched his finger into the buttons as though he was entering a code.

"What the hell—"

A soft electronic beep sounded, and a panel slid open. Vinnie ducked down and shoved his face in the box. After a moment, a metallic grinding noise filled the air and a large garage door slid open.

"It's my garage!" he said with a wide grin. "You said we needed a ride."

I peered into the inky darkness of the void that yawned ahead of us.

"I dunno—"

Vinnie didn't wait for me, he just waltzed into the place like he owned it. Which... he did.

Ugh.

Aching feet and all, I hurried to catch up and huffed in disbelief when I stepped inside. The lights snapped on as we entered and illuminated the cavernous space with an eerie, green-toned light.

"This is your *garage?*" I asked dubiously. The building was the size of a regulation football field except instead of fans and sexy men throwing a ball around, it was filled with cars.

Shiny cars.

Expensive cars.

An absurd number of expensive cars.

"Uh, yeah?" Vinnie looked around and shrugged as if he couldn't understand my disbelief. The only people who shrug at that kind of opulence are people who have lost all touch with the concept of money.

The thought made me irrationally angry.

"Gee, did you ever think to spend some of this money on, I don't know, your community? How many kids could have had new books or donations to the Food Bank! Did you think of them, *Vincent?*"

He just looked at me with confusion written all over his face.

"You want me to give cars to... the library?"

I didn't dignify that with an answer. There's really nothing to say. This place was every gear-head's wet dream. Gross. All I saw was inflated gas prices and douchebags who drove too fast through school zones.

Ugh.

We scurried past the sports cars and tiny sedans and headed towards the back where a fleet of SUVs shone darkly under the lights.

Vinnie was like a kid in a candy store. He stopped every few moments to point out something he wanted me to see, or rub his hand over a shining fender. Each time I said no, he pouted, and I hated myself for finding it the tiniest bit adorable.

But we didn't have time for show and tell, and by the time I had to physically drag Vinnie away from a bright yellow Lamborghini, my patience was well and truly gone.

Time was wasting, and I didn't dare think of what might happen if they caught us. The first SUV we came across was the one I wanted. It looked like a car fit for ferrying around a president or head of state, or possibly the leader of a cartel. Knowing Vinnie, it would be outfitted with all the latest technology and defense mechanisms.

"That one!" I barked at Vinnie, tapping my foot impatiently while he searched the wheel well for the key box.

"This one is great! It has heated leather seats and a snorkel." Vinnie's exuberance dimmed slightly when he saw the look on my face. With a quiet beep, the behemoth was unlocked, and I climbed in. The leather seats were buttery-soft and I let out a satisfied sigh as I settled back against it. *OK, fine. Some luxury is worth it.*

It's the best we can do. It won't stand out as much as the Lambo, but rolling around Seattle in a tricked out rig like this *will* draw some attention. I only hoped that people would assume we're the badasses who shoot first and ask questions later. Maybe then we'd be able to get out of the city unmolested.

Maybe.

Vinnie wisely kept his mouth shut while he carefully backed out of the parking spot and drove down the aisle towards the open garage door.

The digital clock read 04:00 a.m. and gray streaks of dawn already decorated the sky and mingled with the darker black of the smoke that still rose from the direction of Vinnie's destroyed house.

Shit.

"Get in the back. Sun's coming up." I ordered.

I jerked my thumb toward the bench seats behind me. From one glance, I could tell that the window-tints kept the sunlight out. Smart boy.

"We still have a couple hours," Vinnie protested immediately. "I can at least drive us out of the city!"

My vision narrowed, and little black dots of frustration appeared at the edges of my vision. This was not the time to play petulant rockstar.

"Get. In. The. Back." I forced the words through gritted teeth and grabbed for the wheel. If he didn't comply, I'd have to rip the keys out of the ignition.

I had no more patience left.

Vinnie picked up on my tone and eyed me with trepidation before he sighed in defeat and put the vehicle in park.

In a flash, he was out of the car. He tapped on my window with a cheeky grin before he opened it for me.

I slid out of my seat and fixed him with a furious glare. Anger, lust, and half a dozen other emotions churned through me but I didn't have time for any of it. I stalked past him and his hand snaked out and captured me. He hauled me up against him roughly and I grunted in frustration.

"What are you thinking about, Tuesday?" His voice rasped in my ear and I had to stop myself from rubbing up against him like a cat. *Freaking vampire pheromones.*

"Nothing," I lied. Every minute we wasted out here was another minute we were at risk of being discovered and another minute closer to true daylight and vulnerability.

I hardened my resolve as his hands moved over my back. "Look, pal. I did not just blow up a house and fake the death of the most popular pop star on the planet, only to be captured by the bad guys because said pop star couldn't follow some simple instructions. Now. Give me the keys and get. In. The. Back."

His eyelids drooped in defeat and he trailed a single finger down my cheek. I shivered despite myself, caught in his trance.

Vinnie's soft laugh in my ear brought me back to reality and my face flooded red. Thankfully, he didn't press his luck. He smirked at me as though he knew every single one of my secret thoughts and then dropped the keys into my outstretched hand.

He climbed into the back of the rig and I slammed the door shut after him and took a moment to shake out my limbs and stretch my arms.

If Vinnie was determined to throw me off my game, he had another thing coming. I was a woman on a mission.

I climbed into the driver's seat, pulled my tangled hair back, and tucked it up underneath a ball cap I'd swiped from the warehouse before I shoved the keys into the ignition.

It wasn't the best disguise, but it was something.

With any luck, we'll have made it through the city and be well on our way to the Olympic Peninsula by the time any of the dust, literal and proverbial, had settled.

My luck had been in short supply lately, so I had to hope that Vinnie had some saved up.

We were gonna need it.

12

TUESDAY

"I'm going to need blood," Vinnie called out from under his nest of sun-protection blankets in the back seat.

I groaned aloud. I'd forgotten about that. Food was one thing, I could survive on coffee and cookies if I had to, but Vinnie couldn't. *Freaking high maintenance vampires.*

I could probably donate one or two feedings before things got weird. When he fed off me back at the house, it hadn't been *that bad.* Something in the back of my mind also whispered that Vinnie could probably make a feeding much more enjoyable if we weren't in the throes of a full-blown crisis. And that part of me was *very* curious about what exactly that might entail. One hears things... fascinating things...

Shut up, Tuesday. Not. The. Time.

Business face.

"Where do you go to get blood?" I yelled back. It wasn't as though there was going to be a road sign or a symbol on a gas station that meant "Blood Here!"

"Uh, well, Patricia used to get it for me. But a butcher, maybe? Blood banks don't exactly deliver... Maybe a hospital if there's one nearby?" He sounded completely unsure of himself, and I closed my eyes and counted to ten while cursing him again for being a spoiled celebrity.

Also... *Did he really just suggest sneaking into a hospital to steal blood?*

I was mildly horrified, but given our current situation, it's not as though I could lay claim to any moral high ground.

"I think we are fresh out of *hospitals, Vincent.* You're gonna have to hope that the butcher at Food Mart has something for you. Can't you just.... I dunno, suck the blood out of a raw piece of steak or something? Would that work for you?" My mind raced for options, but nothing came immediately to mind. The image of Vinnie attacking a piece of raw beef was entertaining, and I grinned to myself. I should buy him one anyway.

When Vinnie didn't answer my steak question, I sighed and made an executive decision. After all, he's the one who basically employed me to run his life until this was over. I don't spend a ton of time out of the city, but I wagered 24-hour supermarkets weren't super common once you got out in the boonies. The idea of dealing with a crowd was nerve-wracking but the parking lot of the Food Mart was almost empty and I sent up a silent prayer of thanks.

"What else do we need? We'll have time to get more provisions later. But blood, food for me, maybe some toothbrushes? Anything else?" I opened my notes app on my phone and started making a list.

"Condoms. Big ones."

I froze, and every nerve in my body erupted.

"Uh, that's presumptuous of you. Don't vampires need to be invited first before they come inside?" I retorted.

Vinnie was silent for a second before he laughed uproariously from his blanket nest.

"Well played, baby."

I just chuckled darkly and frowned at my phone. *Love that he thought I'm kidding. Ugh. He has to be screwing with me. The last thing either of us needed right now was an... entanglement. No matter how curious we might be.*

"Ok. Stay out of sight, I'll be right back." I held out my hand and Vinnie grumbled something I couldn't hear before he dropped his wallet into my hand. I pulled out a wad of cash and threw the wallet back in the general direction of the blankets.

Without waiting for him to say anything, I bounced out of the car and beeped the lock as I hurried towards the entrance.

Butcher.

Snack aisle.

Wine aisle.

Definitely wine. Whiskey if they have it.

And... headache meds. And shampoo. All of those.

I grabbed a basket and started throwing things in it as I navigated the long aisles toward the butcher's counter and rehearsed what I was going to say.

Blood pudding?

Need it for soup?

Just give me the blood!

Nothing was going to make me sound less like a freak or a serial killer. *Or someone buying supplies on the down low for a vampire in hiding.*

I swallowed thickly, crossed my fingers for luck, and rang the little bell for service.

"Can I help you?" The butcher glared at me from across the counter and I gulped. My skin buzzed with nerves.

"Uh, yes. Can I get... a packet of sausages, two pieces of salmon, some pork chops, a steak, and onegallonofblood, please?" I smiled sweetly at the grumpy old man and tried to stay as calm as possible.

"You want sausage, salmon, chops, steak... and blood?" He repeated as he raised an eyebrow at me.

Nothing beats a 24-hour grocery store at 4:00 a.m. amiright?

"Yes, sir!"

Bright and cheery. Bright. And. Cheery. Totally normal requests.

The man gave me a long measured look before nodding and wrapping up my order. He placed three styrofoam cups with lids next to my order of meat and I handed him cash. He just grunted and slapped a 'paid' sticker on my purchase and went to go back to whatever he did in the back.

My heart lightened considerably.

Maybe everything would be okay.

My hope lasted until I got to the checkout stand with the rest of my supplies.

The TV next to the customer service desk was on and a small crowd of employees crowded around to see what was happening.

My blood froze in my veins as the news camera panned over the destruction left in the wake of the explosion I'd orchestrated. Fire crews were still trying to put the blaze out. To my utter horror, my official Pisces PR headshot had been included in the report, right next to a publicity photo of Vinnie, and a candid paparazzi shot from the vampire support book club meeting. Right before the violence had erupted.

That was fast. Too fast. How had they connected us? So much for that iron-clad NDA Baldwin forced me to sign.

There had been no time to fully disguise myself before we got in the SUV and started driving. By then, there was nothing available except for the battered baseball cap I'd shoved down over my hair when we'd fled the city and the pair of dirty coveralls I'd found hanging in Vinnie's garage and jammed into my tote bag. I looked around the displays for any clothing that I could add to my meager collection, but there was nothing, not even a t-shirt.

Gods help us.

Forty-eight minutes.

Forty-eight soul-sucking minutes of freedom. Gone in an instant.

Worse? It was all my fault. I had been too busy thinking about safehouses and planning the big picture to remember the little details. Necessities like bathrooms, breakfast, and... blood. It was a rookie mistake and I could kick myself for making it.

If only we'd been able to get to one of the official Pisces safe houses within the city. I would have had a network ready and willing to help me buy anything and everything we might have needed. But we were out on our own, and it was becoming more and more clear that our time was already running out. I needed to get my head in the game or we would not survive this.

No one noticed me standing in the checkout line and I weighed my options. I could wait patiently like a normal person, buy my groceries, and walk calmly back out to the vampire fugitive who waited in the SUV. That would be what normal people do.

Or?

Or I could make a run for it. These people probably won't chase me down for some stolen groceries. If I kept my head down, I might avoid most of the cameras. We could just drive out of here.

Drive... In our very recognizable, obviously expensive, SUV.

God, we're gonna die.

"Be with you in a minute, hun!" An older woman slowly made her way toward my station, but my anxiety spiked when her eyes rested on my face just a little too long. I made my decision.

"Oh! No problem, ma'am. Just realized I forgot my... bread. I'll be right back!" I waved her off and turned around with my fingers clutched desperately around the handle of my basket. I headed toward the display in front of the double doors, snagging a pair of sunglasses and a small travel hairbrush from the rotating rack.

The woman smiled and turned back toward the TV as the news blared out the strange events surrounding the suspicious explosion of Vinnie Quake's waterfront mansion and his suspected death in the fiery inferno.

I needed to get out of here.

I counted to ten again during the commercials and watched the employees as they clustered together and talked among themselves. The second the newscaster was back on the screen, their faces turned back to the TV and I made my move.

I strolled as calmly as I could toward the door. When I was within dashing distance, I quickened my pace. My nerves were electric as I closed the distance. I've done a lot of things in the name of fixing things for my clients, but shoplifting from a major grocery chain had not been on that list.

First time for everything.

For my first time stealing groceries, it was decidedly anti-climactic.

No one stopped me.

No one even looked at me.

To be honest, I'm not even sure they noticed the way I walked out the front door of the Food Mart with a full basket of groceries and three containers of blood.

As I walked back towards our SUV, I noticed an older man struggling to load several contractors bags worth of recyclable bottles into a cart.

His old, battered brown van had purple tinted windows and looked as though it had seen much better days. It was a vehicle that would be almost invisible on the streets of any city.

With that thought, a devious, brilliant idea popped into my head. *Vinnie is going to hate this idea. He's going to hate it so much. This gives me so much joy.*

"Sir!" I called out, startling him. "Sir, I have a proposition for you…"

It took ten minutes of haggling, but the man finally agreed to my proposal and it took everything in me not to let out a shout of victory as I ran back to the SUV with my basket of supplies.

I steeled myself for Vinnie's reaction to the plan.

"Took you long enough." He complained as I opened the door, his fangs descending as soon as he smelled the blood, and his eyes widened appreciatively as he saw how much I'd gotten.

I shoved a straw into one of the styrofoam cups and handed it to him.

"Change of plans. Or rather… change of vehicles." I announced.

The choking noise in the backseat was strangely satisfying as I slid behind the driver's seat and pulled our brand-new luxury vehicle into the parking space next to the van with a torn yellow sticker on the dented bumper that read: "I brake for Sasquatch."

Five minutes later we were the proud owners of one 1997 Astrovan that smelled like old burritos, pot, and regret.

If Vinnie had any issues with our change of transport, he said nothing, but I could feel the heat of his glare as he leapt from the SUV's back seat and into the van with his blanket over his head.

I couldn't help but feel somewhat encouraged by the exchange, and even though the van handled a little shaky, it was more than serviceable. Most importantly, no one would look at us twice in this hunk of junk. In the store I'd decided where we were headed. A cabin in the wilderness of the Olympic Peninsula. Pisces had a few on standby. They were remote. The perfect place to get our proverbial shit together while the city sorted itself out.

At least, that was the plan… But as I pulled the van onto the freeway and merged into the early morning traffic, doubt clawed at my stomach. Vinnie huddled against the back of my seat, swathed in sun-proof blankets.

I didn't know what he was thinking, but I didn't want to know, either.

I knew better than anyone that even the most painstakingly organized plans could backfire in spectacular ways whether or not I liked it.

13

———

VINNIE

If I weren't already dead, I'd be seriously concerned about the risk of contracting some sort of virulent disease from the trash on the seats and floorboards of the charming bucket of bolts disguised as a vehicle that Tuesday has acquired for us in the FoodMart parking lot.

The aroma alone was memorable enough, but I'd never been more thankful I didn't actually need to breathe. Tuesday complained it smelled like burritos and regret, but my senses were sharper. It smelled like something much more sinister than that.

It was a potent mix of fear and destruction covered by trash, dust, wet dog and stale laundry. Barely wiped away, dried blood —human, not pig—decorated the rear door and over the small window. I had questions.

The guy she'd got this complete and utter disaster of a vehicle from clearly had secrets. *Texas Chainsaw Massacre*-style secrets. I just hoped they didn't come back to haunt us.

Rationally, I knew why Tuesday had insisted on trading my luxury, light-tight, fully climate controlled vehicle for... *this*, but knowledge doesn't always equal power. This was a choice, and a risky one.

She hit another bump on the road and I gritted my teeth as my head slammed against the side of the van. Shock absorbers were apparently optional on this model.

Lovely.

The only information Tuesday had been willing to give me was that we were on our way to a cabin, and that she had everything under control.

That was Tuesday for you.

Control should have been her middle name.

With my sun-resistant blanket draped over my head, I had no choice but to think. I didn't have a phone to distract myself (Tuesday had confiscated it), and I was pretty sure that I wouldn't like what the news would be saying about me.

The sun was still out, so I couldn't drive or even sit in the passenger seat. The radio didn't work, and I can't exactly sit up and watch the scenery go by. Instead, we rode in silence and my mind drifted to the tension between us.

I hadn't planned to kiss her after we escaped the burning house. It just happened. But the memory was seared into my psyche forever now. After five years, kissing Tuesday felt like coming home after a long time away. There's a familiarity and a comfort there—a shared history. But there's also a newness. Not everything was the same as when you left it.

But that was the epicenter of our problems.

I'd *left* her.

Whatever we had, whatever was between us now, the tension and pain and chemistry—it all boiled down to one inescapable fact: I'd left Tuesday in the worst way possible. When she had needed me most, I'd walked away and ghosted her without a second thought.

My mind shifted to the memories of the night I'd become a vampire.

We had just finished playing a set at a little backroom bar, and it had gone better than anything we could have expected. Young and stupid, we rode that high, drinking and congratulating each other on the gigs that would follow such an epic night. We'd be on tour with Slash in no time, we were convinced of it.

So, when the beautiful woman in the red dress offered to buy me a drink, I didn't think to say no.

We were celebrating, and it was only one drink... Until it wasn't.

In a single evening, that strange woman bewitched me, destroyed me, and then left me for dead.

I never even knew her name.

Once I realized she had infected me, I had tried to find her, but it was as though she had disappeared off the face of the earth. She had left me to fend for myself. A newborn vampire with no clue how to feed myself, how to survive—alone with nothing but my hunger, and the image of her skintight red dress, long blonde hair, and cruel blue eyes that haunted my dreams for five long years.

The temperature changed as we turned away from the interstate and headed deeper into the forest. I dared to move my blanket to the side so that I could glance out the window.

The sky was gray and overcast and, in typical Olympic Peninsula fashion, looked as though it might rain at any moment.

I can't say for sure that Tuesday would have welcomed me back with open arms if I had mustered up the courage to tell her what happened that night, but I had never even given her the chance.

I slammed my fist into the back of the passenger seat. The action caused a small, foul cloud of dust to rise and sting my eyes.

Perfect. Just perfect.

Thud.

Thump.

"Dammit!" Tuesday slammed her palm against the steering wheel in disgust.

She edged the van over to the side of the road. The vehicle lurched twice and then slowly came to a stop.

I didn't need her to tell me our situation. We clearly had a flat tire.

Tuesday didn't say anything to me for a long moment. She leaned forward and rested her forehead on her hands and exhaled loudly.

An uneasy feeling that I couldn't place crept over me, as though we were being watched.

"Tuesday. Stay in the van." I whispered harshly as I emerged from my blanket nest with my fangs out.

She glanced over her shoulder at me with an exasperated look on her face.

"How am I supposed to change the tire from inside the van, Vinnie? I don't even know if this piece of shit has a jack or a spare!"

Something snapped outside the van, and I heard footsteps. Boots on gravel.

Someone had followed us.

"Tuesday. There's someone out there. Crawl back here with me," I said in a low voice. I draped the blanket over my shoulders like a cape and peered out the tinted windows at the forest surrounding us.

Tuesday paused for a moment and I could hear her pulse as it sped up.

Good. She was listening.

"Are you sure?" she whispered. Her gaze darted from one side of the road to the other, scanning for threats.

The footsteps came closer and her breath caught. I nodded silently.

Tuesday unbuckled her seatbelt with a careful motion and eased her body over the center console toward me.

She was just within reach of me when something tapped against the back window of the van.

Tuesday and I both reacted to the noise differently. She fell over in surprise, tangled in my blanket with her foot wedged between the driver's seat and the center console.

I whipped around, ready to defend my territory (and my Tuesday).

But as I focused on the back window of the van, I could see nothing through the smeared window.

Maybe I'd just imagined the tapping sound...

My head whipped from one side to the other as I strained to see through the trees, but I could see nothing.

"I—it was probably a tree branch or something. We're over-reacting." Tuesday muttered as she struggled to free herself.

But her pulse was throbbing, and I could smell her fear.

We both knew the odds were heavily in favor of *not* a tree branch.

The knock came again, this time at the front of the van. Tuesday covered her mouth to keep from screaming.

"Roscoe? That you in there? Looks like you got yourself a girl in there!" A friendly voice was half-muffled by the van.

Tuesday and I looked at each other.

Roscoe?

Tuesday shrugged. The van's former owner obviously had more of a story than I'd expected.

A gangly looking man appeared in the front window. His

black beard was matted with leaves and his red flannel shirt was torn in three places with no attempts made to patch it. He'd clearly seen better days.

"You gotta flat tire there, Ross!" The man pointed vigorously toward the passenger side and Tuesday shrank back to hide herself from view.

"What do we do?" she whispered as she pressed herself against the back of the passenger seat. There was nowhere to hide.

"I don't know? I don't think he's going to go away." I whispered back. We sat in silence for a full minute and watched the unusual man pace outside our decrepit van.

"Ross, c'mon man. Open the god dang door so we can fix yer tire and get outta here! Leslie's making a roast and my stomach's a growlin'!"

"I think I'm gonna go talk to him," she whispered as she struggled to her feet. She waded through the sea of Taco Bell wrappers to get to the sliding door and slapped my hand away when I tried to grab her arm.

"If he turns out to be a bad guy, you'd better save me. Sunburn or no!" She winked at me and threw the blanket over my face before she slid open the heavy side door.

I froze in place and listened to Tuesday turn on the girl-next-door charm. If I remembered correctly, it was a good act. Something she'd perfected in college to get free drinks out of Engineering students.

"Uh, hi," she began. "We just bought this van off an older guy this morning. We don't know any Roscoe but my name is... Suzie. Looks like we have a flat, huh?" I cringed at her overly cheerful tone. She was overselling it. Big-time.

Normally, Tuesday could sell anything, but her nerves were on edge, and if she wasn't careful, those same nerves were going to get us captured or worse.

The man outside smelled wrong too. He smelled like... dog.

"You bought ol' Roscoe's van, huh?" the man replied. His tone was jovial enough, but there was something guarded about it, too. "Never thought he'd let old Vanna go! You must have offered him something real sweet to get him to part with this gal. She's been with him longer than any of his wives." His coarse laugh made my lip curl in anger. He was treading on thin ice and he didn't even know it.

"And what's a pretty little thing like you need with a beat-up piece of shit like this?"

He was way too curious for my liking.

Tuesday laughed brightly. I gritted my teeth and wished that I could see what was happening. "I just needed to get away from the city, y'know?" she laughed. "Mind my business for a while. Fly under the radar, you get my drift?"

The man didn't answer right away and the smell of a lit match, followed by a faint whiff of cigarette smoke drifted into the van.

"You runnin' from someone, girlie?" he asked shrewdly.

I shrank back against the seat and hoped he thought I was just part of the mess in the back. If I had to pop out there and defend Tuesday, I wanted the element of surprise on my side.

"Let's just say, I'm highly motivated to spend some quality time on my own right now." Tuesday replied. I knew she was smiling, I could hear it in her voice. But there was a really good chance that her mask had started to slip. This entire exchange had gone on for far too long.

Thankfully, her answer seemed to satisfy the man. Another whiff of cigarette smoke. Tuesday hated smokers, especially ones who blew it in her face. This guy seemed like the type.

"Ain't no better place to do that then out here," the man said. Tuesday let out a little breath of relief, and I realized she trusted him. She hadn't lied to him—we *were* on the run. "Let's get you fixed up, huh?" the man continued. "Name's Dez. Pleased ta meet ya."

Tuesday thanked him with more enthusiasm than she should have—well, more enthusiasm than I would have used, anyway. But it seemed to work on Dez. His boots crunched over the gravel on the side of the road as he walked back to his truck. I crawled forward to peer out the window and saw him bend over the bed of a battered old red pickup parked just behind us on the shoulder.

How had I missed that?

He pulled a worn but serviceable-looking tire from the bed and bounced it on the road. I ducked back down as he pulled out a jack rig and a tire iron and rolled the tire toward the van.

"It won't get ya out of the country or nothin' but it will suit for whatever else you need to do today," he called out.

Tuesday glanced back through the door at me with a smile on her face that was half smug and half encouraging.

Dez slid the jack under the van, and the vehicle lurched to the side as Dez cranked it up. Something was seriously off about this guy, but I couldn't put my finger on it. The overwhelming smell of dog filled my nostrils.

Werewolf. It had to be. I'd only heard stories about their presence in Seattle. None of those stories were good.

If the mob that had attacked my house was any indication about how people felt about vampires, I knew for sure that how they felt about weres was worse.

The van shook and jumped as Dez worked the tire with seasoned hands. I didn't know how long it took to change a tire. I collected cars but the maintenance? I paid people to do that shit for me.

Dez let out a long belch, and the van slammed back down onto the pavement.

"All set!" he called out. "Now, you promise me you'll be careful out here, missy. These woods are perfect for findin' yourself... But they're also good for losin' yourself, if you know what I mean."

Tuesday thanked him profusely for his help, but she said nothing about his warning. Whatever he'd meant, I didn't like it.

I peeked out of the blankets as Dez's boots crunched over the gravel again as he walked to his truck.

"You're the best," Tuesday called out. I peeked out from behind my blankets and watched as she waved at him energetically. I could see the smile on her face even though her heartbeat was erratic and tense.

My Tuesday became a talented actress in the last five years... I suppose that was my fault. Was she even 'My Tuesday' anymore?

"I hope the roast is amazing!"

The beat-up pickup roared to life, and I huddled under the blanket as the engine revved and it roared by. Dez honked as he passed us, and I bit down on the blanket in frustration. This whole escapade had taken entirely too long for my liking.

Tuesday didn't climb back into the van until the roar of Dez's truck had faded well into the distance. She slid the panel door closed and climbed into the passenger seat.

She leaned back in the chair and let out a long, noisy breath.

"That was so weird." she said in a choked voice.

"You're telling me," I muttered from under the blanket.

I heard the rustle of the map as she consulted her directions again. The van started reliably enough, but the cough of the exhaust wasn't reassuring as she shifted it into drive and pulled the hunk of junk back onto the road.

"Tire feels great," she said cheerfully.

"Yeah, yeah."

***

. . .

Dusk fell before we pulled into the narrow driveway of the cabin Tuesday had promised me. Lit up by our headlights, it looked quaint and rustic, but I didn't like the look of the inky darkness beyond the cabin. Like most of the older places scattered out amongst the trees in the Olympics, it was made of rough-hewn logs, but unlike the other random cabins, this cabin had been built by someone with money and merely styled after the old frontier log cabins instead of haphazardly built like one.

Small mercies were better than none. Maybe.

It had a small porch complete with porch swing, a river rock chimney, and a cherry red metal snow roof.

We stumbled out of the van, eager to get inside.

I carried the supplies Tuesday had stolen from the Food-Mart, an embarrassingly small assortment of snacks and an enormous bottle of wine that was clearly *not* for me, and set them on the swing.

Tuesday searched the porch until she found a small, hideously ugly ceramic cat statue in the corner. She picked it up and threw it viciously against the side of the cabin, shattering it into tiny pieces, and I stared at her in disbelief. *Violent little thing.*

She ignored me completely and focused her attention on rummaging through the pile of rubble. After a moment, she let out a little squeal of victory. "Got the key!" she proclaimed triumphantly as she held it up for me to see.

I grabbed the key, unlocked the deadbolt and pushed her inside. I pulled the door shut, slid the lock home and leaned back against the door.

The feeling of being watched only increased as I peered out the window beside the door and scanned the tiny, darkened yard.

Something was out there, but after the last 24 hours I'd had, I wasn't sure I wanted to know what it was.

14

VINNIE

A sharp pain dragged me out of the blissful blackness of sleep. My hands came up defensively, but they were pushed away and something forced between my lips.

"What the f—"

A weight on my torso kept me pinned to the bed, and I grabbed my attacker in a tight grip and roared my anger into his face.

Whoever it was, they were going to die a painful death. The smell of jasmine and gasoline drifted towards my nose and I froze.

"Tuesday?"

She struggled in my grip like a fish on a hook.

"Let me go!"

I released her immediately, and she glared at me and shoved a cup of deli counter quality blood into my hands. She was straddling my torso, her thighs gripping me tight. *I could get used to being woken up like this.*

"Wh-what were you *doing?* I was sleeping for chrissakes!"

Tuesday pushed her hair out of her face and rubbed at her

arms before rolling her eyes and glaring down at me. "I thought you were dead, ok? God!"

I held up the styrofoam cup and looked at her incredulously. "I hate to break it to you, doll, but, uh, I *am* dead."

She let out an exasperated breath. "You know what I mean! You weren't moving and nothing woke you up."

"Well, I'm awake now, and just the normal amount of dead," I said as I sipped the blood she'd given me and moved my hips beneath her.

"Wise ass," she muttered.

She crawled off me and sat on the edge of the bed.

"Do you always... sleep like that?" Her voice sounded strangled and soft. It made me instantly remorseful for my reaction.

"Sleeping is a little... weird for vamps," I said. "I haven't been on a regular sleep schedule for... well, ever, and I crashed a little hard."

"Sleep like the dead." She chuckled and shook her head. "Never thought I'd see it in literal format."

I rubbed my cheek where she'd hit me.

"I'm not apologizing for the slap," she said. "You scared me."

"Fine," I grumbled around my straw. "So, what happens now?"

Tuesday got up from the bed and I immediately regretted asking the question. I wanted her heat beside me. It was something I hadn't realized I'd missed... the warmth of someone's skin pressed against yours. It used to piss me off that Tuesday was a hot sleeper; I was always pushing her away at night.

If she were in my bed now, I'd never let her go.

Fuck, I'd been stupid.

Tuesday paced the worn carpet, and I propped myself up on the bed to watch her. She was still wearing the t-shirt she'd taken from my house underneath her utilitarian jacket and sturdy jeans. It pleased me to no end that she was wearing something of mine. I wanted to take her shopping and dress every inch of her. A masterpiece like Tuesday deserved fine silks and lace, not cargo pants.

"Stop smirking," she snapped, "this isn't a joke."

"I never said it was," I said. I hadn't realized I was smirking;I knew it wasn't a joke—I had just been busy imagining taking her on a shopping spree and watching her try on outfit after outfit. Pointless extravagance was the absolute best part of being rich. Plus? She deserved it. I owed it to her. But something told me I'd never get to see that through. *Depressing.*

"Someone finally picked up the phone at Pisces," she said. "I was wondering if something else had happened, but... never-mind." Her brow furrowed with worry, but she caught my eye and it smoothed again in an instant. *Mask on. Business-face.* She was too good at that.

"Okay, is that good news?"

"It is. It means we have support now."

That sounded like a good thing.

"And they know where we are?"

Tuesday grimaced. "In a general sense. But I'm still not convinced that Baldwin hasn't got his hooks into anyone else at the agency."

Now it was my turn to frown. Baldwin's betrayal stung. That bastard had been with me since the beginning. I thought I could trust him. He had access to everything—keys to the proverbial kingdom. I still couldn't understand why he'd done it, and I hated not knowing things.

"Great."

"You will hate this," Tuesday warned. "But we don't have any choice."

"Hit me," I said, and then held up a hand. "But not literally, unless you want this to spiral into something else..."

Tuesday glared at me and I bit back my laughter. I loved

winding her up, but only because she made the most glorious pissed off faces.

"Are you done?"

I shrugged. *Not remotely.*

"If you can't take this seriously for one second, I'm going to kill you myself just to make my life easier," she snarled.

"Was that a challenge?"

"Vincent!"

I chuckled and sipped my blood. "Fine, fine. I'm taking this seriously. Please, continue."

"Oh, thank you, you're too kind."

My god, even her sarcasm was cute. I'd forgotten. How the hell had I forgotten that?

"So. Here's the deal. Pisces is going to work with the Seattle PD and the coroner's officer to release a statement saying that you were killed in the blast."

I held up one finger. "Slight problem, kitten. I'm already dead, remember?"

"Did you know the vampire that Baldwin and Zach kidnapped with you?" she asked pertly.

"No. I didn't even ask his name—"

Tuesday shook her head as though she was trying to banish the image from her mind. I didn't need to ask; I knew what she was imagining. I saw him in my mind, too. The bloody gaps where his fangs should have been...

"For now, that's all we need," Tuesday said firmly. "An extra male body was present. It'll be on what's left of the security cameras, and it should be enough to keep the press focused on mourning the life of the *amazing* Vinnie Quake to buy us some time."

"I don't like how you said 'amazing,'" I said dryly.

She shrugged. "You're going to have to get used to that, cupcake."

"Fine," I grumbled. "So, what's the point of all this?"

"Baldwin needs to think that he did what he set out to do. Chances are, he'll slip up. He'll get comfortable thinking that he's fooled everyone. But my boss knows everything. They'll be watching him, and they'll have other eyes on him as well. If he makes a move, leaves the city, spends one penny of any money that doesn't belong to him—we'll know about it."

"You want the rats to come out of the woodwork," I said. I was kind of in awe of what she'd planned out. From the explosion to the social media storm... and now this? "You're fantastic at this, Tues."

"I know," she snapped. "That's why you're still paying me."

"I am?"

"I'm on retainer," she said with a quick smile. "That's why you're still alive, and I'm still here."

I sighed heavily. "So, you're only here because you're being paid?"

"You got it," she replied in a matter-of-fact tone. "You think I wanted to be out in the middle of nowhere with my obnoxious fang-headed ex who was on everyone's kill list?"

"That's partly your fault," I pointed out.

"Details," she snapped. "Baldwin will need to make a statement. Your record label is going to freak out when they hear the news."

"You're not planning on clueing them in on the plan?"

Tuesday shook her head and tucked a strand of loose hair back into her bun. "No way. There are literally four people who know the truth right now, and we're two of them. That's how it's going to stay. I don't trust anyone, and neither should you."

"They are sticklers for rules," I mused. "You don't even know what a pain in the ass my last album was to produce..."

"I literally could not care less." Tuesday resumed her pacing. "Your fans will go nuts. They were already nuts, but this is going to make them insane. Your death... your *murder*... International attention."

"Are you sure this is a good idea?" I wasn't so sure anymore.

"Of course, it's a good idea," she said vehemently. "You wanted a coming out party? Here it is. You can come out in a blaze of glory, having survived an inferno... a literal phoenix from the ashes. New career. New everything. Get it?"

I nodded dumbly. She was good.

"Now, I have to get on the phone with a photographer and a private investigator. I need Baldwin followed."

"Why? I thought you already set that up. Aren't you supposed to be notified the moment he does anything?"

"I will be, but I also want his reaction to the news of your death caught on film. There won't be any pre-prep meeting with him. It'll just be straight to a police press conference. He'll find out about your death at the same time the world does."

I smiled, showing my fangs just a little. "You're sneaky. Were you always this sneaky?"

"I learned from the best."

Her tone stung just a little, but that was the point.

"What about the protestors? Are the cops going to do anything about them? There were cameras everywhere. Those assholes need to pay. Destruction of property — Murder — everything!"

Tuesday shook her head. "Probably not. As soon as the news breaks, the anti-vamp groups will go underground to avoid prosecution. It's what always happens. The dumb ones who got their photos taken might lose their jobs or be arrested, but it won't be anything more than a slap on the wrist. Don't get your hopes up."

"That's bullshit."

"It is what it is, for now," Tuesday sighed. She crossed her arms over her chest and looked out the window. Dawn was on its way. "The crazy ones, the zealots, they'll crow about your death. They will say it was justified and use it as proof for their ridiculous theories. It will make them look even crazier, which will do its work to bring attention to the vamp cause and make them look like villains... That's what we want."

"You've got it all figured out."

"Not everything," she replied, but I heard a touch of pride in her voice. "But most of it. It's my job to be proactive. I can't control the reaction, but I can set up the dominoes so that they fall the way I want them to."

"Except for that little riot..."

"Yeah, well, I didn't make allowance for just how many people you'd pissed off in the last five years."

Touche.

She sighed heavily and leaned against the wall. "Now we just have to wait for Baldwin to do something stupid."

"Have you slept?"

She shook her head. "Not yet. I have more to do."

"Have you had a shower?"

She looked down at the grubby t-shirt she wore and made a face. "Noooo."

"Maybe you should."

She wrinkled her nose at me. "Hilarious."

"I'm just saying it might make you feel a little... clearer."

Tuesday covered her face with her hands and let out a little scream of frustration. "Fine," she said after a moment. "Fine. I'll take a shower. But then I have work to do."

"I — am going back to sleep," I announced. I saluted her with the styrofoam cup. "Thank you for the snack. Now, get out."

Tuesday blinked at me.

"Unless you want to stay?" I patted the bed beside me and she made a face.

"Keep dreaming, pal."

"I don't dream," I said casually as I set the cup of blood on the bedside table. "It's the weirdest thing. I used to dream really vividly—"

"You used to kick me in your sleep, too," she said dryly.

"Like I said, vivid dreams. But now, nothing. Just... blackness."

"Lucky you." She walked to the door and leaned against the doorframe dramatically. "Pleasant blackness, Vinnie."

Now it was my turn to frown at her, and she laughed as she closed the door. This was not going the way I'd expected it.

Although, I wasn't really sure *what* I'd expected.

Seeing Tuesday again had been a shock that I still hadn't quite gotten over. I didn't think I'd ever see her again, or that I'd still have such... overpowering feelings for her. She was fighting against what she felt and was allowing her anger and hurt to do the talking. It was easier for her that way, that was for sure. I just had to let her work through it. Maybe we'd come out of it together —

I smashed my face into the pillow and growled in frustration. I'd done this to myself. To her. To us.

This was my punishment, and I deserved it.

I could have done without the extra drama, but if that's what it took to bring Tuesday back into my life, then so be it.

I rolled off the bed and walked to the window. Another blood-red sunrise. That didn't bode well.

Or maybe I remembered the saying wrong. I think it had to do with sailors so maybe it didn't even apply.

I pulled the curtain across to block out the sight of the approaching daylight. I'd thought it would get easier to block out the light. I'd always spent most of my time staying awake until dawn—that was what musicians did. We were only really alive between 11:00 p.m. and 4:00 a.m. But now that it was my reality, I didn't feel so hot about it.

Everything's different when it's not an option.

My options had changed just a little.

Tuesday's plan — to announce that I died (again) in the blast — was a good one. And it might be the only surefire way to know what Baldwin's game actually was.

If he hadn't skipped town already.

But Baldwin wasn't stupid. It would look hella suspicious if he just disappeared after what had just gone down. He was guilty as fuck, and I couldn't wait until everyone knew the truth.

And what the hell was up with that Zach guy—Tuesday had mentioned that she knew him.

We'd been in the middle of trying to escape the house at that point, and I hadn't given her words much thought... but now that we were out.

I strode back toward the door and grabbed the knob, but it turned in my hand and the door flew toward me as Tuesday stormed back into the room.

She crashed into my chest and stumbled back, but when I reached out to steady her, she slapped my hand away.

"What the hell?"

"Don't you what the hell me, Vincent Quaker," she raged. "What the hell is *this*?"

I hated it when she used my full name. No one ever used my full name. I'd been Vinnie Quake for so long that I didn't even know who that other guy even was anymore.

"What?"

She shoved her phone in my face and put her hands on her hips as I struggled to focus on the image on the screen.

"What am I looking at?"

"You have eyes," she snarled, "use them."

I frowned at the phone, confused by her aggression. And then it hit me. Baldwin. I was looking at a photo of Baldwin.

"Where did you get this?"

"My photographer works fast," she said simply. "Seems like Baldwin has been a busy guy since we last saw him. He's been on the phone a lot." She made a swiping motion with her finger and I pressed my finger to the phone and followed her unspoken instruction.

The next photo was a closeup of Baldwin's face as he sat outside a 24-hour cafe. His phone was pressed to his ear, but he didn't look upset or angry. He looked... elated.

"Who was that with him?" Tuesday demanded.

"Tuesday, what's this about... Where is Baldwin now?"

"You're not answering my question."

I gritted my teeth and looked down at the phone again. "I don't know what you're talking about."

"Yes, you do, Vinnie."

There was something strange about Tuesday's voice that made me look up from the phone. She was wearing her business mask again but her eyes flashed in anger.

Shit.

I concentrated on the phone and swiped my finger across the screen.

Now I knew why she was angry.

Double shit.

She sat across from Baldwin, just out of frame. Her head was turned just out of frame, but I would have recognized that fall of silvery blonde hair anywhere.

My maker.

15

———

TUESDAY

My blood boiled in my veins and I was *positive* that Vinnie could sense how angry I was. When I hired the photographer, I hadn't quite known what to expect. It's hard when you don't know what you're looking for.

Our go-to guy at Pisces PR was an ex-tabloid hack who lacked a code of ethics, was a crack shot, and had an incredible knack to be in the right place at the right time. He was a complete creep, but we could always count on him to get the most damning (or flattering, depending on the request) angles of his targets, and he was fast. Carlyn had something on him that was powerful enough to lure him away from following starlets around, and now he's on call for us.

I never doubted that he'd get the shots we needed. A part of me hoped that Baldwin would be stupid enough to allow himself to get photographed doing something out of character. A nice spread of him in the arms of a high-priced call-girl or spending Vinnie's money on hard drugs? Yeah. That's the stuff a spin doctor dreams of finding on an opponent.

But no.

Baldwin had to go be strategic and irritatingly by-the-book.

He had to know that he would be under scrutiny. Vinnie Quake was a big fucking deal, not just in Seattle, but globally. There was no way Cainin Records would let an attack on their golden boy be swept under the rug.

Baldwin *had* to know the police would be all up in that.

I tried to think what I would do.

If it were me, I would have planned to be very visible with the police response. The model of mournful cooperation. I would have volunteered the information that he believed that Vinnie had returned to his house to take shelter from the incident at the bookstore. While the police were gnawing on that, I would have made some choice comments in front of the media to get a head start on the public opinion piece. If you waited until the actual incident happened with this kind of thing, you were already running behind the curve.

I anticipate things. It's why I'm so good at my job. But every now and again you get thrown a curveball. And this curvy curveball pissed me right off. He was good. Good enough to set us up. But I was better.

Exhaustion hovered on the edge of my anger. Confronting Vinnie had seemed like the logical reaction at the time, but the longer I stood in the room, the more that logic began to slip. Plus, I had never told him that I knew about her. Well, that was about to change.

Goddamnit.

"What does this mean, Vinnie?" I demanded quietly. I just needed answers.

Vinnie shook his head, confusion written all over his handsome face. The same handsome face I wanted to slap for being so stupid.

"I — I don't know. What *does* it mean?"

"Don't you think I recognize her?" My chest burned with the effort of keeping all of my rage inside. "I saw you together,

Vinnie! I saw you with her the night you left me! You were *busy*, or don't you remember."

He was silent for a moment, and my hand itched to slap him again.

I've carried this burden for years and now that we're facing it, he's silent. *Asshole.*

"What do you want me to say?"

His question was plaintive, but I wasn't in the mood for any of that bullshit.

"You. Tell. Me." I exploded, "How should I know? She's not my problem. Are they working together? Are they lovers? Was she part of the record label? Tell me what you know. Secrets will not help either of us right now. I need to know *everything*."

Please God, don't tell me everything. Knowledge was power, but it's also pain. I needed the information if I was going to get him out of this mess. But it was equally tempting to just... abandon him in it.

Unfortunately, I was as deep into it as he was. My life was in danger, too. And now? With Baldwin bringing shithead Zach into the mix? Yeah, it was personal for me, too.

"I think I have a right to know everything, too," Vinnie said as he shoved the phone back into my hands.

I glared at him. "You have *what*? The right to know things? Like what?"

"Who was that Zach guy? You said you knew him."

Fuck. Had I said that? Ugh.

"Answer my question first!"

That would give me time to think about what I actually wanted to say. It was complicated — But then again, it really wasn't.

Vinnie rubbed a hand through his hair and turned away from me. "There's nothing to tell," he said sharply. "It was one night. We were celebrating, she was there. She bought me a drink — And that's all I remember. I woke up alone in a hotel room and I didn't see her again after that night. When I got home, you had already left... And a few days later I was in the throes of the infection. I didn't want to believe it—"

"So, you were a one-night stand," I interrupted cruelly.

I'd struggled with Vinnie's disappearance for *YEARS*, and even though it would have been easy to forget all of my anger in favor of guilt for shutting him out so completely, I couldn't do it. I'd been feeding on my anger for so long that I couldn't replace it with anything else. He could have done anything that night. He could have just come home to me. He could have answered his phone one of the seventy million times I'd called. Answered one text message. Anything.

But he hadn't. He'd allowed a strange woman to buy him a drink, and then let her — No. No, I was going to stay mad. Maybe forever.

Vinnie looked at me over his shoulder, but I couldn't tell if he was angry or just... sad.

"Looks like it," he said flatly. "I was a suck and chuck, does that make you happy?"

It didn't, actually.

I sighed heavily.

This wasn't productive, and it didn't answer my question. "So, you've never seen her with Baldwin, he's never mentioned her... nothing."

Vinnie shook his head. "The only thing I remember about her was a name."

"A name?" I stared at him.

"Apogee."

"That's not a name," I scoffed.

"Says the girl named Tuesday."

"Hey, we've been over this."

Vinnie chuckled, grabbed the styrofoam cup of blood off the

bedside table and sucked angrily on the straw. He still loved pushing my buttons, and I hated that I kind of loved it when he did.

It was exhausting to flip back and forth between hating him and still having feelings for him. I hated it. I hated him. I hated myself for being so... "Ugh!"

"Ugh yourself," Vinnie mumbled around the straw. "You got my answer, so what's your deal with the other guy? Zach? Who the hell was he?"

I pressed my palms against my cheeks and took a deep breath. Vinnie was possessive. Telling him about Zach would definitely provoke a reaction. At least this way, we'd both be upset.

"Zach was a hookup," I said through gritted teeth. "My own suck and chuck."

Vinnie's mouth dropped open. "Wait — That guy? You slept with *him?*"

I threw my hands up in protest. "What do you want, Vinnie? You want me to say he was nothing like you? That no one could ever measure up? Sure. Fine. That's what it is. He was boring. Deadass boring. He's a mortgage broker—"

"Who murders vampires on the weekends?" Vinnie interjected snidely.

"We didn't get that far into the conversation," I snapped back.

I knew I deserved a little pain for all the shit I'd said to him, but the low blows were a surprise.

Vinnie leaned against the wall casually, his eyebrow raised. "So... was he any good?"

"No," I laughed shortly, "Actually he was a colossal disappointment and a complete dickhead who stole my whiskey and wouldn't shut up. I kicked him out before I'd even gotten my bra off."

Vinnie blinked at me, speechless, and I burst out laughing.

"So... let me get this straight. You brought him home for sex and then kicked him out... and now he's in a murderous rage and out to get revenge. Is that about right?"

"I'm pretty sure it's a coincidence," I said with a frown. It would have been arrogant to think that Zach had gone on some rampage because I'd blown him off—or, rather, not blown him at all.

Vinnie looked thoughtful for a moment. "Coincidences don't exist," he said. "It's just... supposed to happen. You thought the night we met was a coincidence."

I took a deep breath and looked down at the worn carpet. "If you're going to tell me some 'romantic' story about how you stalked me for weeks before getting up the courage to talk to me at that club you can forget it."

The night we'd met had been a mess, and we both knew it. I wasn't about to stand there and listen to him put chrome on a beat-up pickup truck bumper.

Vinnie started out as a one night thing... but then he never left. Before I knew it, he turned out to be a fiance and joint-accounts thing.

"Tuesday—"

"I said forget it. I don't have time to go stumbling down memory lane with you right now. There had to be another reason Zach was there. Period."

Vinnie looked down at the styrofoam cup in his hands and smiled briefly. "There was, actually. Baldwin brought him in."

I stared at Vinnie in disbelief. "What now?"

"You were passed out," he explained. "Baldwin told me he brought Zach in. He — He's Patricia's brother. He *was* Patricia's brother."

"Your assistant? The one who got all of that blood for you and..."

Vinnie nodded. "She was the one who suggested we call in a PR company."

With her dying text...

"Bloody hell, Vin..." I groaned and leaned against the doorframe. "Did you know she had a brother?"

He shrugged. "I knew she had a cat. Should I watch my back for a vengeful cat, too? How the hell was I supposed to know? It's not like I was planning for all this to happen."

"Trust you not to think any farther ahead than your own needs," I snapped before I could stop myself. My fingers tightened on my phone. If I'd been any angrier, I would have shattered the damn thing. "This isn't helping anything."

Vinnie snorted and took a sip from his straw. If I hadn't known he was drinking pigs' blood, I would have laughed at him. It was impossible to take him seriously when he was sucking on a straw.

I took a breath to focus my thoughts. "I have to talk to Baldwin... well, not me. But someone at Pisces will have to talk to him. But *after* the press conference. I want to see how he reacts. I also want to find out about his connection to that—"

To that undead bitch in the red dress.

"— to that woman."

"Nice save."

"Shut up. I need to think."

All at once, he was right in front of me. I hadn't even seen him move. His hand was on my jaw and his fingers dug into my skin in a painful, yet maddeningly comforting and possessive way.

"You spend too much time thinking," he murmured.

"That's the only reason we're alive," I said through gritted teeth.

He smiled, and I could see the gleam of his teeth. A shiver ran down my spine at the thought of those teeth grazing over my skin. "I seem to remember it was *me* who hauled you out of that chimney."

"Details."

"But you've always been all about the details, Tues," he whispered.

My eyes drifted closed. I hated him. I still loved him. I was a conflicted mess. I could have kicked him in the face and left him writhing on the floor and felt justified... *Complete shitshow.*

"Things have changed."

I choked on the words.

"Have they?"

He bent forward and brushed his lips over the sensitive skin of my throat, and I bit my lip to keep from moaning. *Fangy bastard.* All I could think about was what it would feel like if he bit down —

My hands came up to touch his chest. Fingers that had always searched for a steady heartbeat now found nothing... just a solid wall of muscle with nothing underneath. We used to lay there after sex reveling in the way our hearts beat in synch. But now — Now there was nothing.

Just my heart hammering against my ribs. Nothing else.

"They have," I said bitterly as I pushed him away. "I have work to do. You said a name — what was it again?"

Vinnie froze, but then he released his hold on my jaw and stepped back.

Good. I didn't need any more... complications.

"Apogee."

Oh, my god. Now that I was thinking more clearly, I was just irritated.

"That is definitely not a name. Dear god, I didn't think you were that dumb."

Vinnie shook his head. "How the hell am I supposed to know?"

"I dunno... Google? It's not fucking hard, Vin."

He shrugged, and I rolled my eyes. *Just like always.*

"You and your S.A.T. words."

"Good to know you're still jealous."

"I'm jealous of a lot of things, Tues."

I laughed, but it sounded more awkward than it should have. This was my worst nightmare. *Literally the worst.*

I tapped on my phone to bring up my boss' number and glanced at Vinnie. I didn't like the way he was looking at me. It made me feel like I was a meal he was waiting to devour. Not happening. Not now. Not ever.

Well... maybe. No. Bad Tuesday. Back away.

"I have to make a call. It's almost dawn—"

"And I should go to sleep, I know," Vinnie said. He turned toward the covered windows. "Are you going to be okay?"

"I've been okay for the last five years. I think I'll last a few more hours."

I couldn't resist getting in another shot, and I smiled when he winced. This was going to have legs, and he would have to get used to the fact that he couldn't charm his way out of it.

I didn't know what I needed from him. But penance like this was a start.

It was easier to walk out of the room that time. The door slammed shut behind me, and it galvanized my will. I needed to call my boss. Carlyn would know what to do.

She picked up the call on the second ring. In my five years at Pisces, she'd never done that.

"Tuesday — what do you have for me?"

"A lead," I said firmly. "Baldwin was meeting with a person of interest right after the explosion. I have photos. We're going to need a meeting with him to find out where his head's at."

Carlyn was silent for a moment. But it was just a moment. "Are you going to provide a script?"

"Oh, hell yeah. That bastard has some explaining to do."

Carlyn chuckled. "So, you're telling me this is going to be interesting?"

"Maybe don't assign an intern to it, that's all I'm going to say right now," I said with a smile I knew Carlyn could hear.

"I'll do it myself. Sounds like fun."

"I'll have something for you in a few hours."

"Do you ever sleep, Matson?"

I glanced back at the closed door behind me. "Not lately."

"That's what I thought. Check in with those scripts in a few hours and we'll talk about coordinating a supply pick up."

"You got it."

I ended the call with a fresh surge of determination. I had scripts to write, and a grocery list to plan. This could actually work...

Now I just needed Vinnie to keep his shit together.

That might prove more difficult to manage.

16
____

VINNIE

I didn't know what the hell I was supposed to do with myself, or with anything Tuesday had said.

Whatever human part of me remained throbbed with need for her. And a frustrated need to punch a hole through a wall.

But that was different.

I pulled back the curtain and frowned at the stubbornly pale silver light of the crescent moon that peeped out from behind a cloud bank. Dawn was coming with steady determination, and it wouldn't go to bed... just like me. Strangling every last second from the sunlight.

We were defiant to the end, the moon and I.

Lit by both the night and the approaching day, a broken picnic table just outside my window leaned drunkenly on the dark lawn. I knew three photographers who would have done nefarious things to get access to this place for a photoshoot.

The thought brought a smirk to my lips.

Maybe I *did that too* much.

If Tuesday's primary goal had been to find some place truly

off the grid for us to hide, she had definitely been successful. Dead leaves rustled along the rough-hewn planks of the porch and gave the whole place an eerily unnecessary horror-movie vibe.

Unlike Seattle, the light pollution was non-existent out here in the woods. Dawn battled with the darkness in dramatic tones and I could have wasted countless hours watching it if it didn't put me at risk of a nasty sunburn...

There was no more comforting buzz of city traffic, or the sound of gentle waves lapping at the shore just outside my boathouse... There was nothing out here. It was just trees, wind, trees, and more trees.

There was no mystery to what I was feeling at that moment.

I hated it here.

Tuesday said that she found it peaceful, but I sure as hell didn't.

There was something menacing about being this far away from civilization. I had never thought that I needed the reassurance of a nosy neighbor within shouting distance, or the easy accessibility of a 7-11 for a 'just in case' ketchup emergency... but I did.

I really, really, did.

The tension between Tuesday and me had risen to almost nuclear levels, but neither one of us had the balls to address it or do anything about it.

If it was possible to drown in confusing, emotional turmoil, we'd both be dead. Well. I was already technically dead, but I'd definitely be dead all over again.

The constant fighting and exhumation of painful memories had left me drained. I was tired, hangry, and confused. But there was no escape.

We were stuck together... at least for now.

Tuesday didn't seem to want to do anything but make an autopsy of my vampiric history... I wasn't exactly willing to go over every detail for the eight hundredth time; probing and poking for details and ignoring the painful memories her questions evoked in me.

The connection she had found between Baldwin and my mysterious maker hurt, but no worse than the undercurrent of malice in her accusations.

I had *never* pretended to be perfect. I'd been a goddamn monster, literally, figuratively, *spiritually?* Definitely.

Effort. Ugh.

I had hurt Tuesday, and I could easily spend a lifetime making that up to her. But with all that considered, it still felt like Tuesday was being unfair.

Maybe.

Slightly.

Maybe I was still the asshole.

If we didn't talk about the whole mass murder aspect of my life and focused on the fact that I was killed, forced to rise again as a member of the living undead, promptly abandoned and left to make my own way in the world as a different person—a different species — she *was* being unfair.

I pulled open the sliding door and stepped out into the very early morning. Enough of the night remained to allow me to walk in the half-light. It was enough... a small blasphemy.

I took a deep breath of the clean woodland air and closed my eyes.

I felt exposed out here. It was dangerous here. Secluded. But it was also... calm.

I heard movement behind me and twisted. I was on edge, I wouldn't deny it. Tuesday leaned against the sliding door frame and glared at me with an unmistakable glint of loathing in her eyes. I wanted to throw things at her or yell or scream, but my monster was itching for a fight and I knew I couldn't lose control.

Not with Tuesday.

Not again.

"Are you ready to talk about this plan or are you just going to stay out here and sulk?" Tuesday called out. Her voice was frosty and tight, and I'd had just about enough of this act.

"I'm so fucking *TIRED* of hearing about plans, Tues. How much of this do you honestly expect that we're going to *plan*. We're trapped in the woods with a band of assholes hell-bent on killing the both of us hot on our tails? You're so busy focusing on the past, you can't see what's coming for us. Really? How about the fucking future, Tuesday? What does that look like?"

I really shouldn't have screamed at her.

Her eyes filled with tears and she slammed the sliding glass door closed hard enough to make it shudder on its track before she stomped out of the room.

Shit.

"Tuesday, I'm sorry…"

My voice trailed off when I realized she wouldn't be able to hear me.

Maybe it was the stress of everything. Or maybe too much time had passed for us to really make a go of it. Tuesday and I were more like oil and water than we had ever been oil and vinegar…

Or, you know, maybe it was simpler. The human and vampire mix wasn't exactly known to be compatible.

Maybe I was a classic dumbass who thought that we could somehow pick up where we'd left off.

Times of crisis bring people together—but they also drive people apart.

Just another thing I can blame my maker, and Baldwin, for.

I still had trouble fully wrapping my mind around that connection.

There was evidence. That had been her in the photo. It couldn't be anyone else.

How had they even met? Had she been stalking me? Keeping tabs on me somehow? Was she taking credit for my stratospheric rise to fame like some clandestine mentor?

But how had I not known what was going on??

Every interaction I'd ever had with Baldwin over the last five years flashed through my mind, but there was nothing that popped out at me that could have tied him to my maker.

Baldwin had found me at a bar.

Everyone found me at a bar.

Back then, I was trapped in an excruciating cycle of trying to pretend as though everything was normal while denying my new nature until I snapped. Tuesday left me—the band and I had just completed a set but it hadn't been well-received. I had been sitting at the bar forcing drink after drink down my throat, determined to get myself drunk enough to do what needed to be done for the second half of our show.

When Baldwin had handed me his card and told me to call him if I was interested in going solo someday, I thought he was just yanking my chain.

I'd forgotten about that interaction for weeks, until one night I felt desperate enough to make the call. I had picked up the phone and attempted to call a dozen times but always chickened out at the last minute, convinced no manager in their right mind would accept a client who could only come out at night.

But I did it.

And he accepted me, very few questions asked.

Baldwin created my persona and he got me in with Cainin Records.

In his own fucked up way, Baldwin had saved me. He had given me a reason not to walk out into the sunrise the next day.

If we were looking for honesty, my mysterious maker created me as a vampire, but Baldwin Kennison created Vinnie Quake, and made me a household name.

I owed him almost everything.

The betrayal—that cut deeper than any stake that had been hammered into my chest in the last 24 hours.

I kicked the rocks on the porch and watched as they crashed into the dirt. I looked back through the window, hoping that Tuesday would come back, but I knew she wouldn't.

It was going to be a long, long day.

We were missing something. I was sure of it.

Baldwin and my maker. That sultry, crimson bitch.

It made little sense... unless it made perfect sense.

Why would they work together? Why me? What did she get out of this? How far does this go? If they were working together, why kill me now?

My head hurt, and there was a pounding starting behind my eyes. What was the point in being undead with superhuman strength if you could still get migraines?

My mother's voice floated into my mind randomly. *If your head hurts, dear, get a drink or something to eat. Gotta keep your blood sugar up!*

Blood sugar.

Hilarious.

But she had a point.

I hadn't really eaten anything aside from the pigs' blood that Tuesday had acquired for me. And there was only one cup of the stuff left in the fridge in the outdated kitchen.

I'd been living off the stuff for the last five years, but if the last few days were any indication, it wasn't enough. Especially now that I was actually doing stuff—physical stuff.

Pigs' blood was fine for a lazy vampire, but all of this... activity was taking a lot out of me. And all I could smell was Tuesday.

However, because of my idiocy, a voluntary feeding was *not* an option. Which left... nature.

I stared at the darkened forest and swallowed hard.

Yikes.

I was definitely a city vampire.

Great. Just great.

All the vampire movies and TV shows I'd seen before I'd been turned always showed these big, badass vampire men taking down wildlife with ease.

However, I'd never gotten that memo, and no one had shown up to lead a training session on bringing down big game—and I was definitely never going near any goddamn bears.

Those... Wild vamps could hunt cougars up the side of a cliff face while I hunted... in luxury. They could lose all the skin on the bottoms of their feet while they were busy running around practicing field craft—I had minions who waited on me hand and foot.

But the hunger was real, and the forest was full of heartbeats.

Full of blood.

If Tuesday was actually talking to me, she'd tell me to get over myself and go hunt a deer. But, knowing Tuesday, she'd probably pull a rifle out of a closet somewhere and go hunt one herself. Tuesday has always been a doer, not a talker.

That thought motivated me.

Commune with nature.

Get yourself a goddamn SNACK.

"I'm going for a walk!" I yelled at the cabin. I didn't care if she was listening or not.

I jumped off the porch and strode toward the woods with determination in my step. There was no answer from the house, but I tried to push away the sudden stab of disappointment when Tuesday's face didn't appear in the window to watch me go.

It shouldn't have, but the sense of disappointment and loss settled deeper into my soul.

I still couldn't shake the feeling that we were missing something big.. It was going to come back and bite us in the butt or worse—stake us right through the heart. Something else was out there. Something bigger than this. I just wish I knew what.

First things first.

I pushed through the pine boughs and inhaled deeply, my first nature walk since I'd been a boy scout.

Snack time.

***

Fallen trees and boulders covered in moss littered the path that led away from the cabin. I picked my way through dark tree trunks and dense branches that waved and swayed in the breeze. I inhaled deeply and the scent of rain, evergreen, rotting leaves, musk, and earth filled my nose.

The trees here came alive at night. Not in a creepy, magical way, but — they stood proud and tall, sentinels guarding the getaway to one of the last great wilderness spaces. They don't make it easy for trespassers. I'd seen nothing like this in the city... They even sanitized the parks in the city. These woods were feral... like the part of me I tried to keep hidden. It was harder to keep it caged here.

The scruffy redneck from the highway's words of wisdom filled my mind as I stepped over another fallen log.

"You can find yourself... or lose yourself—"

Losing myself was looking more and more appetizing with every passing moment.

Dawn was coming faster than I wanted to admit, but I told myself that the pale light that danced across my skin was moonlight that had been filtered through the dense canopy of trees. That was enough to make me push ahead.

My enhanced senses allowed me to see clearly, but the forest still worked hard to keep me out. I tripped over bumpy roots and fell over tangled brush; the barbs dug into my skin and took tiny droplets of my blood as payment.

The branches that scraped across my forearms were still wet from the afternoon rain we'd driven through on our way to the cabin, and for the first time in a long time, I felt truly vulnerable just from being alone.

The darkness swallowed me with each step I took as I moved deeper into the forest's embrace. I knew that the cabin, and Tuesday, were just steps away, but they may as well have been miles away.

Everything was quiet except me. The crack of branches under my feet sounded like gunshots as they echoed through the trees. No matter how hard I tried, I couldn't make myself move more quietly. In the city I could have been a hunter—but in reality? Not so stealthy.

The trees parted suddenly, and I stood in a clearing and strained my ears to detect the telltale *thump* of a nearby heartbeat or the sound of a scurrying creature.

But the silence stretched out and wrapped around me like a blanket.

Every hair on my body stood on end as I looked around the

clearing and peered into the darkness for clues, even though I knew I would find none.

Something, or someone, didn't want me here. That much was clear.

The wind sent a shudder of movement through the trees and I bit back a yelp of surprise. Anxiety made my skin crawl, and I backed up slowly, eager to get back to the relative safety of the cabin. If the woods didn't want me here, who was I to question that?

A single, mournful howl of a wolf broke through the silence and I moved faster and ignored the answering rumble of my monster.

Wolves? Hell. No. I did not sign up for freaking wolves. This is not Twilight: The Real-Life Revival.

My body warred with itself and our dual-nature. The human side of me, if I could even claim humanity still, wanted more than anything to be back in my room. Safe behind the sliding glass door.

But my monster, that powerful apex predator of a vampire, wanted more. He wanted to stalk, to kill, to capture, and — to feed.

My hands shook, and I balled them into fists to keep myself focused as I ran along the path that led back to the cabin. Roots and rocks rose to trip me, and I bumped against the rough bark of the trees as I went.

Graceful predator, indeed.

The call of the wolf had acted like some sort of alarm clock, and the rest of the forest seemed to shake itself awake around me. Overhead, the pale light of dawn crept ever closer.

Where there had been silence, a cacophony of noises surrounded me. Heartbeats, the jarring cries of birds, and the ominous crash of unseen creatures as they moved through the underbrush.

I was a city boy through and through, and I definitely didn't belong here. This nature shit could mind its own business.

The lights from the cabin glimmered through the last few feet of forest and I turned and ran for it, no longer caring what Tuesday or anyone else might think.

I burst through the trees, and a sharp shriek pierced my eardrums. Tuesday had been half-sitting on the broken picnic table. But as I rushed out of the woods, she jumped up. She brandished a large piece of firewood, holding it up over her shoulder like a baseball bat.

She eyed me curiously and relaxed just a little as she registered the fact that I wasn't some monstrous intruder. I mean, I was, but she knew me. That was different. She relaxed her hold on the log and leaned against the bench. It lurched drunkenly to the side and she frowned at it as it shifted under her weight.

"Shouldn't we go inside?" I gestured towards the cabin and shifted my weight from one foot to the other. After my little escapade in the forest, my entire body was on edge.

Tuesday crossed her arms over her chest and looked down at the pitiful excuse for a table that she leaned on.

"Did you hear the wolf?" she asked finally.

"Yeah. I didn't know we had wolves up here."

Tuesday shrugged and pursed her lips as if she wanted to say something but didn't know how. That was weird. Tuesday always knew what to say. Always.

My monster was growling and pressing against my self-control. I felt antsy. The need for action hovered right below the surface. Any action would work.

Feeding.

Sex.

Hunting down that wolf.

All three in random order. It didn't matter. My monster had heard the call of the wild; he was determined to answer it.

I, however, wanted to get back into the cabin.

Not happening, buddy.

"Look. I'm… sorry. We're both under a lot of pressure and for me, it feels like I'm gonna crack at any moment."

Tuesday focused on the lightening sky instead of me while she spoke.

If my heart had been beating, it would have seized in my chest at her words, hope and desire bloomed in my chest.

"I don't know what to do, Vinnie. I don't have any of the answers and that scares the piss out of me." She whispered as she shook her head in defeat.

Everything in me longed to comfort her. To hold her close and tell her that everything was going to be ok, but I couldn't move.

"I'm sorry for forcing you to relive that time with Baldwin and… your… *maker*. I had hoped… I guess I hoped that you might have some small memory or that we'd missed a detail that would help. It's not fair for me to think I'm the only one who hurts —" She finally turned her gaze to me. "You *died*, Vinnie. She turned you into a… a vampire. Your manager and person who basically, I don't know, *built your career*, betrayed you. You're allowed to have feelings about that and I'm sorry I wasn't listening."

The early morning light illuminated her skin and flickered across her anguished, upturned face. I could see the damp sheen of tears across her cheeks. Everything. Every moment, every feeling, every memory crashed down on me and I couldn't stop myself from lurching forward to gather her up into my arms.

Spiderwebs and dry leaves still clung to my shirtsleeves, remnants of my flight through the forest, but it didn't matter. Nothing else mattered but Tuesday.

Not Baldwin, not my maker, or my record label, certainly not the assholes who were hunting us, or the wolf lurking somewhere in the woods.

"Vinnie, I don't know how to do this. You and me. I don't even know if we should." Tuesday pressed herself into my embrace and whispered her words into the collar of my shirt.

"I don't know either," I whispered back. I pressed a kiss into her hair and inhaled deep. She still smelled so fucking good. My fangs itched to taste her as the memory of her jasmine scented blood forced its way into my thoughts, but I ignored them.

"I excel at fucking things up, Tuesday, you know that. You've always said that it's like my dominant life skill. I will make you angry, I will probably ruin things in a dozen different ways, I might even scare you. But right now, all I want is to hold you."

Tuesday stilled at my words and then she moved against my body, her breasts rubbed tantalizingly against my chest and I closed my eyes to savor the moment.

There was no way to hide the physical effect she had on me, and I didn't bother trying. She felt my arousal pressing against her and she froze for a second; the decision playing out in her head and across her face.

I stayed silent. Whatever she decided, it was her choice to make and hers alone.

"You only want to hold me?" she finally asked, looking up at me from underneath the dark fringe of her eyelashes. Her hips ground against mine and a small growl escaped my lips.

"Don't toy with me, Tuesday. My control has limits." I growled back through clenched teeth.

She studied my face and then reached up to run a single finger down my jawline and then rested it on my lips.

Her eyes were serious as she looked at me, and then she glanced up at the sky above us. I didn't care if the sun was rising. All I cared about was right here.

"We need to get you inside," she said, and then she bit her

lip. "One time. That's it. One time to indulge whatever this is... But after that it's time to get back to work."

I didn't wait to hear the rest of her rules, I just picked her up and raced back into the cabin.

If 'one time' was all we had, then I refused to waste a moment of it.

17

TUESDAY

One minute I was standing in Vinnie's arms, wishing that I could press pause on the batshit crazy that had become my life, and the next minute I was unceremoniously lifted off the ground and carried into the cabin.

His vampiric strength was on full display, and I hated how much I loved it.

When he ripped the door to the cabin open with such force, the whole damn door frame shook. My nipples hardened and I may have even moaned a little.

I'm a freak. That's new.

He heard me, too, and I giggled at my absurdity.

A single, smoldering look that went straight to my nether bits silenced my mirth. When he looked down at me those familiarly strange burgundy eyes promised pure sin.

Yeah. There was no time for laughter. This was deadly serious.

This would likely rank in the top ten worst ideas I'd ever, ever had and I didn't care.

You hear rumors about sex with vampires. It's not really a brunch topic, even among the progressive crowd. It's still too taboo and misunderstood. But you hear whispers here and there. Women and men with vamp lovers—they're different. They walk differently; they stand differently... Once you knew someone who'd taken the plunge, it was impossible not to notice.

Sure, they'll recount bits and pieces of the experiences to those who will listen, and each time they do it's with a certain... reverence. Mysterious things. Magical things. Things that make you squirm in all the best ways.

People might whisper about it, but it was impossible to ignore the fact that it intrigued me. *Obviously.*

I would finally get to find out if reality matched the myth.

I already knew I liked sex with Vinnie, but that was before all of—this. But getting to find out if he's learned any new tricks since he became Vinnie the Vamp? Yeah. I'm allowed this single, brief lapse in judgment.

He kicked the front door closed and strode across the cabin to the room I'd banished him to. Even if it was lumpy, the bed was large, and there was more than enough room for the both of us. He threw me on the bed and I bounced a bit, coming to rest propped up on the pillows and my elbows.

Backlit by the red light of the dawn that came through the cabin windows, he looked like some sort of demon prince as he leaned against the door. My entire body was on high alert as I watched him slowly unbutton his shirt and reveal the chiseled torso underneath.

Eager to get this epic show on the road, I mimicked him and reached down to pull the stained, dirty t-shirt over my head, but he was by my side in a flash.

"Don't." He ordered, surprising me with intensity.

I let my hands drop back to the bed and arched a single eyebrow at him.

"I've waited too long for this, Tuesday," He murmured. He

lifted the hem of the shirt and eased it slowly up my body and over my head. He undressed me with exquisite gentleness and it blew me away.

This was a new side to Vinnie. He looked at me like I was something priceless. It took my breath away and threatened to thaw an icy corner of my heart.

For one frozen moment in time, I saw the possibility of a future together.

It was beautiful and passionate and perfect and... *Definitely outside my emotional price range.*

This was a one off. It had to be.

A night for fantasy and vampire fuckery.

An exorcism of sorts to get it out of our system.

I can't afford for my heart to thaw. I wouldn't survive it.

Tomorrow morning has to be business as usual.

"Strip for me, I need to see you," I ordered. I pushed my palms under his open shirt and palmed his ice-cold pecs. *God, he's jacked.*

Vinnie's eyes narrowed, but his shirt was on the floor in a flash and his pants soon followed. Gotta love the efficiency of superhuman reflexes.

His thumb darted out and rasped against a hardened nipple, and I bit my lip to keep from moaning. *Keep it together, Tuesday. You call the shots here.*

"Lay back," his voice was husky and rough with desire and his burgundy eyes were wild.

I obeyed without thinking and met his heated gaze with my own. He growled his approval and moved to kneel between my splayed legs.

"You are so fucking beautiful." His eyes roamed over every inch of me and I preened under the attention. I have always loved a confident man in the bedroom and Vinnie left no doubt that he was in complete control of the situation. He would follow orders, but only if they suited him. It was both profoundly annoying and sinfully delicious. *And oh, so familiar.*

"Will you let me taste you, Tuesday?"

I froze for a moment, weighing my options.

On one hand, biting and rough sex? 10/10 recommend. Big fan. Huge. On the other hand, uh, vampire.

He said nothing, just traced the lines of my body with his fingertips while he devoured me with his eyes.

I gulped. *What kind of vampire sex would I even be having if I didn't let him bite me? It's not like he hasn't bitten me before...*

"Um. Yes. But not where anyone can see and I want a safe word." I blurted out. My cheeks burned as he looked up at me and flashed his sharpened smile.

"Of course," he inclined his head and moved his hand up the inside of my thigh. *Just a little higher... Mmph.*

"What's your safe word, dollface?"

I screwed up my face at that and rolled my eyes.

"Fang-head," I smirked at him.

Vinnie tackled me and pressed me into the mattress with his body weight.

Every touch of his cool skin against mine sent a sizzle of pleasure through me. He peppered me with small kisses as he moved down my body until my breath came in jagged gasps. He made hungry, growling sounds in the back of his throat and it thrilled me.

The knowledge that I could make a vampire squirm with desire was a powerful and unexpected aphrodisiac, but it was nothing compared to the liquid fire that consumed me at the first bold swipe of his tongue.

My back arched, and I squirmed on the bed, but he rested his forearm on my hips and held me down, teasing me and driving me to new heights impossibly fast.

If this was the foreplay, sign me up for the whole damn ride.

The cool touch of Vinnie's fingers made me jump before I sank into the pleasure of his touch. He stroked me deep and slow while his tongue worked in tandem and brought me higher. The white-hot pleasure of my orgasm was building steadily and I held onto the sheets with a death grip.

Vinnie growled in approval and moved his lips to my inner thigh. His fingers moved faster and I let out an anguished moan. I was so close and every second of delay made me feel like I could die.

"Come for me?" Vinnie murmured, his voice muffled against my thigh.

I wanted to. Badly.

I scrunched up my face and concentrated on my pleasure, imagining it a ball of energy radiating outwards. Just as I had the visualization in my mind, a sharp pain struck my inner thigh, followed immediately by a cataclysmic wave of pleasure that drove me backwards into the bed. I rocked and writhed as he drank deeply, Vinnie's fingers still buried inside me and wringing every ounce of pleasure from my body. The force of my orgasm drove all rational thought out of my brain.

Ring.

Ring.

Riiing.

The sound broke through my subconscious, and I struggled to remember why I cared. Something was making a ringing noise? Should I be concerned? *Go for it, little something. Make all the noise you want, I'm busy dying.*

Vinnie looked up at me and grinned. His fangs were stained red, and there was a smear of blood at the corner of his mouth.

Without breaking eye contact, he withdrew his fingers from my pulsating core and brought them to his lips. He sucked each of them and my eyes almost rolled back into my head again.

He sat back on his knees and casually stroked his cock, and I swallowed shakily. *No wonder they talk about vampire sex in hushed tones. It's dangerous! You have to be superhuman to keep up!*

Gathering my thoughts took a supreme amount of effort, but I managed it. The ringing noise. That hadn't stopped yet. What rings? *Oh. Shit.*

"PHONE!" I croaked out. I rolled away from Vinnie and scrambled over the bed in the search for my cell phone.

"Can't you call them back?" Vinnie asked. He still had his dick in his hand while I hopped around the room and looked under our scattered clothes for the source of the ringing.

"Uh, no. No, I can't. We're in a crisis situation here. I have to *always* answer my phone." I snapped back.

Where the hell did I put that thing?

The ring stopped and Vinnie patted the bed next to him but I scowled at him instead. The afterglow of my heart-stopping orgasm had already taken a backseat to the desperation of finding the goddamn phone.

"Ugh, Where is it? Have you seen it? I have to find it and call them back!"

"That's it? You're just going to leave me here?"

I stopped at the foot of the bed, grabbed Vinnie by the back of his neck, and pressed a searing kiss to his bloodstained lips.

"You were great. Really. Superb. Best I've ever had. But I have to go save your ass so you can keep doing... whatever that was and not get staked on sight."

The ringing began again, and I grabbed Vinnie's discarded flannel shirt before I ran through the bedroom door to find it.

The job always has to come first. It just does. I don't make the rules.

I stubbed my toe on the hideous antler horn and glass coffee table and hopped on one foot, swearing viciously through the living room. By the time I finally found my phone on the charger in the kitchen I was in an... excited state of mind. I looked down at the tiny screen and sighed at the number of missed calls.

Four from Carlyn.

Damn it. You don't just miss calls from Carlyn without a very, very compelling reason. I doubt she would take 'being fingerbanged to oblivion by my ex/our client' as particularly compelling.

Two from my best friend, Adrienne.

One from the photographer.

I needed to call him back.

At least in the mountains I had a valid excuse for missing the calls. Even with my signal boosters, the coverage up here was spotty.

Vinnie's flannel shirt was filthy, but it smelled like him and I shoved my arms through the sleeves, anyway. A part of me longed to throw my phone into the woods and run back into that bedroom to finish what I had started. Leaving him like that felt weird and for the first time since we started this mess, I actually missed him more than I wanted to stab him.

That was progress, right?

"It's better this way." I whispered forcefully before moving to the window to look out at the sunshine that peeked through the heavy clouds.

Rain today.

"Is it?" Vinnie's voice behind me was low and controlled. He tried to hide it, but I could hear the edge of pain there too and it almost broke my heart. *Almost.*

I turned around slowly. I'd been a fool to assume he would just hide in there forever to avoid this awkwardness. We're fugitives together. We don't have the luxury of hiding from each other.

Gone was the demon prince with the burgundy eyes who looked at me like I was a gift from the gods. In his place stood a man with ethereal beauty and a flat, emotionless expression. This version of Vinnie freaked me out a little. *Ok, a lot.*

I remembered Vinnie referred to his battle with his vampire side as trying to stay in control of his monster. When I looked into his eyes this time, Vinnie wasn't looking back at me. It was his monster.

Oh, shit.

"Was this a *game* to you?" He spat the words out as he crowded me up against the wall. A shaft of early morning sunlight seared the flesh on his forearm, but he didn't flinch or pull away.

"It's revenge. Don't deny it, Tuesday? I can see it in your eyes. You want to make me hurt the same way I hurt you."

Fear crept up my spine as I watched him warily. I flinched when he slammed his palm against the wall to one side of my head. Trapped between the wall and an angry vampire. Not my best moment.

"Vinnie, let me go. Please."

I dared to bring my palm up and rested it lightly on his bare chest.

He froze at my touch and snarled as he looked down at my hand and then back at my face.

His mouth twisted into a cruel grin that made every brave thought in my mind scurry for cover. I'd never been so scared in my entire life.

Sharp fangs gleamed white in the pale daylight and I braced myself for how it would feel when they pierced my skin and my blood would flow hotly over my neck and into his mouth.

"You forget yourself, Ms. Matson." Vinnie's voice was soft like velvet, but that didn't mask the cruelty behind his formal words.

In one motion, he grabbed my wrist and spun me around, pressing my face into the rough wood of the cabin wall, my arm twisted painfully up behind my back while he leaned against me and pinned me in place.

"You work for me." His breath was icy cold against my ears and I shivered as terrified goosebumps rose all over my skin.

"If you recall, Tuesday, you're the one who came up with our little plan. Something simple that involved disguising the cold-blooded murders of eight people and at least one innocent vampire under an explosion that could have leveled the entire neighborhood. That makes you, at the very least, an accessory to murder, does it not?" He placed a cold kiss on the top of my shoulder that I could feel through the thin fabric of the flannel shirt I'd grabbed from off the bedroom floor.

Accessory to murder? What now? Is he... threatening me because I didn't fuck him? Oh, hell no.

Anger coursed through my veins, and I welcomed its familiar warm embrace. Asshole wanted to play this game? Fine. Let's play.

"You're missing some key points there, *Vincent*." I sneered. I swallowed a gasp of pain when he grabbed a handful of my hair and yanked it hard to tip my chin back and expose my throat.

Nope. I'm not going down like this.

I lifted my left foot slightly and brought it down as hard as I could on the top of his foot. He grunted in surprise and I took advantage of the moment to swing my free elbow around toward his face as hard as I could, allowing my momentum to turn me slightly.

There was a satisfying crunch when my elbow hit his nose, but the burning pain in my arm intensified as he twisted it tighter against my back.

I had been successful in injuring him, an accomplishment when your opponent is a vampire, but I had not yet freed myself. Completing my turn, I yanked my wrist down against his thumb and brought my knee up into his groin. Luckily for him, this time he was wearing boxers. But the sound of his agonized voice as my knee connected with his balls for the second time in the few weeks since we'd reunited was heavenly.

The moment his hand left my wrist, I dropped and ducked under the table, crab crawling toward the kitchen door.

Vinnie was still doubled over, both hands clutching at his crotch, when I reached the door but he heard me move and he looked up. Thick blood dripped down from his nose and a fearsome grin spread over his face.

He looked every inch a monster who had stepped straight out of my worst nightmares.

I shoved a chair in his path, darted through the door, and slammed it shut as hard as I could behind me.

A door wouldn't delay him long, but it was long enough for me to leap over the couch and grab the keys to the shit heap of a van we'd arrived in and get within two steps of the front door.

A tremendous roar of rage shook the house, and I heard the kitchen door splinter as Vinnie came after me.

There was a small notepad and pencil cup next to the door, and I grabbed the first pencil I found. As far as stakes go, it wasn't the best, but beggars can't be choosers. I grabbed a small ceramic cross that had been hung on the wall and scrambled to open the door.

I will not die for this asshole.

He was too fast.

That vampire superspeed thing was not a myth.

One second he was standing in the kitchen doorway, the shattered remains of the door scattered over the parquet and peeling linoleum. Blood covered his chest from his broken nose. The next second he lunged at me with a fresh roar in his throat and his fangs bared.

I acted on instinct.

Screaming at the top of my lungs, I jammed the pencil into the side of his neck and pressed the cross against his face.

Vinnie snarled in rage and swung at me, but the crucifix I'd slammed into his face made a disgusting sizzling noise that made him lurch back and jerk away from me.

I'm not dead. Holy shit, I'm not dead!

He groaned and held a hand up to his face. Burned, blistered flesh was visible between his fingers and I felt a small twinge of victory to see how deep I buried the pencil in the side of his neck.

For a moment, we regarded each other cautiously, and I laid a hand on the doorknob. If I pulled it open, I could escape into the sunlight.

It was an impasse. A pause. We were both breathing heavily, injured, angry. Vinnie was covered in blood and I was sure I didn't look much better.

My wrist throbbed, and I didn't need an X-ray to know that the sharp grinding pain I felt meant that it was broken. *And for what?* Adrenaline, fear, pain, and pure unadulterated fury ran through me like an electrical current. I debated what to do. All the books said to never turn your back on a wounded or angry animal. They told you to make yourself big and scary.

Does a vampire count as an animal?

My anger decided for me. "What in the actual fuck is your problem?" I screamed at him. I brandished the small cross in my good hand and advanced a few steps in his direction.

Another pencil rolled across the floor and I crouched quickly to pick it up with my other hand. My wrist screamed in pain and I gritted my teeth against the jolt.

He didn't answer me.

I expected him to lunge at me, or scream back, or—I half-expected him to kill me without hesitation.

He dropped his hands and looked at me, his perfect face marred by the purple blisters that the cross had given him.

There was something to be said for mythology and movies.

Vinnie's eyes had cleared, and his deep burgundy gaze was tortured.

Vinnie. Vinnie's back in control.

He grimaced as he pulled the pencil out of his neck. It lay flat on his palm and he stared at the crimson droplets that added to the mess on the floor.

"I — I don't know what to say," he whispered, meeting my eyes once more he staggered backwards, putting as much space as he could between us. But he didn't account for the blood and debris on the ground. A sense of unease started at the base of my spine.

"Vinnie," I warned.

It happened in slow motion. One minute he was standing, and the next minute he was falling, arms flailing wildly.

His eyes widened in surprise right before he crashed onto the antler coffee table.

A sickening crunch echoed through the room and we both looked down in horror.

Vinnie's face creased in a brief half-smile. "I'm sorry," he whispered.

"Vinnie!" I grabbed for his shoulder, but he was too heavy for my broken wrist to support, and he slipped out of my hands and slumped over onto the floor.

The sound of my own screams echoed in my ears as I watched a pool of blood grow underneath him, a broken piece of antler sticking straight out of his chest.

18

TUESDAY

ust. Breathe. In. Out. In. Out.

So much adrenaline was pumping through my body that it would not surprise me if I could suddenly see sounds. It was like standing in the middle of a serial killer's basement while jazzed on a half dozen red bulls. Fear, anxiety, adrenaline—it was a potent mix that made me aware of every single nerve ending in my body.

Vinnie just fell on an antler. ON AN ANTLER. Did he stake himself? We don't know. Fucking hell. Did that seriously just happen?

I nudged Vinnie's body with my foot and shuddered when he didn't move. A pool of blood, dark and thick, was slowly accumulating under his body. The asshole had attacked me. I should have been relieved that he was out of commission, but the sight of his motionless body made my chest hurt.

This was... Wow. I did not anticipate this.

This was all so *unnecessary*.

Vinnie was a lot of things.

Selfish. Rude. Vain. Arrogant. Moody AF. Painfully inept? Sure.

But vicious? No. Not really. Vinnie had always been a lover, never a fighter.

Does that sound like a cold-blooded killer to you?

No.

For all his asshole tendencies, and despite his talk of his 'monster' and his 'darkness,' Vinnie's soul was still bright. Homicidal wasn't his default setting. I should know. I've made a career out of cleaning up after the ones who have given in to their own darkness.

He wasn't evil but the vampire in him was trying to be.

I felt another wave of deep-seated hatred run through me for his maker. He referred to her as the 'Crimson Lady,' but that made her seem almost folksy. An innocuous vampire who had accidentally turned him into her little pet and then abandoned him on the side of the road. I referred to her as the fang-faced homewrecker who broke Vinnie. That crimson bitch ruined everything.

She destroyed him when she turned him into this monster and forced him to live in the darkness. This was all her fault, and she needed to pay.

But first: to the problem at hand: Vinnie and the damn antler.

The tang of blood filled the room and I choked on it as I tried to decide what to do. Vinnie lay on his side on the linoleum floor and I could see the end of the antler protruding from his chest.

The wound had stopped bleeding, but the pool of blood was thick and dark and I swallowed hard to keep from panicking.

I walked toward him slowly and bent down to confirm what I'd seen from across the room. The bleeding had slowed to a trickle.

That was good... right?

Forming a plan, even if it was an extra crappy one, would be reassuring. Plans anchored me when I wanted to give into the complicated feelings that filled my body.

Anger. Worry. Horror.

Soul-crushing anxiety.

I didn't have the bandwidth for any of that right now, so I built a small box in my mind and shoved each feeling into it and locked it shut.

I picked up my phone and called the one person who would have answers.

"Pisces PR Agency, Elena speaking," The tension released from my shoulders when I heard the bright, business-like tone of my favorite researcher at the firm.

Elena and I got along well. I understood her hatred of social interactions more than most, and she understood my need to ask questions without judgement.

"Elena, this is Tuesday," I hesitated, suddenly unsure of how much to reveal over the phone, "I have a research request. It's for a Level 10 client situation."

"Go ahead, please."

I bit my lip and looked at the pool of blood next to Vinnie.

"What are the indicators of death in a vampire?"

Elena didn't answer for almost a full minute, and I held my breath.

"It says here that individuals who carry the vampiric infection, or are susceptible to vampirism through blood-borne pathogens, are deemed immortal. Sacred objects, silver, blessed water, and wooden stakes can wound them. Those with vampirism have perished through specific incidents such as beheading, fire, and a stake through the center of the heart. Death is indicated through sudden exsanguination of the infected individual, desiccation, or, with fire, combustion."

I let out a breath. I'd caught maybe six of those words. "Could you say that again with smaller words, please?"

"Which ones?"

"The perishing parts."

Elena only paused for a moment. "Sudden blood loss, drying into a husk as all the moisture leaves the body... and bursting into flames."

I'd know the last one.

"Are you sure? What if the vampire was, hypothetically, staked *near* the heart with a non-wood object? Do they die then or just injure themselves for a while and take longer to heal from their stupidity?"

Elena sighed, and I heard the clicking of the mouse through the fuzzy connection.

"I do not see any research showing death of an infected individual through partial staking of non-wooden objects without showing significant exsanguination."

Hope soared through me, and I thanked Elena politely before putting her on mute.

There was so much tension in my body

"You selfish, stupid *jerk*!" I yelled at Vinnie's prone body. "You don't get to just *die* by antler. You don't die unless I tell you to!"

Unmuting Elena, I thanked her again for her time and asked her a few more questions about vampiric first aid, which she dutifully answered.

I ended the call and set the phone down carefully on the broken table.

Pisces PR's contract with Cainin Records would end as soon as I delivered Vinnie into their care. They could work out all the messiness of what to do with his undead career without me. I was just the chaos coordinator, someone else would have to manage him.

After that, he'd be filed away as just another case that went awry. Vinnie and I would go our separate ways, and I would conveniently leave out a few of the juicier details in the debrief report. Carlyn would assign me a new client and send me off to solve a new crisis. It would be business as usual. That would be it.

"I'll fix this, Vinnie. I promise. Even if I have to go rogue," I muttered.

The cabin was a disaster all around me. Shards of glass, splintered wood, the broken crucifix... I made a mental note to tell Carlyn that we would need a special clean-up crew out here. It looked like a murder scene and you can't outsource that kind of clean up to just anyone.

If it was the last thing I ever did, I was going to make sure that the Fang-Faced Homewrecker died screaming for what she'd done to Vinnie.

Now, I'm no expert on vampire mythology, but according to most of the movies I've seen, there was a way to partially reverse some effects of vampirism. Dark magic was part of it, but it was the link with the senior blood link in the afflicted's chain that had to be severed.

Cut the cord. Cure the vamp.

It sounded easy enough. And who's saying that I wouldn't be doing a bunch of vamps a favor? I hardly believe that crimson bitch wouldn't have started (or stopped) with Vinnie.

I wasn't a witch or familiar with magic—dark or light. But the work I do means that I have access to all kinds of people who, for the right price, would *sever* just about anything you want.

One in particular stood out and I closed my eyes in dread, knowing what I had to do. I hated asking for help. The cost of asking was often too high to pay. But this situation was different and Carlyn had trained me well.

If you want something done right, you have to surround

yourself with the best. Don't fuck around with the ones who are still learning their craft, just go straight to the master. My pulse rocketed as I reached for my phone. Everything in me screamed that this was a bad idea.

I looked down at Vinnie, my most recent bad idea, sprawled out on the floor. It gave me strength and I took a deep breath.

I've worked in this world long enough that I've accumulated a few IOUs and favors to various people. That's all this was. Calling in a favor.

My bloodstained fingers were steady when I gripped the phone and dialed a number I knew by heart.

My eyes were locked on Vinnie's prone frame, and I swallowed hard. This could be beyond the favor owed. But if they asked for payment, I already knew that I would give them whatever they asked.

"Answer the phone. Answer the phone. Answer the freaking phone." I chanted as I tapped my toe on the sticky floor.

"Tuesday," the voice greeted me with warmth and my skin immediately started crawling. If I wasn't careful, I would be in over my head before I'd realized I'd left the shore.

"To what do I owe the pleasure?"

Ugh, so slimy. Shudder.

"I — I need a favor," I said firmly. "There's a person of interest that I must locate and I only have a name: Apogee. I'll send the file. This is... personal." I tried to convey confidence. These kinds of people only respected force. Any sign of weakness would see me eaten alive.

The silence on the other end of the line was charged, and anxiety crept up my spine while I waited for a response. I never asked for favors. Ever. But this one—this one was worth it.

Vinnie was worth it.

"Apogee is outside the realm of a favor, little bit. I can get you the information you seek. You know the price?" The voice on the other end of the line sounded almost gleeful, and I swallowed the bile that rose in my throat.

Sometimes you have to deal with scary players to find scarier players. Pull it together, Tuesday.

"I do," I whispered and closed my eyes against the sudden feeling of panic that washed over me. There was no turning back now.

"We will begin immediately. Send the information the usual way. I'll look forward to seeing you in person soon to collect. It's been too long, Tuesday."

The line went dead and I let out a shaking breath as I slumped against the wall

OK.

That Fang-Faced Homewrecker would be taken care of in the future. We *would* find her and I *would* free Vinnie from her clutches. This I vowed. Now, I just had to get him awake.

According to Elena, the biggest issue for injured vampires was the blood loss. If they lost too much blood, they didn't *die*, but they sank into a coma until they received an infusion of blood.

I pushed at Vinnie's shoulder with my foot.

"Drama queen."

Blood.

Everything always comes down to blood. We had at least a pint on the ground. I wondered if there was a way to somehow sop it up and reuse it somehow. The idea of being on my hands and knees wringing a bloody washcloth out into a teacup made me gag.

Nope. That plan would not work.

My hand drifted to my inner thigh and caressed the two puncture marks he'd made. I hadn't even given him the chance to heal me properly before I'd bounced out of bed and launched this total mess into motion.

I *could* donate some blood to this effort, but I have no idea how to safely do that.

The regular method wouldn't work... for reasons.

Merde.

Elena had mentioned that it was imperative to render some form of basic first aid to a vampire if they were severely injured. I wasn't up on all the latest vampire health directives, but I was pretty sure that 'antler embedded in chest, currently unconscious and bleeding out' qualified as a severe injury.

That's a plan. It's not a good one, but it's a plan, and that was all I needed.

Satisfied that I had a starting point, I carefully made my way back to the kitchen for a bottle of whiskey and a roll of paper towels. Looking down at my sticky, scratched, blood-streaked legs, I figured a pair of pants might be a good idea. I was still naked under Vinnie's shirt. I desperately wanted a shower, but getting Vinnie into some kind of recovery was my priority.

Vampirism was, at its core, an infection from a blood-borne pathogen. You usually couldn't get it if a vampire bit you. It was usually shared through repeated ingestion of vampire blood, or through blood transfusion. I was covered in more blood than Carrie on prom night, and that worried me.

As a human, I have more blood supply than a vampire so it would stand to reason that most of the blood that covered me was my own. But when I threw an elbow and crushed Vinnie's nose or when he leaked out blood after falling on that stupid, hideous table... that blood could have risks.

Bandaging, cleaning, and covering my wounds had to come first, in order to stay on the safe side.

The first aid kit in the bathroom was woefully inadequate for the aftermath of a vampire attack, but I made it work.

I turned on the tap, ran the water as hot as I could manage it, and plunged my cut leg under it. I gritted my teeth as the scalding water cleansed my wounds. The cuts weren't nearly as deep as I had initially thought, and I slathered them both with antibiotic ointment and some colloidal silver. I did not know if the silver would help prevent a vampiric infection, but it couldn't hurt. Bonus? It would definitely prevent any vampire biting for a while.

I found a small brace in the first aid kit and a bottle of acetaminophen and almost cried with victory. Wrestling the cap off the bottle, I poured four tablets into my hand and swallowed them with a generous shot of whiskey. The soft brace barely fit over my wrist, but I was thankful for it.

Once bandaged, I chanced a look in the mirror and gasped in horror at my reflection. I looked like a shadow of my former self. My complexion was deathly pale with deep purple circles under my eyes. My hair, normally shiny and thick, hung limp and matted. Fingertip bruises decorated my upper arms and a long scratch traced its way from the top of my shoulder to the underside of my breast.

I looked like I had literally been through hell. All that was missing was a burn mark or two, but it was still early in the day.

I took another swig of whiskey straight from the bottle and choked as the amber liquid burned down my throat and warmed my chest.

Ok.

I could do this.

Clothing. Clothing helps. If nothing else, clothing made one feel a little more human. After everything that had happened, I desperately needed some human time.

Except clothing was in short supply. The cabin came equipped with necessities like bedding, towels, and coffee but it did not have an extra stash of clothes. We only had what we had been wearing when we escaped Vinnie's house, plus a few odds and ends we'd stolen on our journey here. My spare set that I normally kept in my tote bag was taken by our foray to Vinnie's penthouse. I kicked myself for not restocking before we went to the book club meeting but it's not as if I could have predicted all of this.

I had to be strategic about this, so I had something acceptable to wear out to the grocery store if needed.

Vinnie's flannel shirt was shot to hell, but it was cozy and warm, so I kept it and rolled the sleeves up as far as I could. Vinnie's jeans were still on the floor of the bedroom, and they wouldn't fit me if I tried. Those weren't an option. I still had his t-shirt from the other night before the apocalypse of our own making, and my fleece jacket. My jeans were missing, probably somewhere in the bedroom. That wasn't a lot to go on.

The coveralls I had snagged from the garage when we'd left Seattle (to match the hat, of course) peeked out from my bag in the corner. *Perfect.*

They were three times too big and smelled strongly of diesel, cheap cigarettes, and motor oil, but they were sturdy and would cover me. *My* hair was hopelessly tangled and matted and I didn't have the time it would take to fix it, so I just swept it up in a messy bun on top of my head. *Out of sight, out of mind. Maybe I will just chop it all off at the end of this. It can be a cleansing moment.*

Even cleaned up, I still looked like some sort of lost soul from a horror movie, but at least this time I looked more like the serial killer and less like the victim.

Channel your inner Dexter, Tuesday. You can do this!

I saluted my reflection grimly and gathered my supplies—including the shower curtain and the loofah from the tub. *Better to be over prepared than under-prepared, I always say.*

Vinnie was in the exact spot I'd left him in, and that was comforting.

I moved the lamp from the side table to the floor and spread the shower curtain out on a relatively blood-and-glass-free section of the floor. With a grunt, I grabbed Vinnie by the ankles and dragged him to the shower curtain. It was like moving a boulder with one hand, but inch by inch, I maneuvered him enough to have most of his body on the plastic.

Good enough for me.

Cleaning the dried blood off his battered body felt more intimate than anything else we had done in the years we'd been together. I would swear under oath that I was only doing my due diligence for a client, but caring for Vinnie, even in the aftermath of one of the scariest moments of my life, was unique and special.

God, I needed therapy.

I gently wiped the blood off Vinnie's face and neck, carefully taped his broken nose, and put cream on the blisters the crucifix had left on his cheek.

It was easy to fall into a rhythm. Wipe off the blood, bandage, repeat. By the time I was done with him he looked largely the same as he had before, with the giant exception of a two pronged antler sticking out of his chest.

Truth be told, I was terrified of ripping it out of him. He was unconscious now, and that meant I didn't have to worry about Vinnie or whatever he called his monster coming out and wrecking things. If the pain from removing the antler woke him, I'd be at his mercy again, and I never wanted to be in that position again.

You did it before, it's exactly the same.

Just get a good grip, pull, and it's over! Easy.

Except the last time I'd pulled a stake from Vinnie's body, I had distracted him with my blood and he was with it enough to know when to stop. I had no such guarantee this time around.

I glanced at the blood on the floor once more and contemplated the teacup idea again. Short of going out into the woods and, I don't know, hunting down a deer with my bare hands or finding some conveniently located roadkill, I was shit out of options.

"Vinnie," I used my sternest voice and pressed my hands to his cheeks. "Vincent Quaker if you're in there and you can hear me, listen up. I'm going to hurt you when I yank this antler out and you are going to let me. You will not move a fucking muscle, you hear me? Do not move! And for the love of God, don't attack me or I will toss you out into the yard to work on your tan!"

His face remained expressionless, but I felt confident that somewhere in his subconscious he had heard me.

The antler was slick with blood, and it was jammed so far into Vinnie's chest that I wondered if he had slammed it into his ribs. I braced my palm on his chest and my foot on the floor as I leaned against the antler. I pulled as hard as I could and even punctuated my efforts with an unladylike grunt that usually worked on heavy bookcases.

The antler didn't move a single inch, and my broken wrist throbbed and burned.

Ring.

Riiiiiing.

My phone was currently 0/3 for appropriate times for a phone call. I wiped my hands on the coveralls and reached for it.

Adrienne Georgatou Requests FaceTime.

Oh no.

My head fell forward, and I rested my forehead on my arm. I had two choices: answer and talk to my very nosy best friend, or hit ignore *again* and risk her calling my boss for a status update.

Adrienne was my ride or die, and that translated into a complete lack of acceptable boundaries, personal or professional. Normally, I found her behavior endearing, but showing her the shitshow I was currently in the middle of wasn't exactly an option.

Swiping the request, I quickly turned my video off and turned the phone face down on the table.

"Hey! What's up?"

"Why is it so dark?" Adrienne asked, amused at my antics.

"Listen, is this an emergency? Kind of in the middle of something here." I tugged on the antler again, but it didn't move.

Maybe I needed a different angle.

Adrienne sighed dramatically. "If by emergency, you mean 'do I miss my best friend and am trying to catch up with her?' Then, yes, Tuesday Matson, it *is* an emergency. A friendship emergency. I'm worried about you. You work too much, don't do enough self-care, and let's not even talk about your lack of orgasms." Adrienne was on a roll and her Southern drawl was coming out with each word.

I wonder what she would think of my current attempt at self-care. I had tried to have a no-strings attached orgasmfest with my ex who was now a vampire, and now I'm straddling his blood-soaked body trying to remove a fucking antler from his chest. Yay self-care.

"Kinda busy right now, Renny. Can we catch up later? Maybe over the weekend?"

I moved, so I was standing straddling his chest and wrapped both hands around the nub as best I could. With my entire body weight, I pulled and the antler finally moved and with a gross sucking noise, it slid free from the wound.

"Augghhh! Take that! You owe me so big, asshole!!" I shouted in victory as I waved the bloody antler over my head.

Worryingly, Vinnie didn't so much as twitch a toe when the antler was removed. He looked even paler than usual.

He needed blood.

Thinking fast, I held the teacup to the trickle and collected it. If given the choice of floor blood or fresh, I would always choose fresh. I'm sure Vinnie would agree.

"Uh, take *what*?" Adrienne's prim and proper voice made me

laugh, and I stepped over Vinnie's prone body to pick the phone up off the table.

"Just work stuff. Listen. Do me a favor? Can you please let yourself into my condo and pack a warm-weather bag? I'm going to have a quick turnaround on this one and will need to jump on a plane right away."

"You owe me some explanations, Tuesday. Something is going on and my inner eye is giving me all kinds of terrible visions every time I think about you! Be. Careful."

Adrienne was a worrywart, but her 'inner eye' bullshit was accurate—most of the time. I took her warning seriously. It was nice to know that someone worried about me.

"I promise, Renny. I'll see you soon. We'll catch up. I swear!"

When Adrienne hung up, a heaviness settled on me. Sunlight shone through the window and I brushed the loose strands of hair out of my eyes. For the first time since I started work with Carlyn and Pisces PR Agency, I wondered if I was really on the right side of things.

Sure, we cleaned up messes, and we solved problems, and we also made an ungodly amount of money while we did it, but was it worth... all this?

I sighed and walked back to the kitchen to scrounge up some caffeine. There was a zero percent chance I could survive this day without coffee.

The curtains on the small kitchen window hung crookedly on their rail, and I reached out to fix them and then froze in place.

At first, I thought it was just a shadow or a trick of the light, but when I looked again, the image was still there.

There was a grey wolf in the yard and it was sitting next to the van, staring intently at the door. The hair on the back of my neck prickled, and I ducked out of view.

Maybe it smelled the blood?

Could this day get any worse? Probably. I wasn't about to dare anything else to happen.

When vampires went public a few years ago, there were rumors that other paranormal creatures existed as well, but no one had told me anything about werewolves. I made a note to check in with Elena at my first opportunity. I crept to the door and flipped the deadbolt into the lock position.

One killer supernatural creature is plenty, thanks.

Plus, wet dog smell. No, thank you.

With a cup of coffee in hand and a laptop beside me, I sat down across from Vinnie and waited for him to wake up.

"You *would* make this virtually impossible to fix, wouldn't you?" I frowned at Vinnie sourly, "Wake up and face the music, fang-head... Please."

When this was all over, I was going to need a very long, very alcoholic, vacation. Surely there's some sort of sunny vampire and wolf-free beach somewhere.

19

VINNIE

Tap.

Tap, tap, tap, tap, tap, tap, tap.

The sound invaded the darkness, and I tried to turn away, but it just drove farther into my brain.

Everything hurt. Every inch of my skin, the bones in my feet, tendons in my arms. All of it.

Am I dead? Again. This version of dead sucks hairy balls.

One eye opened slowly, cautiously, as I struggled to remember what had happened when my monster had taken the reins. When Tuesday had left me sitting on the bed with her blood singing through my veins, a red fog had dropped over my eyes and I couldn't hold him back anymore. That bastard had almost killed Tuesday. He felt justified, but I just felt sick.

I tried to roll over, but all I could do was groan as pain rocketed through me.

Warm hands put pressure on my shoulder.

Tuesday.

"Slow down," she whispered gently.

"I—"

"Hush," she commanded. "You don't have to do anything but

just lie there." She eased me down onto the floor and I grimaced as another shooting pain lanced through my torso.

"You really did a number on yourself. Looks like I can't trust you around furniture or antlers, either."

"What's that supposed to mean," I croaked.

"You got lucky," she said.

I could hear the smile in her voice, but there was only a hint.

Of all the mistakes I'd ever made, and all the pain I'd ever caused—the times I'd hurt Tuesday (purposefully or not) were the ones that hurt the most. But this... This was a thousand times worse than anything I'd ever done.

"I—"

"If you're trying to apologize to me, you can save it," she muttered. "Drink this."

The smell of blood filled my nostrils, and I opened my mouth obediently as she pressed something to my lips.

"This is the last of our supply," she breathed. "We need to think of something else to get you back to strength, but this will do for now."

The blood was cold and thick, but the moment it hit my tongue I felt some pain ebb away.

Tuesday knelt behind me as I drank and propped me upright with her comforting warmth. This was all I'd ever wanted, and I'd ruined all of that. First the bloodlust, then the guilt — *How could I have been so fucking stupid.*

The monster inside me was coiled and ready to strike at any moment. Even now, weakened but not defeated, he was there. Waiting. I couldn't trust myself to keep any kind of control. Especially not around her.

I drained the cup and fell back against Tuesday. Her fingers pushed through my hair and I tried to smile.

"You are the dumbest vampire I have ever met," she murmured.

Was that a compliment?

"Do you know many?"

"I don't. But after this, I don't know if I want to."

I tried to chuckle, but it hurt so I just lay there instead.

"Go back to sleep, you big dumbass. I have work to do. There's a press conference happening in a few hours that I want you to be awake to see."

The blood had helped, I could feel things knitting together.

"Did you break my nose?"

"I did," she replied with a hint of pride. "But you deserved it."

I gritted my teeth. "I deserved way worse."

Tuesday's hands slid down to my shoulders, and she pressed her fingers gently into my tingling skin. "Well, lucky for me, you're still a clumsy ass when you're not on stage with a million people watching you." She eased herself away from me and I laid back on the floor.

Whatever I was lying on crinkled beneath my fingers. "What is this?"

"A shower curtain," she replied briskly. "Just in case I had to wrap you up and bury you in the woods."

"What?"

"What? Sleep. You've got three hours to get your vampiric shit together, and then I'm going to need that back so I can take a shower."

I forced my eyes open and flinched at the brightness in the room. Tuesday had pulled me into the shadows of the living room so that it protected me from the worst of the sunshine. "One day of sunshine a year and it had to be today," I grumbled.

Tuesday walked across the room, grabbed her laptop and folded herself gracefully into a chair.

"What are you wearing," I croaked.

Her hair was in a strange knot on top of her head, and the

coveralls she wore were... heinously large. I could smell the oil on them, and the guy who had worn them. "Did you take those from my garage?"

"It's called fugitive fashion," she snapped as she opened the laptop. "Look it up."

"Trust you to make something like that look good."

Tuesday pointed an accusatory finger at me. "Don't get started with me, pal. You just... do your healing thing. I have work to do."

I had very little interest in doing what I was told. The vamp virus hadn't changed that about me. In fact, it had probably made it worse. "Work? What kind of work?"

"Sorting this out," she muttered. "Pisces PR is going to handle the press conference. Y'know, the big one where they announce you were just a pile of ashes in the house? Very tragic, your fan club is already in pieces over the fact that you haven't made an appearance yet."

I winced and pushed myself up on my elbow.

"They are?"

My fans were reliably insane and followed my every movement like rabid lemmings hurtling toward the edge of a cliff.

I adored them almost as much as they obsessed over me. Every rockstar should be so lucky.

Tuesday nodded. "There's been a vigil outside what's left of the gate at the end of your driveway since it happened."

"Do you have a photo of it?"

Tuesday glared at me. "Glad to see you're feeling better."

I struggled to sit up and grabbed for the styrofoam cup that held the last of the pigs' blood. If we were truly on the last of our supply, things could start to get dicey, real fast. But Tuesday always had a plan, I could count on that. And after my little... display... I didn't think she'd want to chance that it could happen again.

"Do you have a photo or not?"

Tuesday groaned loudly and rubbed a hand over her face. "Yes, I have photos," she grumbled from behind her hand.

"Show me."

I rolled over and grabbed the edge of the table to pull myself up to my feet, but the table gave way under my weight and crashed to the floor as I stood up.

"Shit."

"Nice one. You've single-handedly assured that Pisces will have to buy this cabin. The damage deposit won't cover the actual damage you've done to it."

"Shit. I can buy it—"

"I know you can, but that's not the point."

"Then what was the p—" I stopped mid-sentence as my eyes finally focused. Strange shadows streaked through the room from the crooked curtains that hung on the windows and I wished immediately for the massive blackout curtains that had filled my home.

But they were all gone too.

"Holy shit."

Smears of blood covered the floor, as though a classroom full of toddlers had spilled fingerpaint everywhere and gone nuts with it.

The table was broken beyond repair, and shards of a smashed mirror littered the threadbare carpet.

"Did I do—"

"Did you break the table in half? Yes, yes, you did," Tuesday said calmly. She pointed to the remnants of the kitchen door that hung crazily on their broken hinges.

"And that."

A coffee table that had been constructed of antler horns, a tacky monstrosity that only a bona fide hunter could love, had been shattered over the floor. It was covered in blood, too and I resisted the urge to press my fingers against the steadily healing wound in my chest.

"Was that—"

"Yessir, that was the culprit. Honestly, it's my hero. I don't know what I would have done if you hadn't been clumsier."

She was trying to keep her voice light, but there was something else beneath it.

She was afraid of me.

That hurt worse than any other wounds I'd sustained. To know that Tuesday feared me—

"All right you egomaniac, come and see your legion of adoringly desperate fans," she said dryly. She turned the laptop toward me and I staggered through the smeared, drying blood toward her.

"Children of the Night," I blurted. "That's what I'm going to call them after this."

"What?"

"My fans. Every good rockstar has a name for their fan base."

"You're ridiculous," Tuesday snorted. "Can't you think of something a little less... obvious?"

"Tuesday, I'm a vampire. I can afford to be a little obvious."

"Well, if that little *escapade* was any sign, clearly you can't."

"Fans dig gimmicks."

Tuesday stared at me incredulously. "You're a vampire, Vinnie. That's not a gimmick!"

"Sure, it is. It makes me different. Dangerous. Johnny Cash never shot a man in Reno just to watch him die, but it worked for him, didn't it?"

"You did not—"

It wasn't worth it to argue with her. This was a great idea, and I knew my record label would agree. But I didn't actually care what they thought, either. I focused on the screen instead of Tuesday's angry glare. "Was that it?"

The photo gallery that Tuesday had found was from a gossip site. They always seemed to have photos of my house, and I wasn't convinced that they'd actually followed the restraining order I'd put on them a few years ago. *There's always some motherfucker with a drone —*

My fans were very... dedicated. I could only imagine what they'd be saying online. The rumors would fly thick and fast. Not even Tuesday could have seen this firestorm coming.

They had brought flowers, balloons, stuffed animals, candles —it was touching, really.

As I clicked through the gallery, it was hard not to smile. These people actually cared about me. They didn't want my money, they just wanted *me.*

Wasn't that all anyone craved? To be wanted?

"Children of the Night," I whispered.

"*Don't* call them that," Tuesday snapped.

I made a face at her and clicked another photo. This one was a closeup. Women and men clung to the twisted metal gate. Tears. Mourning. They already thought I was dead. This press conference was going to be epic.

"Wait. Who the— That's one of the bastards that staked me!" I stabbed my finger into the screen. "How do I make this bigger?"

"Give it to me," Tuesday demanded. She pulled the laptop from my hands and enlarged the photo. I pointed again.

"Him. That's your suck and chuck! Zach?"

"I should definitely *not* have said anything about that date," Tuesday muttered.

"Yeah, well, maybe not. Or maybe you should have found out that he's a fang hater!"

"And how was I supposed to do that? Just... casually drop it into conversation? 'Oh, how do you feel about vampire rights in today's society?'"

She was mocking me. That part was obvious.

"If he's there, that means he's doing reconnaissance for Baldwin," I said firmly. "They want to know that they did the job right."

"Oh shit," Tuesday whispered.

"What?"

"If you were supposed to die in the blast, that means they'll expect me to be dead, too. They left me there with you."

I let out a chuckle. "Yeah, that might be awkward if you just showed up to a meeting when you're supposed to be mixed in with the wreckage of my house."

"Funny," she said dryly, the same as she always did when she thought I wasn't being funny in the slightest.

That small nugget of familiarity between us was comforting. Maybe she could forgive me, after all.

"I need to call Carlyn," she blurted. "The press conference goes down in two hours. You need to get in the shower. You stink, and it stinks in here."

I shrugged. "You don't look so great, either."

She looked down at her coveralls and touched her hair self-consciously. "Yeah, well... I just... I need you gone so I can work."

"Fine," I said airily. I could use a shower. Especially after spending so much time in that heinous van the day before.

"Vinnie," Tuesday called out as I walked across the room. "There's something else. Apogee isn't a person."

I froze in place and looked back at her. "It's not?"

She shook her head. "It's a company."

Confusion spiralled through me. "A company— But that doesn't..."

"It makes no sense, I know," Tuesday said. "I've got my best people looking into it. We'll have something soon. If it's anywhere in the U.S., we'll be able to find them."

I shook my head. "It doesn't matter," I said. "They won't have any answers... I have to talk to Baldwin."

"Have you forgotten something?" Tuesday demanded. "You're *dead*! As far as Baldwin knows, he's succeeded in whatever he set out to accomplish. Zach got his revenge and Baldwin got—"

"What?"

"I don't know," Tuesday sighed. "There has been no activity in your accounts except for your usual expense withdrawals. Do you *really* keep a Reiki instructor on salary?"

"He helps keep me grounded," I said with a shrug.

"You're ridiculous."

"I will not argue with you about my personal expenses, Tues. But I need to talk to Baldwin. I have to find out the truth. He's not going to just admit it."

"And how are you going to do that without alerting the press to the fact that this was all a massive lie?" Tuesday's voice was desperate, but I was determined. I needed answers from that little weasel. "It's not like you can just kidnap him and interrogate him!"

That wasn't a bad idea.

"Actually," I said. "That's exactly what I'm going to do."

"What?" Tuesday screeched.

Her phone rang, and I took that as my cue to leave the room. She wouldn't ignore her phone, and I could percolate over my little idea in peace. The press conference would be starting soon, and I didn't want to miss the show.

20

VINNIE

Tuesday paced the kitchen and kicked at the peeling linoleum as she argued with her boss. She had her phone pressed tight to her ear and even though I could only hear half of the conversation, it sounded like Tuesday's alternative plan might work...

My knee bounced under the hastily repaired table. It was a little rickety, but serviceable. I just had to be careful not to knock into it too hard.

The task at hand did not hold my interest. I needed to get back to the city so I could put *my* plan into action.

Pisces PR kept a basic laptop at the cabin and we set it up so we could watch the press conference. I tried to be excited for Tuesday's sake but all I wanted to do was high-tail it out of there. I didn't actually care about a press conference. Sure, they would talk about me, so it might not be too boring, but I was a man of action!

Cainin Records had sent out word less than twelve hours ago, but it looked as though everyone on the West Coast had gotten the memo. All of my favorite publications had sent reps, I recognized a few of the best interviewers and personalities, and some disreputable ones too. I used to hate the rag publications —not much had changed, but I've grown momentarily tolerant of their presence because of what Tuesday had accomplished with their unknowing assistance. They were still shady as hell, but they served their purpose.

They trained the camera on an empty podium that was emblazoned with Cainin's logo. Photographers and journalists jostled for position in the pit.

Tuesday had assured me that this would be quick and painless.

Announcement. Pause for shock and horror. No questions. *Thank you very much, minions.*

That was the plan.

Well, that was *Tuesday's plan.*

Pisces PR's Director would be on site to make sure that nothing would go south, but I had my doubts. Press conferences could be unpredictable.

A few of my own had gone off script a time or two and caused a bit of a stir—but that had been the point. *Sorry, not sorry!*

"That's right," Tuesday sounded impatient. "No, do *not* let them answer questions. All questions should go through Pisces PR staff... that's it. Give the script to Ricardo and make sure he doesn't deviate. I don't know, be scary. It usually works on industry guys. They're all afraid to look like dumbasses in front of the camera. Once you're a meme, that's it. They don't want to be memed. Trust me."

Ah, Ricardo, I thought. She wasn't wrong. Ricardo Russo, Cainin's CEO, hated looking stupid, especially in front of the press. That was why I had a ten-year contract. It was just easier and less embarrassing for them. Well, it had been. Until I'd gone and had my little... accident.

Baldwin had negotiated that contract for me. He was vicious

in the boardroom. By the time he finished, they hadn't even batted an eyelash when I made my list of demands.

"Okay. No, that's perfect." Tuesday smiled; she was winning. She loved winning. "Keep Baldwin in sight of the cameras. His reaction is everything."

I still wasn't sure what we were looking for, but Tuesday seemed convinced that she was going to get some kind of damning evidence out of this press conference. I hoped she was successful, but I had my own plans to get information out of my manager.

Play stupid games, get deadly prizes, asshole. By the time I'm done, you'll wish I only fired you!

"You bet, we'll be watching."

Tuesday stabbed her finger into the phone screen to end the call and practically ran back to the table. Her business-face was cracking and pure, gleeful excitement showed through. She was made for this.

"They're starting. Carlyn is going to take care of everything. The script is all prepared."

"Does Ricardo know what's going to go down?"

Tuesday shook her head, and her eyes practically glowed in excitement. Shifting her weight from one foot to the other, she hopped around in anticipation. "He'll know at the same time everyone else does. The only information we have given him is that we're having a press conference for a very important Vinnie Quake update, and he's speaking at it."

"His priorities are correct," I said with a wink.

She rolled her eyes and looked back at the laptop, but I saw a hint of a smile on her face, too.

The cocky asshole side of me was confident that it wouldn't be long before she'd want to give that "one time only" thing a go again. Even my monster was sure of that. The chemistry we had together was explosive, volatile... and addicting.

But the rational side of my brain. The one that frequently had to redirect my decisions away from my dick urged caution. The last time we crossed that line, a lot of other lines almost got crossed. Maybe that's what Tuesday and I are. The ultimate in star-crossed lovers. I cursed us so now each time we get close, disaster unfolds. I scoffed to myself and kicked the edge of the couch in frustration.

"When it's done, you'll take a shower, right?"

Tuesday glared at me briefly, a single eyebrow raised in protest of my tone. *Yeah, ok. I was being a jerk.* But then she looked down at her grease-stained coveralls and grimaced instead. "Yes. Fine. God, you're obsessed with my hygiene. I'll take a shower, but for now I need you to shut it. The adults are about to speak."

Cameras flashed on the laptop screen and there was a low buzz of conversation in the conference room as Cainin's executive team filed in. Ricardo led the group, and a woman I didn't recognize followed close behind him.

"Carlyn has everything under control," Tuesday said. There was the slightest hint of awe in her voice, and I realized that she genuinely admired her boss. *What was that like?* I'd never needed a mentor... people aspired to be *me,* not the other way around. That was all about to change.

Ricardo took his place at the podium and I glared at Baldwin's image as he stood to the left and folded his hands behind his back. *I hate him.*

Cainin's CEO cleared his throat and Carlyn handed him a manilla envelope. They were really keeping this under wraps... *Deep breath. Here we go!*

Tuesday impulsively reached over and squeezed my hand under the table. I could hear her heartbeat racing in her chest. She was really, really excited for them to announce my death. I wasn't sure how I felt about that—suddenly; I wasn't sure how I felt about any of this.

"Uh... Tues, are you sure this is gonna work?"

She stared at me incredulously. "It's a little late for that, Vin."

"Ladies and gentlemen of the press... welcome. I've called you all here today for a very important announcement regarding Cainin Records' star recording artist, Vinnie Quake."

The low buzz in the room increased in volume as Ricardo opened the envelope.

Tuesday was right, it was way too late. Even if she called her boss and pleaded with her to rip the paper out of Ricardo's hands and shred it in front of all the cameras... it would never work. There were too many rumors, too many questions left unanswered. The gossip rags would spin whatever story they wanted and my reputation would be—well, I'd ruined it myself about a hundred times.

Fuck it.

Let it ride.

I tried to relax, but I was too focused on Baldwin's face. I knew Tuesday was looking for some kind of reaction, but I had no idea what my manager was going to do—my *former* manager.

Another ex.

I was racking up quite the body count. Literally and figuratively.

Ricardo's face paled as he read the words on the page, and he glanced at Carlyn with a desperation that I could feel through the cameras. Flashes went off like wildfire as Ricardo stared at the press and back at Carlyn.

"Is it true?" he asked.

Oh, no. Abort!

"Talk," Tuesday muttered. "Just... read the script."

On the screen, Carlyn's tight smile was encouraging and Ricardo's expression hardened.

"Ladies and gentlemen of the press, I called you here today to confirm rumors and reports about Vinnie Quake. I have received word from the Seattle Police that evidence of human remains were discovered in the debris of his home after the tragic events following the violent incident with anti-vampire protestors."

"Where is Vinnie Quake?" someone shouted.

I chuckled, and Tuesday glared at me.

Ricardo shifted on his feet and looked down at the paper again. He didn't want to say it. He didn't want to believe that it was true. I'd gone rogue on more than one occasion, but it had always been something that Cainin could handle.

This? This was different. I didn't even know if *I* could handle it.

Ricardo cleared his throat and tried to continue. "Vincent Quaker—known to all of you, and to the world, as Vinnie Quake, is believed to have perished in the blaze along with members of his household staff. Police are still working on identifying bodies and notifying next of kin."

The room erupted in noise and shouted questions as Ricardo kept reading. "The Seattle Police Department has confirmed nine bodies in the house. On behalf of our client, we condemn this violence." He paused and swallowed hard.

Was he crying? Hoo boy, I'd have some serious apologizing to do when I got back into the city.

"In honor of our beloved client, and the innocent lives lost on that fateful night, Cainin Records will open a charity to provide advocacy and support to the families of those lost and work to build bridges within the vampire community both here in the Puget Sound area and nationwide."

I looked at Tuesday in surprise. "They will be?"

She nodded. "It was the best way to give some closure to the families of your victims," she said. "Without saying they were your victims, of course. Cainin has also offered to cover the cost of repairs on the bookstore that was ruined during the... incident."

"On my behalf, of course," I said. I'd had every intention of paying for it myself, anyway. This just cut out the middleman. Which was a good thing, seeing I was officially dead now.

"Of course."

We dragged our attention back to the press conference and took in the chaos.

Ricardo looked utterly lost and his expression was tight as he folded the letter and tucked it into his suit jacket. His handlers were edging closer to the stage, shielding him from the hell that had broken loose.

In all the hubbub, we took our eyes off Baldwin.

This was a mistake. I scanned the tiny screen and the people milling about, but he wasn't there.

"Where is Baldwin?" I snapped.

"He was right there," Tuesday replied. "He was... What the...."

She grabbed for her phone and punched in a number. On the laptop screen, the press conference had descended into chaos as reporters jostled for position and tried to get an exclusive interview or have any of their questions answered.

Madness.

The live feed froze, and I stared at the screen, scanning the crowd for anyone I recognized.

"Tuesday," I hissed.

"Carlyn, what's going on?" Tuesday said into her phone. "Where is Baldwin? Someone needs to get eyes on that weasel. If he gets away, everything goes to hell. He's the one behind all of this. We need to know where he is!"

"Tuesday."

She whirled toward me, her eyes wide and angry. "What!"

I pointed to the screen. "He shouldn't be there."

Tuesday frowned at me, and then her gaze followed my finger.

"No way."

She leaned forward and held up her phone to take a photo of the screen. "What the hell are you doing there?" she whispered.

Zach.

That smug, murdering bastard.

His smile was hard and cold. He looked vindicated. As though he'd dealt out some righteous justice and gotten away with it. *Not today, Satan.*

Tuesday's phone rang, and she picked it up instantly. "Do you have him? Good. Stay on him. I don't want him to know that we suspect anything. I'll go back through the footage to see what happened. He's a slippery one. We can't let him skip town."

She listened to the voice on the other end of the phone, and then her eyes widened.

"Are you sure that's a good idea?"

I stared at the laptop as the feed came back online. The conference room was emptying, but it was a disaster. Overturned chairs littered the floor, and someone had knocked over a light in their haste to follow the CEO and executive board out of the room. Ricardo was a pro. He wouldn't answer questions without consulting with Cainin's army of high-powered lawyers.

I smiled faintly. Of all the press conferences Cainin had to give to explain some of my wild behavior, this was, by far, the most intense.

When Ricardo was finally told the truth, he would lose his freaking mind. I only hoped that I would be there to see it. He never, ever lost his cool, and if he was ever going to—that would be the moment.

"Right. I'll be in touch."

Tuesday set her phone down on the table and took a breath.

"What?" I asked.

"We're going back to the city."

"You don't sound very enthusiastic about it."

She sighed. "I'm not. But if we're going to get this straightened out, we need to be there."

Her phone rang again, and Tuesday answered it. I could hear the woman on the other end of the line shouting before Tuesday even lifted the phone to her ear. She winced as the shouting continued.

"Adrienne... hey." She got up from the table and walked over to the kitchen. "No. Obviously. You're talking to me right now, aren't you? I'm not dead. Seriously. Stop."

More yelling.

"Promise me you won't say anything, Renny. Promise me!"

Subdued yelling.

"Good. This will all be over soon. I will need a LOT of mimosas to get this out of my system."

I chuckled just a little. Overprotective friends could be the best and worst accessories. Here, I hoped Adrienne could keep her mouth shut.

Tuesday came back to the table and sighed heavily as she sat down beside me again. She leaned against my shoulder briefly as she reached out to rewind the video.

I grabbed her hand and squeezed her fingers. "Looks like we're in the deep end now," I said.

She nodded and pulled her fingers out of my grasp so that she could start the playback. "Hope you remembered your water wings," she said briskly.

Ricardo's voice interrupted my next thought as the video began again.

"Watch Baldwin," Tuesday said.

Ricardo was the focus of the camera's attention, but Baldwin was visible in the background just to Ricardo's left.

"Vincent Quaker—known to all of you, and to the world, as Vinnie Quake, perished in the blaze," Ricardo said again.

The words rippled down my spine. I couldn't even imagine what was going on as they broadcast the news around the world. Vinnie Quake. International bad boy and charismatic performer —gone. The victim of anti-vampire violence. I would be a martyr for the vampire cause.

I wasn't ready to be any kind of martyr. All I'd wanted was to keep performing, keep my little secret hidden, and preferably stay out of jail.

Now I wasn't sure what was on the horizon.

"There, did you see it?"

Damn. I'd drifted again.

"What?"

Tuesday pointed at the screen. "Baldwin. Did you see his face when Ricardo read that line?"

I shrugged, and she let out a frustrated noise. "Will you just watch it this time?"

She started the video again, and I hit the mute button. I didn't want to hear him say it again. Tuesday looked at me strangely, but I didn't acknowledge it. I was focused on Baldwin's pale face.

His expression stayed the same throughout the video, and I wondered if Tuesday had just imagined it. But then Baldwin's eyes darted toward the crowd. Just for a moment, and then his focus shifted back to Ricardo at the podium.

"Did you see it?"

I nodded grimly.

"Do you think he was looking for someone?"

"Zach," I said. "He was looking for Zach."

A reporter stood up and blocked the camera to shout a question, and when he moved away, Baldwin was gone.

"But where did he go?" Tuesday muttered. "And why didn't anyone stop him?"

"Baldwin has his own security team," I said. "They're not affiliated with Cainin. It was part of his contract." I hadn't thought about it much—but it didn't concern me, so why would I?

"So they would get him out without a fuss," Tuesday mused. She unlocked her phone and texted quickly before attaching the photo she'd taken of Zach. "I'm going to have Carlyn put out a call to find Zach. He was at that press conference for a reason, and we need to get ahead of it."

"You promised me you'd take a shower," I said. If I didn't stop her soon, she would keep going until she exploded, and I needed her to get me into the city. Now that I was officially dead, I couldn't risk being seen.

Tuesday's face had been on the news. But people could forget her... they hadn't forgotten me. Especially not when hundreds of news articles were hitting social media by the hour all speculating on the circumstances surrounding my untimely and tragic demise. Speculation was rampant and conspiracy theories were in full swing.

I could definitely write a song about this. Something obvious and phoenix related for sure... It could be my redemption saga. Every pop star needs one.

They'd eat it up.

She glared at me but didn't argue.

"Fine. Then it's your turn. Carlyn wants us back in the city before midnight, so we have to get on the road sooner than later."

"You might even have time for a nap."

"Don't push your luck," Tuesday growled. "If I even think about sleeping, I won't wake up for a thousand years. Shower, get dressed, on the road. Deal?"

I smiled, showing my fangs, and she drew back slightly.

"Deal."

21

TUESDAY

Horns honked all around us and rain beat a staccato tempo onto the roof of the van as we navigated the rush hour traffic back into the city.

Maybe it just always felt like rush hour.

You would think, in a city where it rains over 150 days out of the year, people who had lived in the city all their lives could drive in it.

Spoiler alert: They totally fucking can't.

Between the log trucks barrelling down the road with no thought for the other cars around them, and douchebags in zippy little sports cars that wove in and out of traffic, my anxiety level was reaching 'spring in Chernobyl'-esque levels.

This entire case had been one disaster after the other.

Murder. Hidden Plots. The reemergence of the fang-faced homewrecker, that crimson bitch.

The toll of the last few days weighed heavily on me. *What's the level of tired after exhaustion? I'm about 25 steps beyond that.*

I slammed on the brakes to avoid a merging cement truck and hit the horn as hard as I could.

A wall of water cascaded off the truck and hit our windshield hard. I gripped the wheel tight to avoid hydroplaning or sliding off the road. This week could go straight to hell. I cursed under my breath and heard a chuckle from the pile of blankets behind me.

Vinnie. Captain Disaster.

He has his *plan.*

It's really cute that he thinks I'm going to let him do it. He thinks he can play with the big kids... Ruining lives and spinning stories.

He's been pretty tight-lipped but the whole thing seems to hinge on finding Baldwin and torturing him to get information, and a reason for his betrayal.

So original.

Considering this masterpiece of a plan, and Vinnie's determination to be a dumbass about getting his own way, I declined to tell him that Carlyn had already worked with the Seattle PD to set out an APB for Zach so he could be arrested in connection with the explosion. The screenshot I'd taken from the press conference feed should match up with CCTV footage from Vinnie's security cameras.

If everything goes according to *my* plan, Zach is going to shoulder the blame for everything from the attack on the bookstore to Vinnie's (second) death and the murder of the other eight people in the house.

Vinnie's desire to do something different was understandable. He had always compulsively needed to control the surrounding environment, that much had been clear from our first 'date.' It didn't surprise me one bit that he wanted to seek his own brand of justice. He'd always complained that the police took too long to do anything.

Vinnie was a rebel. Albeit, usually a lazy one. I was surprised he was taking such a personal interest in this quest for vengeance. Getting his hands dirty was not his strong suit.

If he hadn't been who he was, they may have pushed some things under a rug or explained away with some other reasoning—choked in red tape and bureaucracy—I just needed to keep everything legit. Pisces PR's name and fingerprints were all over the place, and if there was anything out of place, the magnifying glass would come down on us. I had no intention of being burned alive like an ant.

But this desire to go vigilante wasn't unfamiliar territory. One in ten clients wanted to take matters into their own hands and tell us how to do our jobs—or demanded their money back because they didn't think we were using all of our options.

What they didn't understand was that we had our own asses to cover getting them what they needed to get the job done.

I could tell Vinnie he wouldn't be successful.

I could even tell him that he might ruin everything we had just spent agonizing days putting into place.

But it wouldn't matter.

He wouldn't believe me until he figured it out for himself. I just wasn't sure if all of *my* plans would survive his brief journey of self-discovery.

The only thing on my list at the moment was to get us back to the Pisces PR headquarters and into the protective orbit of my team.

My fingers tightened on the wheel as another car changed lanes in front of me without indicating properly, sending a sheet of water spilling over the guardrail and into oncoming traffic. Horns blared, and a headache pounded behind my eyes.

Getting back into the city in one piece would be key.

Judging from the way people were driving, that would be an accomplishment all on its own.

I blinked hard and focused on the road. The sun was setting over the water, and it painted the buildings along the side of the interstate red and gold. I couldn't imagine never looking at the sun again... I'd never asked Vinnie what that had been like.

Later. Maybe.

"Tell me the plan one more time, Vinnie. I need to know you understand what we're trying to do. And I need you to promise me you will not deviate from the script."

I looked into the rear-view mirror and saw movement under the sun-proof blankets before his dark head appeared. He met my accusing stare and made a big show of rolling his eyes like a petulant teenager.

He ticked off each item on his finger as he recited the steps of the plan.

"We arrive at Pisces HQ and you get out to go play catch-up with your boss. I get a new babysitter named Frankie. Frankie cuffs me to the passenger seat and makes sure I get to a safe-house. You go to a meeting. Someone brings me blood. I wait. You do your fancy-pants PR thing. This ends."

My eyes narrowed at him. "Frankie is a good person. Don't try anything with him, dickhead. You hear me?"

Vinnie flipped me a single-finger salute, and I chuckled despite myself.

Frankie and Vinnie.

In another life, they would probably be the best of friends. We'd be lucky if they both survived the night unscathed. I noticed that Vinnie had made no promises about sticking to the rules, and I sighed heavily. It was a good thing I knew Frankie could hold his own and didn't take crap from anyone, not even world leaders. He was the perfect choice for this assignment.

With one hand on the wheel, I fished around in my bag for my cell phone and scrolled down to Olivia's number. The head of Pisces PR's security department consulted on every case, and she was rabid for this one. I was pretty sure she was a member of the Quake Squad, but she'd never admit to being a fangirl.

I balanced the phone on my knee, popped the Bluetooth headset into my ear, and hit the call button.

Olivia's no-nonsense voice answered on the second ring.

"Pisces PR, Security Team. Olivia speaking."

"Olivia, Tuesday. Listen, I'm en route to HQ with a Level 10 and there's the potential for a repeat of the Cabo incident. Be advised and prepare accordingly."

Olivia sucked in her breath. "Are you sure?"

"Dead serious."

There was an infinitesimal moment of silence on the other end of the line.

I hated invoking Cabo, but sometimes it needed to be done.

"I'll order a second unit to stand by and alert our agents," Olivia said. I could hear people talking behind her, Cabo always got people's attention.

Satisfied that I had at least one surprise in store for Vinnie's absurd foray into sneakiness, I ended the call and pulled my attention back to the road.

"Cabo incident?" Vinnie asked from the back seat. "Care to share with the rest of the class? Planning to get an unfortunate tattoo and make questionable life choices like a spring breaker? I'm down. Just say the word, cupcake."

I smiled sweetly but didn't answer him.

The steady stream of traffic into the business district had lessened somewhat, and we were finally making progress.

Business face. Check.

***

.   .   .

The shiny, black glass of the Pisces PR building reflected the sunset and the city lights as I pulled the beat-up van into the small turnaround driveway. A few pedestrians hurried along the sidewalk, huddled against the rain, but otherwise the area was dark and empty. *Just what I had requested.*

A lone figure in a navy blue jacket jogged out from the entrance to the parking garage, and I waved when I recognized Frankie.

"Hey, Tuesday!" He smiled at me and lifted a hand in greeting to Vinnie, who crawled awkwardly over the console to take the passenger seat. Frankie laid his hand on the driver's side door and peered inside. "What's the story with this van?" His nose wrinkled as he got a whiff of the van's interior. "No offense, but it smells like ass."

"Thank you," Vinnie said in an exasperated tone. "Now you understand what I've been dealing with." He glared at me briefly before turning his focus to the examination of his nail beds. "*She* traded out my fully loaded Escalade for... this. I still haven't forgiven her for it."

Frankie raised an eyebrow at me, but made no comment.

Smart man.

"Decisions were made," I said briskly. I turned to Vinnie. "You don't get to sit up front. Remember? You're *dead*."

Vinnie growled something I couldn't hear and slunk back to his blanket pile without argument. I turned back to Frankie, but I suspected Vinnie's motives. He hated being told what to do, especially by me. But there was nothing I could do about that right now. Time was running out, and I had shit to do.

I tossed the van's obnoxiously large keyring at Frankie and opened the door to slide out. "Here are the keys. He stays in the back. The sliding door doesn't open from the inside and the back is locked. Don't take your eyes off him, he's an escape risk and I don't trust him."

"Hey!" Vinnie protested from the backseat. "I heard that!"

Frankie caught the keys easily and stifled a laugh. I stepped close and laid a hand on his shoulder as I leaned forward so my lips were next to his ear. "Seriously. Watch him. The world thinks he's dead, but he's plotting something."

Frankie beamed as I stepped away and got into the driver's side. He handed me my battered bag and gave me a thumbs up.

"You're the boss, Tuesday," he said.

"Good. Get on the road. I'll check in with you in an hour."

Frankie nodded, and the van roared to life behind me as I shoved the Bluetooth headset back in my ear, and strode away from the van as quickly as possible.

At the top of the escalator, I chanced a glance over my shoulder. I'd heard the tires as they squealed over the asphalt, but I needed to see that they were gone.

The feeling of unease that had hovered around me all day intensified.

This was going to be... interesting.

I'd half expected Vinnie to pull some murderous vamp maneuver and leave Frankie lying in a pool of blood. Frankie knew what he was in for. I couldn't let him go into the night without knowing what Vinnie was. It hadn't bothered Frankie— just another assignment.

On some level, I was morbidly curious who would find Baldwin and Zach first. If the police or the feds got them, they might serve justice. If Vinnie somehow got his way... I'd probably have another mess to clean up.

Definitely.

A figure appeared out of the darkness and handed me a plastic bag full of dry cleaning.

Anna was always here, I was starting to wonder if she lived in the building.

"You're late," she said briskly as we walked down the corridor. "And you look like a drowned cat. Change. Immediately."

She looked down at my poorly wrapped wrist and sighed before pulling out her walkie.

"I need a medic upstairs. Now."

Always a charmer. Maybe that's why Carlyn had chosen her for an assistant. No one messed with Anna. She'd cut you. Happily.

"Thanks," I said as I took hold of the hanger.

"The meeting will begin in four minutes. Carlyn is in her conference room waiting for you and a medic is on their way up to attend to your injuries. Do not keep her waiting."

"Do I ever?"

Anna's perfectly sculpted eyebrow rose slightly.

Fair.

I laid my hand on my office door. I could change out of these clothes lightning fast. Carlyn wouldn't even notice if I was a few seconds late.

"We just got the call. Zach Edmunds was spotted trying to board a ferry to Canada. He has been detained."

I swept my rain-soaked hair out of my face and pushed open my office door. "Tell Carlyn I'm on my way."

One slimeball down, one more to go!

But right now, I had to help the CEO of Cainin Records plan a funeral, and break the news to him that their deceased star was actually a vampire. This little side step was Carlyn's idea, and I could only hope that Ricardo would be on board with our plans.

First things first.

Get the hell out of these clothes and into something more uncomfortable.

Business face.

With Zach in custody, we only had one more jerk to catch, and a rockstar's funeral to plan.

22

VINNIE

I didn't know where this Frankie character was taking me, and I didn't care. The fact that Tuesday had handed me over without even saying goodbye stung more than I thought it would. More than I wanted it to.

She'd just... abandoned me with this guy and peaced the hell out without so much as a backward glance to make sure I was going to be a good little vamp and not eat her co-worker the minute the driver's side door closed.

"So, you're deep in it, eh?," Frankie said conversationally as the van pulled away from the Pisces PR building and onto the narrow street.

"Save it," I snapped.

I was sitting on a pile of blankets in a van with no back seat surrounded by fast food wrappers and other dubious mess while being shuffled around like a piece of furniture from a thrift store.

Not in the mood.

My mission had a single name and a single aim: Find Baldwin. Take him to the cabin. Make him talk.

I wasn't stupid. There wasn't a snowball's chance in hell that

Tuesday had left me with this guy without employing some sort of backup surveillance. She made it really clear that she doesn't trust me as far as she could throw me, and that's probably smart.

I remembered the phrase she used during her impromptu phone call in the car and debated on asking Frankie. We'd started off on the wrong foot, but curiosity killed the cat... and I was already dead.

Fuck it.

I turned around and leaned against the driver's seat. Frankie smelled like aftershave, beard oil, and hotdogs. Maybe we could get along. "Say, Frankie," I began casually, "Tuesday was going to tell me about one of her other cases, but she didn't get a chance because we arrived at HQ too quickly. What's the Cabo Incident?"

The van swerved dramatically to the right and came to a screeching stop. Car horns blared and someone shouted an obscenity as they careened around us.

I wasn't sure a van in this kind of condition could even start again after a stop like that.

Frankie reached into his jacket and pulled out a small vial of clear liquid before he turned to face me. His expression was unreadable, and even though the vibes he was giving off screamed danger, his heart rate hadn't increased.

Interesting.

"This is Holy Water, Mr. Quake. Combined with the taser I carry, I could make you piss yourself and swallow your own tongue at the same moment." He held up the bottle so I could see it clearly. Like brandishing up a squirt bottle at a misbehaving puppy. His tone was conversational and, despite my bitter mood, I liked Frankie.

"You won't die, of course," he continued, "After all, you're already dead. But I could make it hurt, Mr. Quake. I could make it hurt for a very long time. Now, I'm not trying to threaten you, you're a client. We rarely threaten clients. But Tuesday, Anna, Carlyn, Elena, Olivia—all these women who work for Pisces PR Agency? They're my *family* and I *will* protect them. You keep your nose out of their business, do I make myself clear?"

He waited until I nodded before he put the bottle back in his pocket and turned back to the road.

"We don't talk about Cabo. Ever. And we don't discuss it with clients, or strangers. Tuesday would never have shared information about it. I don't know how you found out about it, but this will be your *only* warning. Never mention it again."

Balls. This guy was serious. I obviously have to know what the hell happened in Cabo now. I will make it the only goal of the rest of my undead life if I have to.

I raised my hands defensively as Frankie glared at me in the rearview mirror. "Uh, understood. I probably misheard her. I'm sure she was actually going to tell me about something that happened in... Cleveland. Ohio. I'm sure that's what she actually said."

Frankie gave me a long, measured look in the rear-view mirror before he pursed his lips and nodded.

"Cleveland. She was probably referring to the territory dispute she negotiated among the residents of the Old West Cemetery. That one took a while to sort out."

I blinked.

"I'm sorry... did you say the *residents* of the cemetery?"

Frankie chuckled and jerked the van back onto the road and then changed lanes violently. The man who had uttered that stern threat only moments ago was gone, and Tuesday's jovial co-worker was back in his place.

I totally had to know what Cabo was all about.

"This world, man... It's full of surprises."

Understatement of the century.

I narrowed my eyes as Frankie pulled the van toward an underpass.

I knew where we were!

"My garage," I said excitedly. "My garage is—take a left!"

Frankie did as I commanded, and the van veered to the left. I brightened at the idea of potentially getting a vehicle that smelled less... pungent. I leaned forward and pointed Frankie in the right direction. He didn't seem to have any complaints, which could only mean that this had been part of Tuesday's plan all along, otherwise he would have pulled out the vial of Holy Water and told me to go fuck myself.

I'll take it.

The brown, nondescript warehouse loomed in front of us and Frankie put the van in park and slid out of the driver's seat. He came around the van and slid open the door to let me out.

"My babies!" I jumped out of the van and kicked the tire for good measure, "Daddy's home!"

Frankie gave me some impressive side-eye, but shrugged and followed me to the keypad. I rubbed my hands together, punched in my code, and bent down for the biometric scanner to read my eyeball.

The machine glowed with the green light of the laser and then beeped. *Entry Denied.*

"What the hell? Did I enter the wrong pin?" I shook it off and cracked my neck before leaning down to try again.

The machine beeped again. *Entry Denied. No such user.*

Balls! The alarm would be tripped if there were three false attempts to enter. The last thing we need is the Seattle PD coming here to investigate a dead rockstar breaking into his own garage. But who the hell had shut off my access?

"Baldwin," I growled. My manager was still pulling the strings with my accounts and assets. *That bastard better not have helped himself to any of my cars.* He'd had his eye on one of the Corvettes, and if I found so much as a fingerprint on it—

"Any windows or anything? I'm pretty handy with a crowbar." Frankie offered as he stepped back to squint up at the building.

I shook my head. One reason I'd chosen this building over a hundred others was the remote location, and the security. Millions of dollars' worth of vehicles were behind those steel-reinforced doors and no one was the wiser.

The only people who had access to this door were myself, my lead mechanic, Omar, and Baldwin.

"Damn it!" I kicked the door and stomped over to where Frankie was studying the garage door.

"Baldwin changed the biometrics on the door. We can't get in."

Frankie stroked his beard thoughtfully and then pointed at the bottom of the door.

"Maybe we can't walk in, but we can wait until he walks *out.* Or rather, *drives out.*"

I stared at him incredulously and then back at the garage door.

Sure enough, a faint sliver of light glowed through the tiny gap between the steel door and the cement ground.

"He's in there?" I asked, gesturing towards the warehouse with renewed fury.

Frankie shrugged. "Someone definitely is."

If Baldwin was in there, he was unlikely to be alone. The man traveled with security most days, and stealing a car from his former undead employer seemed like an activity one might want to have backup for.

Even with my vampire-enhanced strength, getting through the door would be next to impossible without outside help. If we set off the alarms, we'd have approximately four minutes to get in, grab Baldwin, and get out before the cops got here.

"Walk with me," I ordered Frankie. Together we prowled around the entire building, staying in the shadows to avoid detection. I knew where every single security camera was and pointed them out as we pressed ourselves against the building.

When I concentrated, I could hear the beat of another heart inside the building. Frankie was right. Someone *was* in there.

Suddenly, I had an idea. I skidded to a stop and turned to face my bearded babysitter.

I placed a hand on his shoulder, but lifted it away when he reached for the vial of Holy Water. Fine, we weren't there yet, but he wasn't jumpy or afraid of me. I could work with that.

"Frankie, I need you to do me the very biggest favor in the world. Tuesday will not like it, but I need you to do this for me. Man to man."

Frankie's eyebrow rose, but he said nothing, which I took as a good sign.

"I need to get into that garage. And we're going to have to do something drastic." I couldn't believe I was even going to suggest it.

"Drastic?"

"Not 'you're going to get fired and Tuesday is going to dance on your grave' drastic, but... yeah... pretty drastic."

"Like what?"

I pointed to the van that stood under the single floodlight that lit the front of the warehouse. "We're going to drive that rolling death trap into the garage door."

"We?"

"Ok, you. You are going to drive the van into the door. I mean, I could do it, but I'm pretty sure I'd be breaking Tuesday's 'vamps stay in the backseat' rule."

Frankie frowned and looked between the van, and the garage

door before he shrugged. "Sure. Why not. I've always wanted to see what a rockstar's secret garage looked like."

"Of course you do," I said with a smile. He flinched slightly at the sight of my fangs, but recovered well. He'd been a solid choice for my babysitter.

But I wouldn't be telling Tuesday that; she already knew.

"If we get in, I'll let you pick our getaway car."

Frankie's eyes lit up, and he grinned at me. "I'm in."

I knew he would be.

"After you," I said graciously as Frankie loped toward the van. I leapt into the back and held on to the passenger seat as Frankie slid behind the wheel and the engine roared to life.

He slammed the van into reverse and grinned at me over his shoulder. "Gonna take a run at it," he said. "If I hit it at the right angle, the door should buckle."

"Should?"

"Give or take."

I glared at the door, knowing that the man I needed was behind it. "Hit it."

Frankie stomped on the gas and the van lurched forward. I wasn't convinced that we'd be able to get enough speed to do any damage to the door, but if it caved just enough, I'd be able to rip it open the rest of the way.

"Hold on," Frankie said through gritted teeth.

"Does this thing have airbags?" I wondered aloud.

Too late.

Frankie's foot was pressed to the floor and the thrum of the van's engine was deafening. We were doing it. We were actually going to do it—

I'd never crashed a car before, but I'd always imagined that it would be more... dramatic.

I'll never forget the sound of metal twisting and warping, or the hollow BOOM of the garage door as it rippled under the weight of the van. The force of the impact threw us forward, and an airbag exploded out of the steering wheel as the windshield cracked and then exploded into a thousand squares of shatter-proof glass.

"Are you okay?" I gasped. My cheek burned where a piece of glass had cut into me, and my shoulder was dislocated... but I'd be healed in a matter of minutes. "Frankie?"

A soft chuckle emerged from the airbag. "That was fun."

His arm came up and the blade of a knife flashed in the orange light that spilled into the van. He stabbed it into the airbag, which deflated noisily and allowed him to sit upright.

Frankie's face and beard were covered in blood, and he touched his nose gingerly and sniffed. "Damn thing broke my nose."

I laughed and tried to ignore the smell of blood in the air. I hadn't eaten yet and my stomach lurched. My monster lurked just below the surface, and I was way overdue for a snack.

My shoulder tightened, and I flexed my fingers. "Ready?"

The garage door had buckled just enough that I could pry it open.

Frankie popped the van into neutral, opened his door, and spat a mouthful of blood onto the gravel. "Ready."

I jumped out of the van and strode to the garage door. Frankie had wedged the van against the steel, but it only took a push from me to send it rolling away from us.

It came to a stop, dragging its bumper and sitting at a strange angle on its snapped axle.

RIP Van. I hope never to smell your like again.

"How are we gonna—"

I grinned and grabbed the steel doors with both hands. There was a metallic squeal of protest as I applied pressure to the bend in the door, but it widened and buckled under my strength until there was enough space for us to fit through.

"I can only hear one heartbeat," I said through gritted teeth. "I didn't expect him to come alone."

"He obviously felt pretty confident that he wouldn't be disturbed," Frankie said. "You are dead, after all."

"*Undead*," I corrected him. My monster reared up as I heard a noise in the garage, and a low growl started in my chest as I ducked through the opening in the door and into the warehouse.

Lights snapped on overhead, and I immediately regretted my move.

So much for the element of surprise.

23

VINNIE

A shot rang out and clanged off the garage door.

"He's armed, get down!" Frankie shouted.

"He can't kill me," I growled. "*You* stay down."

Another shot slammed into the wall.

"You're a terrible shot," I shouted. My voice echoed off the cars and sounded strange in my ears.

There was a *crash* from the rear of the garage and I crouched down near Frankie. "You get the door open... and find our getaway car. I need to get that bastard."

"I have to tell Tuesday what's happening," Frankie said firmly. He pulled his phone out of his pocket, but I snatched it out of his hand.

"You don't tell her anything!"

Frankie grabbed it back, and I growled at him. "I have to tell her. This is my *job*, pal. So smarten up. I don't have to help you. I could call in backup and have you taken to that safe house whether or not you like it."

I remembered the Holy Water and the taser he'd mentioned. *Fine.*

I let out a disgusted noise, but didn't argue. If that's how he wanted to run things, that was fine with me. Tuesday would not stop me from getting the justice I deserve. .

Frankie fixed me with a meaningful glare before he nodded and stayed low as he ran toward the console that controlled the door. He'd be able to get it up far enough for us to get a car through. That's all we needed.

Right now, I needed to grab that weasel, Baldwin. Before the night was over, he would beg for death and I'd have to decide how merciful I wanted to be.

With my teeth bared I crouched behind the wheel of a band new Limited Edition Mini Cooper. I'd never intended to drive it, I just... liked it. I'm a collector, after all.

All I needed was for Baldwin to give his position away.

His heartbeat was loud in my ears, fast and dramatic. He was close, but I couldn't be sure where.

"Come on out, Balders," I crooned. "You know you're not supposed to be in here without my permission."

"You're supposed to be dead!"

I smiled as I pinpointed the source of the noise and moved toward it.

"But I already *am* dead," I laughed. "I know you didn't miss that meeting."

Another shot zinged over my head and I looked back at Frankie. He ducked, but didn't make a sound. *Good man.*

"You're a shitty shot," I called out. "Remind me to challenge you to a darts game sometime. I like winning."

"Why are you always *such* an asshole?" Baldwin yelled desperately.

"I'm an acquired taste!" I called back.

My tone might have been light and jovial, but inside I was planning just how I would take him down. Every step brought me closer to where he was hiding.

How many bullets was that now?

One plus two, plus one...

The gun cracked again and a metallic clang echoed through the garage.

I jumped up from behind one of the SUV's. "You shot my car!" It didn't matter which car the bullet had hit. It just— "What the hell, man? What did the Camaro do to you?"

Maybe it did matter which car had been hit.

Baldwin didn't answer, but I'd given away my position—but I didn't care. Baldwin had gone too far now. Sure, he'd brought in a lackey to have me murdered and put Tuesday in danger, but this? This was too much.

I leapt on top of the SUV I'd been hiding behind and located Baldwin's wispy blond hair as he ducked behind a tool box as tall as he was.

The cars were parked close enough in the garage that I could run across them like stepping stones over a river, and I took advantage of my speed to cross the distance between us with a few long strides. Ordinarily I would have been screaming in pain as the hoods and roofs of the cars were dented by my heavy boots, but Baldwin had shot the Camaro.

I didn't even need my monster for this phase of my haphazard plan. I was going to rip that sorry excuse for a manager apart without any help from that asshole.

I saw the flash of the muzzle before I heard the shot.

The bullet slammed into my shoulder and spun me around as I leapt toward Baldwin's hiding place.

I landed awkwardly, but caught my balance before I fell.

Baldwin was pressed against the spare tire fixed to the back of a Land Rover I'd planned to take with me to South Africa. That trip wouldn't be happening now, obviously, and the remembrance of it pissed me off even more.

"Wait— Please!"

I hated begging, except in the bedroom.

"Wait for what? You wanna shoot me again and see if you can get it right this time?" I sneered. I pressed my hand to my shoulder and frowned at the tear in my jacket. The bullet was lodged in the meat of my shoulder, I could feel it there.

Itching.

I dug my fingers into the wound, pulled the bullet out, and stared at it for a half-second before flicking it at Baldwin's face.

He flinched and cowered as it bounced off him.

"You're pathetic," I snarled. "I should kill you right here, but I don't want to stain the concrete... Omar still has to work here, you know."

"Get away from me," Baldwin cried. His voice shook with fear. I didn't think it was possible to hate the guy any more than I already did, but he was making it real easy.

"*Now* you're scared of me?" I said incredulously. "I could have gutted you anytime in the last five years. I almost did it when we were overseas last summer—that tour was an embarrassment."

"And you were a trainwreck," Baldwin blurted out before he raised his arms to protect his head.

"How fucking *dare*—"

Baldwin turned and ran.

I watched him with an amused stare. It's not a good idea to run from predators. But the prey always tried to make a break for it.

With a growl, I launched myself after him and grabbed his shoulder. The expensive suit tore under my fingers as I hauled him back toward me. He let out a small cry of pained surprise as I lifted him into the air, turned, and hurled him toward a tower of all-weather tires.

He struck it hard and I laughed as the pyramid broke apart and sent tires bouncing among the parked vehicles. I didn't even care if they slammed into the closest SUV's or dented the doors.

All I cared about was the groan of pain that came from Baldwin as the tires fell down on top of him.

Behind me, Frankie let out a whoop of victory as the garage door made a horrifying grinding noise that made me flinch.

I kicked a tire out of the way and grinned as it bounced off the wall and left a black mark as it struck and veered away. "That's our cue, pumpkin," I said brightly.

I reached into the pile of fallen tires and gripped Baldwin's shoulder.

He groaned thickly as I pulled him to his feet, but I didn't treat him any gentler. He deserved every misery that came his way.

"So, which one were you going to take?" I asked in a conversational tone.

"Vinnie—" Baldwin choked out and I shook him.

"What?" I pulled him close and bared my fangs. "Why shouldn't I just crush you like a cockroach right here?"

A loud wail that I had only heard on one other occasion when I'd tried to get into the garage while drunk and couldn't stay standing long enough to let the biometric reader get a clear picture of my eye... or maybe it was the code.

"Is that the alarm?" Frankie yelled over the din.

"Obviously!"

I dragged Baldwin forward, but he stumbled and let out a scream of pain.

"You big baby, I didn't even pull you that hard," I grumbled. But Baldwin wasn't being melodramatic. The brightly printed shirt he wore under his khaki colored sport coat was stained dark with blood.

"Seriously?" I groaned.

Baldwin touched his side with a shaking hand and looked up at me with fear in his eyes. "I—"

"Save it," I growled and then whistled sharply to draw the attention of my babysitter. "Frankie, pick a car!"

The big man nodded and grinned like a teenager walking onto a car lot for the first time as he ran through the rows of parked cars.

"Any of them?" he shouted.

I dragged Baldwin with me and tried to ignore his obnoxious groans as I approached the wall-mounted metal box that held the maintenance keys that Omar used.

"Frankie," I shouted as I punched the code that opened the box.

Baldwin moaned and leaned against me, but I pushed him into the wall and held him there.

"The Jag!"

I closed my eyes and took a breath. "I am not letting this weasel bleed on my Jag! Pick again!"

"Alfa Romeo!"

"Which one?"

"Blue!"

"Fine," I muttered, but I glared at Baldwin as I grabbed the key. "If you bleed on that leather, I'll drop you off the Space Needle and I will not feel bad about it. Do you hear me?"

The wail of police sirens put extra urgency in my steps as I pulled Baldwin away from the wall and shoved him ahead of me. He stumbled and cracked his hip off the hood of an SUV, but my growl in his ear kept him moving.

Coward.

Five years. Five years of working with me. Organizing every detail of my life.

Only to betray me at the drop of a hat.

He didn't deserve any mercy.

But our cover was about to be blown and we needed to get the hell out of there.

Frankie stood at the driver's side door of a beautiful blue Alfa Romeo Stelvio. I threw him the keys and told myself that I'd be able to get a newer model soon. That was my only comfort as I opened the door and shoved Baldwin into the back seat.

Frankie slid behind the steering wheel and rubbed his hands over it with a reverence reserved for holy relics.

"Nice, huh?"

"Oh, yeah."

"This was my birthday present to myself last year," I sighed. "I liked it so much that I bought two..." I pointed to the silver one beside us.

"Good choice," Frankie said as he hit the ignition. The engine revved to life, and the lines in Frankie's face smoothed as he relaxed into the seat.

"We have to go," I urged.

"Yeah..." Frankie glanced at the garage door he'd managed to raise just high enough to accommodate a vehicle. "Are you sure about this?"

"Dead sure," I replied gravely.

He bit back a laugh. "Funny. Tuesday didn't tell me you were funny."

"That's rude. I'm hilarious."

Baldwin groaned from the back seat.

"Shut up," I snarled as Frankie eased the Alfa into drive.

We only had a few minutes until the cops would be at the warehouse and I'd have a lot more explaining to do than I wanted. Seattle's finest wouldn't take kindly to being made to look like fools when they had already declared me dead only a few hours before.

Frankie squared the Alfa up to the half-open garage door. I could see the lights of the approaching police cruisers on the overpass above us.

"Frankie— Get moving!"

"You got it," he said through gritted teeth. He stomped on the gas and the engine roared and launched the car forward. *Sport package. Of course.*

The door was too low, and we both winced as a shower of sparks rained down on the car and our ears filled with the sound of metal on metal.

"Sorry," Frankie muttered.

"It's fine," I replied in a strangled voice. It wasn't okay. Nothing would ever be okay after this. I needed to tell Tuesday to make sure that my cars weren't impounded as evidence or anything.

The Alfa rocketed through the gravel yard and hit the pavement hard. The tires squealed and spun and we took off through the darkened streets.

I spun around in my seat to watch the cops scream past the sacrificial van and lurch to a stop in front of the mangled garage door.

It would take a few hours for them to figure out what had been taken—that would buy us some time. We'd be at the cabin by the time they put the pieces together.

Frankie dug into his pocket and pulled out his cell. He punched a meaty finger into the screen, but I couldn't see who he was dialing.

"Tuesday— Vinnie and I... We have Baldwin."

"Hey!" I grabbed the phone out of Frankie's hand and pointed to the road. "You, drive."

"Vinnie!"

Tuesday's angry shriek echoed in the car and I smiled fondly as I held the phone to my ear.

"You can't do anything about this, Tues. I've got Baldwin, and I'm going to get the answers I need one way or the other."

"Vincent Quaker, you get back to Pisces HQ right now! Put Frankie on the phone! You're being—"

"An unreasonable bastard? A rockstar? I know. I'll catch you later, cupcake."

I ended the call abruptly and tossed it back to Frankie. He caught it awkwardly and glared at me as the car swerved slightly before he tucked it under his thigh.

"Tuesday has done enough," I said by way of explanation. "She doesn't have to have any part in this."

"And I do?" Frankie demanded.

I shrugged. "You're my babysitter. You're being paid to be here. So... sit. Drive. I have work to do and we're running short on time."

Frankie glared at the road while Baldwin groaned in the backseat.

"Don't bleed on anything," I said in a bored tone. "We have a bit of a drive ahead of us, and if you keep it up, I'm going to give you something else to focus on, and you won't like it."

Baldwin shut up and I smiled as Frankie turned the Alfa Romeo toward the Interstate. Everything was falling into place.

24

TUESDAY

My phone buzzed in my hand and I glanced down at the notification.

Motherfu—

"What is it?" Anna had noticed my face. Carlyn and Ricardo turned to me in surprise. This could not have happened at a worse time.

The Cainin Records CEO's eyes were red-rimmed, and he was teetering on the edge of a professional and personal breakdown. The funeral planning was not going well.

This was just... not ideal.

"Frankie. He just activated his location tracker."

Anna's eyes widened slightly, and Carlyn leaned forward. "What?"

I rose from my chair and smiled apologetically at Ricardo. "I'm so sorry, please excuse me."

His expression of sorrow was mixed with confusion now as he turned to Carlyn. "What's going on?"

"Nothing you need to worry about," Carlyn blurted. "Another case that needs Tuesday's attention."

Ricardo's eyes narrowed. "What could be more important

than this? This funeral is a nightmare, and I need every available resource at my disposal!"

"And you will have it," Carlyn soothed as she waved me away. "Tuesday will advise on whatever we decide. You still have the full power of Pisces PR behind you. This funeral will be nothing but a good thing for Cainin."

I smiled gratefully at my boss and fled the conference room as quickly as I could without giving away the panic that gnawed at my guts.

Anna caught the door before it could close and stepped out into the corridor after me.

"What's going on?" she asked.

I pointed at the notification on my phone. "You heard what I said. This was one of our 'just in case Vinnie is a predictable jerk,' scenarios. I need to get to Olivia."

"It's late, do you think she'll still be here?"

I tightened my grip on my phone. "She'd sure as shit better be."

The moment those words left my mouth, my phone rang and I answered it immediately.

"Do you know where Frankie is?" Olivia's stern voice was comforting and I willed myself to relax just a little. But high-alert Tuesday hovered just in the background.

"Nowhere near the safehouse?"

"Nowhere near the safehouse," Olivia repeated grimly.

"Where is the beacon?"

"Heading northbound toward the 5. They're in the... warehouse district right now? In Belltown?"

"The garage," I growled.

"What?"

"They will not be in the van anymore. Get your people updated, they're not watching checkpoints for a shitty Astrovan anymore. Dammit, Vinnie!"

"How long has it been since he's fed?" Olivia asked suddenly.

Oh, no. That hadn't even occurred to me.

"Way too long."

"Fantastic."

Olivia's dry response was all I'd expected from the Pisces security officer.

"I know."

"What are we looking for now?"

I looked helplessly out the window at the city lights. It was late enough that Vinnie had time—but it wasn't much time. ""A really fast car that shouldn't be going fast through the city, with three morons on board."

Frankie was a great guy, and I'd known that he and Vinnie would hit it off—but I hadn't expected one of Pisces' best security agents to turn into my ex-finace's road trip sidekick. I'd given Frankie one job: deliver Vinnie to the safehouse and make sure he didn't leave until Baldwin had been located.

He was not doing that job at the moment, but at least he'd had the presence of mind to turn on his phone locator.

I could hear the excuses now, the justification for going against every protocol we'd set out for the mission. *Did he still have his vial of Holy Water? Ugh!*

"This is fine. We'll find them," I muttered into the phone.

"Tuesday, I'd prefer to take matters into my own hands on this one," Olivia said.

I leapt on her words immediately. "I'm coming with you."

"I don't think—"

"This is non negotiable. Meet me in the garage in five minutes."

Still in my suit, I dashed for the fire escape.

"Where are you going?" Anna shouted after me. "Carlyn will want to debrief—"

"Have her call me when she's ready," I called back. "I'm going to catch a vampire."

***

I had never left a meeting before, especially one as important as the one I'd just literally run away from. Our fake funeral for our fake dead rockstar was the center point of this whole debacle. The lynchpin to re-launching Vinnie's afterlife career, and that moron had the balls to do something like this?

If I could have burst into flames. I would have. Unapologetically.

Unfortunately, self-immolation isn't one of my strong suits. I'd have to settle for yelling in Vinnie's face the moment I saw him. That would have to be enough for now.

I slammed open the door to the parking garage and felt a wave of relief wash over me to see Olivia standing next to an idling SUV.

"Have you got the tracker going?" I asked.

She nodded shortly. "GPS tracker is already engaged. They're moving fast."

"Of course they are," I said through gritted teeth. Vinnie didn't have a collection of sports cars because he liked to follow the speed limits.

I jumped into the passenger side of the SUV as Olivia took her place behind the wheel. "I have other members of the security team en route," she said. "They're all following the same tracker."

"Good. We need to cut him off."

Olivia looked at me strangely. "Do you know where he's going?"

I nodded. "I have an idea."

The security officer rested her hands on the wheel and raised an eyebrow. "Are you going to tell me where that might be?"

Right. I didn't have to keep these things a secret from my team.

"Vinnie's headed back to the cabin in the Olympics. I'm sure of it."

Olivia nodded shortly and grabbed for her walkie. "Unit 17, unit 2—I need to you get to Location #450 immediately. Wait for the client to arrive and take them into protective custody. Separate Mr. Quake from whoever he is with and get him secured until we arrive."

"You don't think we're going to catch him?"

Olivia clicked off the walkie as soon as the affirmative responses she needed crackled through.

"I'm just covering my assets," she said. "You've said that Vinnie can be unpredictable."

"Predictably so," I said with a wry smile.

"Then I'd say it's necessary."

I focused on the tracker that displayed on Olivia's GPS. "We might catch them before they get on the 5."

"We might."

Olivia shifted the SUV into drive and pressed her foot down on the gas.

As we roared through Seattle's dark streets, all I could think about was wrapping my hands around Vinnie's neck and giving him a good shake.

He knew better than this. I thought we were a team. But I should have known that he'd be looking out for Number One. That had always been his game. His car. His apartment. His career. Everything for him.

Fame hadn't changed him.

Hell, even becoming a vampire hadn't done anything more

than amplify who he truly was. A selfish asshole who was only concerned about his own needs.

I hated how much a part of me still loved him and needed his touch. I'd spent five years running away from what I'd felt for him. It was easier just to shove it all into the freezer and pretend that I'd never cared—I hadn't even taken any days off work when he disappeared. I just... kept on going. It was easier than giving in.

But when we'd been together... in the cabin... I had given in. And it had felt so goddamn good.

No.

Shut up, Tuesday.

"You're thinking real loud over there," Olivia said crisply.

"Just preoccupied. There— we're closing in on them. Why are we closing in?"

"Because I know a few shortcuts, and they didn't have too much of a head start on us, which is a good thing. Frankie did his job."

"Kind of," I muttered. "If he'd been doing his job we wouldn't be on a wild vamp chase across the city. I feel like I'm in a badly written heist movie."

Olivia chuckled and turned the SUV sharply.

The location tracker beeped and I stared at the screen incredulously. "How... how are they just ahead of us?"

"I have my ways," Olivia said primly.

"I can see that."

"Which car is it?"

I squinted in the darkness. It was hard to make out what cars were what in the orange glow of the streetlights, but I was looking for something expensive. Well, expensive for me, anyway.

A silver BMW was a possibility and I pointed it out, but as

we pulled up and an older man leered at me from the driver's side window. *Wrong-o.*

An Audi— no. Vinnie hated Audi. I couldn't remember why.

"Oh shit. There."

I pointed ahead of us to an electric blue Alfa Romeo. It was the newest model—a birthday present to himself. I'd seen the gossip articles about it. It was almost impossible to avoid seeing reminders of who my ex was everywhere in this town. Every ten minutes another "Vinnie Quake smash hit" played on the radio, which was why I only listened to podcasts. At least I could escape him there.

I'd pondered leaving Seattle *many* times. But I stayed out of spite. I would not let him win. No way. *I have an Olympic medal in petty and I'm not afraid to flaunt it.*

"That's it."

"Only two people in the vehicle," Olivia observed.

"Baldwin is probably in the back seat."

The SUV pulled closer, and I saw the outline of Vinnie's head... I'd recognize it anywhere. And the collar of his over-priced leather driving jacket.

You brazen idiot.

The moment that thought streaked through my mind, whoever was in the back seat sat up, and the figure in the passenger seat turned to push him back down.

Subtle.

Subtle as a freight train.

"Gotcha," Olivia muttered. She pulled up beside the Alfa and I rolled down my window with fury. Frankie glanced over and blanched slightly as he recognized my face.

"What the hell do you think you are doing?" I shouted at him.

He looked to the passenger seat and then back to me, and Vinnie's face appeared as he leaned forward.

"Vincent Quaker you turn around right now!" I shouted.

Vinnie's face disappeared and Franke's panic stricken profile filled the window instead.

"Quaker? His name is Vincent Quaker?" Olivia asked incredulously.

"Yup." I glanced at her over my shoulder, but her eyes were on the road. The tracking beacon beeped softly—target acquired. "Don't you read the gossip columns?"

"Can't say I have time," Olivia replied in a dry tone. "Or that I actually care."

I glared back at the Alfa Romeo that sped along beside us. This was dangerous. He could easily outpace us if he got to the open road. I never yelled in traffic. But there was a stoplight ahead, one that they couldn't run.

The cars rolled to a stop and I leaned out and slammed my palm against the driver's side window of Vinnie's car. "Open the goddamned window, Frankie!"

Obediently, the window came down and Frankie treated me to a sheepish look as I pointed a finger in his face. "You pull this car over right *now*, do you hear me?"

I sounded like my mother.

All that was missing was my father's chuckle as he realized he wasn't the one being yelled at.

"Tuesday, I can explain—"

"You don't understand," Vinnie shouted from the passenger seat. "I have to do this, Tuesday! You can't expect me to let the police handle this!"

"I can and I do!" I shouted.

Behind us, horns started honking as other drivers wondered why I was hanging half out of the window of an SUV at a stoplight that was about to change.

"Pull that goddamn car off the road," I shouted. "I'll have your gun and key card for this, Frankie, don't think I won't do it."

"Unit 6 is approaching from the northeast. They will box him in if he tries to run," Olivia whispered to me, pointing at the tracking screen. I nodded and saw there was another industrial area one block over. *Perfect place to lose the audience.*

"Frankie," I warned, "If you know what's good for you, you'll pull that car over in the next parking lot you see. It's half a block down. This ends now. Don't make us use force. You know we will."

Frankie looked pale and he glanced at his irate passenger before giving an infinitesimal nod in my direction. The light turned green and I pulled myself back into the SUV in time for Olivia to hit the gas and go peeling out after the Alfa.

True to his word, Frankie slowed the car and swerved into the dark parking lot of an empty big-box store. He sped up, aimed the car for the darkest corner and, at the last minute, cranked the wheel sharply and slid the car across the wet pavement. It came to a stop parallel to our SUV. Dramatic movie-quality parking job? Check. *I had to remember to review Frankie's resume to see if he'd been a stunt driver before he started at Pisces.*

My heart pounded in my chest.

Vinnie was screaming at Frankie from the passenger side. He lunged for the keys but Franie blocked him.

"Olivia, make sure this parking lot is sealed. And check for cameras." I ordered as I jumped down onto the pavement and marched over to Vinnie's side of the car.

"Hey. Asswipe. Get out of the car."

Vinnie's eyes were deep, blood red, and his fangs were fully descended. I shouldn't have been surprised by how quickly he opened the door and loomed over me, but it was hard to get used to seeing him like... this.

I made eye contact with Olivia over his shoulder and glanced down at the car. I hoped like hell that she could read my intention. We needed to *get Baldwin out of the car and away from Vinnie or he wouldn't survive the night.*

I took a small, relieved breath as Olivia acknowledged my cue and then I turned my attention back to the vampire who stood over me and crossed my arms over my chest.

"What the hell do you think you're doing?" I demanded. I had to show him that I wasn't afraid, but the memory of what he'd done to the cabin when his monster took hold still lingered in the back of my mind. That monster was staring down at me— all passion and fury. He hadn't fed in hours, this was a desperate vampire; hungry for revenge and everything else he couldn't have. I could handle this.

At least, I hoped I could.

25

TUESDAY

"**I** could kill you where you stand," Vinnie threatened. He loomed over me in all his furious glory.

But I wasn't impressed.

We'd been down this road before.

"Yeah, yeah. The last time you tried to do that you ended up playing 'pin the antler on the vampire' and almost killed yourself. You wanna try that again? I'm sure I could find a speed bump for you to trip over."

Vinnie blinked at me and a growl started in his chest.

I was already pushing my luck. Why not lean in?

"You're not going to kill me, Vin," I continued. "You know why? You *can't* kill me. You just don't have it in you." I jabbed his chest with my finger to make my point and he hissed at me menacingly.

Olivia's team crept closer and closer to the car so I decided to take a risk.

Vinnie was incensed and I briefly questioned the logic in provoking him further. *Ah well, in for a penny...*

"You think I still love you? That love will save you?" He sneered, the darkness casting shadows over his cold face.

I grabbed his wrist and yanked him forward, dragging him deeper into the shadows and away from the car.

"Love *will* save me, Vincent. You know how I know? Because if you killed me? It would hurt me for a second and then I'd be free. But you? You would suffer for the *rest* of your miserable, afterlife with the knowledge that you killed me. It would hurt you. You're too selfish to carry that. You were a terrible boyfriend, and now you're an embarrassment of a vampire."

The last part wasn't true... He hadn't been terrible. Not all the time.

Vinnie looked at me incredulously.

"You know why I have to do this, Tuesday," he pleaded quietly. He looked down at his feet.

Did this mean I'd won?

"No, Vinnie. I really don't know. This is *wrong*. We had a plan and people—so many people—have put their asses on the line to cover your mistakes. Going rogue like this? Not part of the plan. Proving all the haters who think vampires are just violent psychopaths right by kidnapping and killing someone? Not part of the plan. You do this and there's no more Vinnie Quake. No more garage full of cars. No mansion on Bainbridge... It all goes away, and you get staked out at the airport waiting for your last sunrise. You get me?"

Vinnie paced back and forth in front of me. I could hear his teeth grinding and the growl that he couldn't hide rumbled in his throat and made goosebumps ripple down my arms.

"Vinnie— Do you *get* me?" I repeated.

"Baldwin has to die, Tuesday. He has to..." He stopped pacing and stepped close to me. He towered over me, but I tilted my head up defiantly and held my ground.

A sense of sadness filled me as we regarded each other. My team was waiting for my cue to take Vinnie down... By force, if needed. Baldwin would be taken into custody, and Frankie?

Well, I sensed there would be a few more training sessions in his future. *Maybe more than a few.*

I'd have to do some explaining as to why I chose him for the job. I'd chosen a little too well. Then again, Frankie might have a future as part of Vinnie's personal security detail... if I could get the fanged moron to calm the hell down.

"And what does that get you? Does it get you any answers?" I demanded. "If you do this, if you get your way... where does that leave you? With a body on your hands and a lot of paperwork on mine."

Vinnie glared down at me, but I could see his resolve crumbling.

"I can give you a million reasons why this is the worst possible idea," I said. "You know I'm right. Don't throw this all away for a crumb of revenge..."

"I can't just let him get away with it."

"He won't," I promised. "He'll be taken into custody. They already have Zach—there's CCTV evidence of him entering your house before the explosion. Baldwin, too. It's already in the works."

Vinnie's hands balled into fists at his sides and I glanced at the security team as they approached the car out of the darkness. They were moving slow, but there was no other way to do it. If Vinnie knew what they were doing, he could turn on them in an instant. And I didn't want to be responsible for any death tonight.

I had to keep him distracted until Baldwin could be taken out of the car and moved to safety. Frankie's door opened and I saw the big man get out and move slowly to the rear door where Baldwin was waiting anxiously for him to help him out. *He must have been injured.*

Vinnie, what have you done?

"The cops aren't going to do anything to Zach," Vinnie raged, ignoring my distraction. "They'll call him up on some bullshit charge and he'll get to sit in a secure cell with three meals a day and all the TV he can watch... If he even gets convicted. It's his word and Baldwin's against mine and the bitch of it is? I *am* a vampire. I can't hide that anymore. Crimes against vamps are nothing more than an anomaly. You know that as well as I do. He could claim any defense and be out in six months, earlier with good behavior. And those shitweasels you stirred up will call him a hero."

"But if you kill him, or Baldwin, they'll be martyrs. Is that what you want instead?" I demanded. He wasn't wrong. The judicial process didn't favor vampires any more than it favored anyone else who challenged the status quo. But if I let him do this—everything would come crashing down. I couldn't let that happen. There was more here than met the eye. This was bigger and far-reaching. I would stake my career on it."

"You have to think of someone other than yourself for once and trust that we have a plan," I said. I couldn't keep the anger out of my voice. His betrayal, manipulations... every single article I'd ever read about him; every exposé about the 'real' Vinnie Quake; every photo of him canoodling with some starlet —I couldn't let it go.

"I think about you all the time," he said softly. He reached for my hand and held it gently. The blood red in his eyes had faded as his monster retreated into the shadows. It was Vinnie again, but at the same time, it wasn't. He wasn't mine anymore.

I pulled my hand out of his grasp. "It's a little late for that, Vin," I said. "But I'm going to get you out of this, you just have to—"

"Hey!"

A strangled shout from behind us made me turn. Frankie lay stretched out on the pavement, his face was strangely pale in the parking lot lights and the sight of him made my stomach tighten.

More shouts filled the air and I realized that Baldwin was nowhere in sight.

"What happened?" I shouted, my heart in my chest.

Frankie was here on *my* orders. The idea of anything happening to him on my watch was abhorrent to me.

I dragged my eyes away from my friend and colleague and turned back to Vinnie.

"You let him get away?" Vinnie cried out, enraged.

My mind was racing. I wanted to be with Frankie and help him, but Vinnie was losing his shit. An out-of-control vampire would not help Frankie at all.

I leapt forward and clung to Vinnie, holding him back as best I could.

"Vinnie. You can't! *Please.*"

He growled in my ear and tried to side-step me.

I knew if Vinnie caught his former manager that he would most certainly kill him on the spot. Rightfully so. He had set this entire mess in motion. But I couldn't let that happen. Not yet, anyway. We still needed information that only he could give. I squinted through the dim light and could just make out a figure running towards the street.

"Olivia! Northeast quadrant!" I yelled, gesturing wildly.

Vinnie lunged again but I held on, my nails digging in. He could easily overpower me if he tried and I was thankful he had not.

Olivia barked orders into her walkie and pointed into the darkness, tracking Baldwin. In the blink of an eye, Baldwin was on the street. Olivia's security teams ran toward him, boots thundered over the pavement, but before they could reach him, a car screeched up to the curb and the door flew open.

Baldwin cast a desperate look over his shoulder at the

approaching security officers and his face twisted into a grin before he lurched forward and dove into the car's back seat.

"No!" Vinnie roared. He broke free of my grip and ran with long strides toward the road, but the car had already screeched away from the curb and disappeared into the darkness.

He stopped at Frankie's side and stood there for a moment, staring at the empty street before he crouched down to lay a hand on the fallen man's shoulder.

Brilliant. Just brilliant. That was definitely not part of the plan.

I ran over to Olivia who was speaking quickly into her phone.

"What the hell happened?" I demanded.

Olivia ended the call and shook her head in disbelief. "One minute Frankie was helping him out of the car, the next minute he had Frankie's sidearm in his hand and Frankie was on the ground."

"Is he okay?"

Other members of the security team were at Frankie's side and helped him sit up.

"Looks like it. I think Baldwin smashed him with the gun and then made a run for it." She shook her head. "You gals sure know how to pick 'em."

"What's that supposed to mean?"

Olivia leveled a serious gaze at me. "It means, I like to know that I can trust my clients not to double cross me."

"You and me both," I sighed.

"You knew this would happen," Vinnie shouted. He charged toward us and I took an instinctive step back. Olivia moved in front of me and pulled her sidearm on Vinnie. He didn't stop.

"Bullets can't hurt me," he laughed. "I've already been shot once tonight."

"Not with silver bullets you haven't," Olivia called out. "Stop where you are, Mr. Quake. I don't want to shoot you, but if I have to put you down and make you behave yourself, I will."

Vinnie snorted, but he slowed his pace. "Why did this happen?" he demanded as he pointed into the dark. "He shouldn't have been able to get away! Why wasn't someone watching him!"

"Someone *was* watching him," Olivia retorted. "He looks like he's going to need stitches for his trouble." She hadn't lowered her weapon yet, and Vinnie eyed her with a little more respect.

His shoulders dropped slightly. "What happens now."

Good boy.

"Now, you and Frankie are going to go on to the safe house," I said firmly as I glared at Vinnie over Olivia's shoulder. "I'm sending you back to the cabin. Keeping you in the city is out of the question."

"Why?"

"Because you can't keep your fanged face out of everyone's business. What if someone saw you on your little joyride today? A Vinnie Quake sighting would be like an Elvis sighting. We can't risk it. Your funeral is in two days, and I need you *reliably* out of sight."

"Frankie's coming with me?" Vinnie looked almost hopeful. He looked back at where the big man was seated on the pavement. A medic leaned over him and secured a bandage over his eyebrow.

"I've re-assigned him," Olivia said briskly. "He'll be your personal detail. But he won't be driving you anywhere."

Vinnie grinned and shook his head. "Too bad."

"Can it, chuckles," I snapped. "You have to get moving. We've been here too long, and I have to get back to Pisces. You have no idea how much shit I'm in for leaving that meeting."

"Tuesday, I—"

"Step away, Mr. Quake," Olivia said firmly. Her weapon was

still raised. She wasn't fucking around, and she certainly didn't trust Vinnie in the slightest. Even though I would have liked to talk to him alone, this was probably for the best. "You'll be going with my team. Get into the SUV."

"Can I say goodbye?" he asked softly.

"I'll be in touch," I said. "You'll be fine. They'll look after you, and you'll have Frankie for company. I hear he's great at Gin Rummy."

"I am!" Frankie called out. Two members of the security team helped him to his feet and patted him on the shoulder. He'd be fine.

Vinnie locked eyes with me, nodded, and then turned away to walk back to Frankie.

Olivia didn't lower her weapon until Vinnie was escorted to a waiting SUV.

"Thanks," I murmured.

"No problem. That wasn't part of the plan was it?"

"Not by a long shot."

Olivia smiled briefly. "Good to know, I'd be worried if it was."

"Thanks for the vote of confidence."

"Anytime."

***

I stood beside Olivia's SUV as the one that carried Vinnie pulled out of the parking lot and back onto the road. As the taillights disappeared over the hill, my eyes stung with unexpected tears and I drew in a shuddering breath.

This hadn't been a simple choice. I knew that Vinnie would see all of it as the ultimate betrayal. I had denied him justice and forced him to follow the plan. That wasn't something a man like

Vinnie had accepted before he was turned, and he certainly hadn't changed.

My team would take good care of him. He would be entertained, catered to, whatever it took to keep him in one place until all of this blew over, they would do it. Vinnie would be safe and sound and as happy as they could make him until it was time for him to make his re-emergence as the biggest vampire rockstar on the planet.

This wasn't goodbye so why did it hurt so bad?

Carlyn had already told me that I was being reassigned. Something about being 'too close' to the client. *If she only knew.*

I sniffled and pulled my battered cell phone out of my pocket and re-read the text from my mysterious contact for the hundredth time.

We found her.

Three paltry words that held so much power. I'd have to beg Carlyn for a Vegas-based assignment. Or maybe I should just be honest and tell her that I was in desperate need of a break before I could get my head back in the game. I hadn't taken a real vacation in years. I was overdue.

Besides, there was always a starlet or two in need of help undoing a hasty impromptu marriage, or a high-stakes gambler on the brink of a scandal. Vegas always came through in a pinch.

I'd take a few days off, then knock out a couple straightforward cases, get back in the groove, so to speak.

It would thrill Carlyn.

She'd been talking about opening a satellite office in Vegas for years.

. . .

I may not be on this case anymore officially, but I'd made a promise to myself that I would see it through. Not just for Vinnie, but for me, too. For all that we'd been through, I couldn't bear the thought of Vinnie finding his next sunrise at the bottom of a tequila bottle.

I had a plan. A new one. A good one.

I brushed the tears off my face and punched my autodial.

As soon as the line picked up I started talking. There was no room for arguments or negotiations.

"Pack your bags, Renny," I said with a smile. "We're going to Vegas."

Day or night, there are always people in Las Vegas. Everywhere. The airport bustles with people coming and going at all hours.

Tourists with brightly colored t-shirts and sunscreen-slathered faces, and the convention goers with their lanyards and laptop bags are arriving for a fresh week of revelry.

Gamblers, families, and the hungover convention crowd from the previous week are headed out. It's a great transfer of people and moods. Exuberant enthusiasm meets with exhaustion and defeat—all in one airport.

Normally, I would enjoy watching the ebb and flow. There were little tables set up next to the concourse slot machines that would be perfect to sit at and just watch.

Perhaps in another life.

My heart pounded in my chest and anxiety buzzed along my skin. Escaping Seattle was supposed to be simple but it turned out to be an almost catastrophic failure.

Vinnie was alive.

Vinnie and that stupid, meddling, heartless *bitch* that they forced me to hire.

I should be grateful that I was even here but I'm too keyed up to be grateful.

The burner phone I'd bought at a kiosk in the SeaTac airport was burning a hole in my pocket and I couldn't stop looking over my shoulder, constantly scanning the breezeway for threats.

I'd followed my orders. This wasn't my fault. Dread filled me when I looked down at the tiny screen clutched in my hand.

It was 12:04, and they told me to expect the call at 12:00.

They're never late. Which meant I'd done something wrong. In their eyes, this *was* my fault. I started to shake.

It was never supposed to be like this. This wasn't what I was promised.

As if on cue, the cheap little flip phone vibrated, and I ripped it out of my pants pocket and answered in a flurry.

"Mr. Kennison."

My blood froze in my veins and I swallowed hard, a wave of dizziness threatening to overtake me. There are two individuals I'd been dealing with during this whole... Debacle.

Her and him.

She was as scary as she was beautiful, like a deadly cobra who liked to toy with her victims. But him? *He* was a mystery that oozed malice. His clipped accent and impersonal voice demanded immediate obedience and loyalty. He gave no quarter. They called him The Director, and I wasn't sure I wanted to know anything else about him.

"Yes, sir?"

I leaned against a column for support. Despite the relative coolness of the airport, I could feel sweat dripping down my face.

"Tell me, Mr. Kennison, do you think so little of our... association, that you couldn't be bothered to at least put on a clean shirt before meeting? I hold my associates to the highest standards of professionalism. My dog is currently better dressed than you. If we are to finish our business together, you will be dressed appropriately. My driver will collect you outside of Terminal 1 in exactly 15 minutes. You would be wise to be waiting for him when he arrives."

The line went dead and I stared at the flip-phone in my hand for a moment. I stood there, the flat soles of my Chucks frozen to the polished airport floor.

The wound in my side spasmed. I reached down to put pressure on it and my fingertips came away stained with blood. *Holy Mother— This hurts.*

He made it sound like I was here on purpose. I didn't pack for this meeting. How could I? I'd barely made it out of Seattle alive. Vinnie and his little bitch had seen to that. The mysterious car that had sped out of the darkness to collect me from my attempted kidnapping? I had no idea who they were. But I knew who they worked for. They'd dumped me at SeaTac without saying a word. I knew I had to get out of town, fast. This was my only option. I was just lucky that my sport coat covered the wound in my side well enough to get me on the plane without the flight attendant giving me a sideways glance.

Lucky.

Hah.

I didn't believe in luck. I made my own luck.

They'll regret getting in my way. There are people who will pay for the information I have.

The memory of Vinnie spurred me to hurry back down the breezeway and head to the prime airport shopping area. These people were not known for their patience, and I knew I wouldn't be given a second chance if I missed the driver. I was in Terminal 3, but the airport was small, so I should be able to make it in time.

I ignored the pain in my side, pushed my small backpack on my unhurt shoulder and sprinted through the crowd toward the airport tram. The people I had admired for their ebb and flow closed in on me as soon as I needed to hurry. With each passing second, my anxiety rose until I finally couldn't take it anymore.

I barged through the crowd, uncaring of who I pushed out of the way in the process. The doors to the tram were just closing as I slid in and breathed a sigh of relief. The other travelers looked on, unimpressed, while I breathed heavily and pressed my backpack to my side to cover the dark stain on my shirt.

My time had dwindled to a measly 8 minutes by the time we converged on the platform at Terminal 1. I flung my body out the door and ran until I saw the familiar logo. I skidded to a stop in front of a stern-looking salesperson who looked as though he was ready to call security before I shoved three crumpled hundred-dollar bills at him.

"Shirt. Black. Sport Coat. Black. Tie. Black. Hurry."

The man looked me over for a second, holding the cash delicately between his fingers.

"Size?" he asked frostily. He glanced at my side and I pulled my jacket over the wound. I could feel blood trickling down my side, itching as it soaked into the waistband of my boxers.

"39. 15 ½. If you get me something in the next 2 minutes, there's another hundred in a tip for you."

The man strolled over to the mannequin and pulled a charcoal colored sports jacket off it and grabbed a black dress shirt and tie and held it out to me expectantly. I nodded my thanks and shoved more cash at him.

The bell for the tram rang, and I darted forward, clutching my new purchases in my arms as if they were my newborn child and leapt into the car. A single seat in between two retirees wearing matching pastel colored visors was available, and I sat down gratefully and ripped open the shirt packaging.

Four minutes to ride an airport tram to the next Terminal, change my entire outfit and meet someone at an as-yet-determined meeting spot.

There's no way. This is the end. You'll never make it.

"You're in a hurry, dear," The woman on my right looked over at me with interest as I plucked pins out of my shirt and tried to unbutton it as fast as possible.

"Uh, yes. I'm, uh, late. Gotta change so I'm not *too late*." I chuckled miserably.

The woman on my left patted my knee.

"Wedding?"

I stared at her blankly but nodded. It's as good a reason as any. And I must have looked terrified enough to sell it.

With a deep breath, I pulled off my linen sport jacket and tugged the printed button down off my torso. I winced as the cotton fibers ripped away from my wound. The two women, along with the rest of the car stared at me with a mixture of horror and amusement on their faces.

I didn't care.

We were approaching the terminal platform, and I at least had my shirt on. I hurriedly buttoned as many buttons as I could before stuffing the stained shirt and torn jacket in my bag and prepared to disembark.

"Your tie, dear?" The old woman on my right held out my new tie, perfectly tied in a Windsor knot.

I took it gratefully, thanked her, slipped it over my head and cinched it tight.

The second the doors opened, and I was out of the car like greased lightning. I tucked my shirt into my pants as I ran towards the ground transportation door.

The map showed two locations for ground pickup, two levels apart, and I almost smashed my fist into the stupid lit-up map in frustration. My time was up and I had no idea where I was meeting my contact.

I slipped the tattered sport coat on and picked my backpack back up.

Shoulders squared, I walked toward the outside doors and my fate.

When I stepped out onto the cement, the little phone in my pocket vibrated again.

I opened it and answered, not daring to speak another word.

"Mr. Kennison." The Director sounded even colder than before. "You are late. I do not abide by tardiness. Consider your agreement with Apogee - and the protection it afforded you - terminated. You're on your own."

Before I could answer, the phone line went dead. I felt another buzz, and I saw I had an incoming text.

It was a grainy picture of a person standing in the dark, crouched next to a body that had been staked to the floor. There was a strange smile on my face, and the body on the ground was unmistakably Vinnie Quake.

An icy shiver ran down my spine, and I squinted, looking at the picture again. It had to be from a security camera. How else—

Another message came through and I clicked the link, my heart in my throat.

It was another picture of me, only this time I was standing outside an airport terminal wearing a blazer and a backpack. A red target had been superimposed on my chest. Terror bloomed in my gut and I found it hard to breathe.

One word accompanied the message.

Run.

I took off like a shot.

People like Apogee? They don't ask twice.

To be continued in Double Stakes: A VamPR Gamble

DOUBLE STAKES: A VAMPR GAMBLE

Sometimes PR work was like fighting a hydra—as soon as one problem was solved, three more would rise in its place. And my sword arm was getting tired.

After several brushes with death in a very short amount of time, the only thing on Tuesday Matson's mind is getting out of Seattle for a mini-vacation. One week of margaritas, low-maintenance clients, and living life on the wilder side is exactly what she needs to recover from the chaos of Vinnie Quake.

With her best friend Adrienne in tow, Tuesday heads to Sin City determined to get her head on straight and refocus on her goals. No worries. No stress. No responsibilities. Just relaxation.

But plans have a way of derailing themselves at the worst possible moment, and Tuesday's attempt at relaxation becomes a race against time when the powerful Sin City Underground takes a deadly interest in her extracurricular activities.

It's Vegas, baby! But there's more at stake than a little ill-advised slot-machine action. If she has any hope of leaving Vegas alive, Tuesday has to play her cards right. But which matters more? A chance at revenge, or unlocking a secret that too many people have died to protect...

Double Stakes is a dark paranormal/urban fantasy thriller featuring a strong-willed PR agent who is committed to her clients—no matter the cost.

Perfect for lovers of True Blood and Scandal, scroll up and one-click now to continue your journey to the truth with Book 2 in the Pisces Paranormal PR Agency series!

Grab your copy at www.books2read/VamPRVegas

AUTHOR'S NOTE

Dear Readers:

That was a ride. Thanks for giving us a chance and picking up our book!

We hope the idea of a paranormal PR agency is as intriguing to you as it is to us. At Pisces Paranormal Relations (PR) Agency, they deal with clientele who are complicated, sometimes undead, often violent, and *always* in need of a fixer. Fast. Vinnie and Tuesday aren't done yet. The adventure continues in *Double Stakes: A VamPR Gamble*, out this summer.

As indie authors, we rely on our reviews and reader recommendations to reach our audience. Loved it? Hated it? Somewhere in between? Consider leaving a few words in a review. We appreciate your honest feedback. If you loved it, tell a friend and then come tell us! Come be part of our Book Club and geek out with us about vampires and some of our more mysterious characters. Find us on Facebook at Bee Murray's Book Club and, while you're there, make sure you're following our series page for exclusive updates: Facebook.com/PiscesPRAgency

With stabby love!
    Bee & Niobe

ABOUT BEE MURRAY

Bee Murray is a USA Today Bestselling author who writes romance with a side of mischief. She refuses to be constrained by just one niche so expect anything and everything from PNR rom-com to dark, gritty, contemporary romance!

You can join her in shenanigans on Facebook at facebook.com/ beemurraybooks or on Instagram at instagram.com/beemurraybooks. Unlike Vinnie, she doesn't bite. *Usually.* Come say hi!

Want to be the first to know about new books? Like to collect random facts? Sign up for the sporadic-but-usually-monthly newsletter and get sneak peeks, book recs, and sassy commentary from Bee: sendfox.com/beemurraybooks

ABOUT NIOBE MARSH

Niobe Marsh is the USA Today Bestselling penname of a prolific romance author writing in several different genres. Here you will find monsters, supernatural lovers, dark heroes, and dangerous heroines in search of their happily ever after—whatever that means.

Follow Niobe on Amazon, Facebook, or on Instagram, or sign up for her newsletter for new releases, giveaways, and more!